A Novel

Tina Ann Forkner

Waking Up Joy

Print Edition

The Tule Publishing Group, LLC

ISBN: 978-1-940296-72-2

This book is dedicated with much love
and respect to my husband,
Albert Forkner.

"Into that world inverted
where left is always right,
where the shadows are really the body,
where we stay awake all night,
where the heavens are shallow as the sea
is now deep, and you love me."

—Elizabeth Bishop, from *Insomnia*

Chapter One

Joy Talley—At the End of Her Rope
1982

I'M STILL BREATHING, so I obviously didn't kill myself. I just want to say that right now. I know what it looked like when my brothers and sisters found me dangling from the roof over the balcony, but—did any one of them ever think to ask why in the world I would have tied a rope around the crumbling chimney and jumped off the roof, especially when there was a perfectly stout and sprawling apple tree growing right next to Momma's front yard?

The magic apple tree, as some people still call it, would have been the perfect hanging tree, but, of course, they didn't think of that. I could have even removed the cover from the old well next to the orchard and tossed myself down into its murky depths; or worse, let myself be washed away in the so-called Spring of Good Luck that spiraled deep into the ground behind our house; but I didn't, because killing myself, accidentally or on purpose, wasn't ever part of my plan.

My plan was to bid farewell to the past and live free in

the present, to let go of the one person who knew the truth about me. For years, I had been clutching the memory of us to my heart like a bride clutches her roses, although I would never be his bride. That much was certain, since he had let go of me a long time ago and married someone else. So, I decided to be brave as I stepped onto the roof. It was time to let go . . . time to trust the future. It was just my luck that my leap of faith landed me dangling in a tangle of rope.

Undeniably, I am a Talley and sometimes our luck is good and sometimes it's bad, so I shouldn't have been surprised when I fell, or that my brothers and sisters thought I jumped off the roof on purpose. They had no idea why I was up there, although it probably wouldn't have made a difference if they had. When a family relies on luck to explain anything and everything, they'll naturally leap to the most horrible conclusion at the absolute worst time. This was one of those times.

When they saw me dangling over the balcony, they thought the worst, and all dashed into the house and up the stairs. If any one of them had a lick of common sense, they would've looked at the grimy soot on my hands and known I was up to something more important than trying to kill myself, but I guess it was the easiest conclusion they could come up with as they spilled onto the balcony and reached out past the railing to pull me in.

Rory, the taller of my two brothers, wrapped his arms around my limp noodle legs and lifted me up, while River pulled out his pocket knife and cut the rope, thank goodness, loosening what they mistook for a poorly tied noose and pulling it over my head.

"She never was good at tying a knot when we were kids," River said.

"I wonder why she did this." Carey's pitiful weeping made me want to scream, but of course I couldn't.

"Bless her heart; did she think we didn't love her?" I couldn't see her, but I already knew Nanette was digging through her purse for a used tissue.

It's funny that I heard my brothers and sisters speak every day, but the way their voices echoed around me in that moment, their Okie accents rolling around in their mouths, they sounded like a bunch of hillbillies. I reckon I sound just like them, but I hope I sound a little bit smarter. Now, I'm not putting them down, just because I made the honor roll my senior year and they didn't, but to be honest, they weren't always the brightest bulbs in the chandelier. Take my sisters, for instance. Each got her GED and husband, then, had passels of kids; and I have to admit seemed to be happier for it at the time.

"Do people who do this still go to heaven?" Rory. I had to feel sorry for my baby brother. He sounded like he might cry, even though he was the bigger and the stronger of the two boys. He'd always had a tender heart—and the worst grades in school. I'm not really surprised he thought I tried to kill myself. To be honest, I'm not shocked that either of my brothers came to that conclusion. I'm just annoyed. They never were book smart, but now, they were definitely tool and dye sharp like Daddy. Those boys didn't even bother with a GED. They could rebuild any engine around and nobody knew how they first learned it, so they opened an auto shop called The Greasy Wheel where I worked as their secretary, just around the corner from Momma's house.

"Momma would say, no," said Carey. "People who kill themselves don't go to heaven."

I heard a gasp. Nanette's voice whispered back, thick with indignation. "You don't know what Momma would say."

"No matter if I do or not," Carey said, her voice hitting a high pitch, like she had gone a little nuts from all the stress. "Knowing Momma, she'd make some kind of charm and then turn around and try to pray Joy into heaven. Because we're lucky—except when we're not. Am I right?"

Nanette's voice turned sharp. "She doesn't need to be prayed into heaven. And besides, she's not dead!"

Before I knew it, I was stretched across Carey's and Nanette's laps in the backseat of the truck headed to the hospital, instead of to the funeral home to see Momma laid out in her Sunday best, which is why they'd all come to pick me up in the first place.

Momma.

My heart leapt toward Momma's memory, but then I realized it was just the truck lurching. I felt the hands of my sisters preventing me from rolling onto the floorboard.

"Be careful, man," Rory said.

"I'm in a bit of a hurry, dimwit."

"It won't matter if you jostle her to death 'fore we get there."

I wished I could rub away the prickling pain in my neck, but my arms were as heavy as the musty bricks in our chimney. Nanette moaned, as if she was in pain, too, and I imagined her pretty olive complexion turning sallow right up to her thick brunette ponytail. I've always been a little bit jealous that she wasn't made to suffer my frizzy red mane.

"Can you two please get along?"

My brothers never have been able to agree on anything. Not even on how to run their shop. Eventually, they had to hire a manager to manage them because they couldn't manage to get along with each other. Of course, it was me they hired, so I wondered what they were going to do if I didn't come out of this alive.

"We probably shouldn't have moved her," Nanette said.

"I guess we could've just let her hang from Momma's roof a few more days," River said. "That's how long the ambulance would've taken to find her."

I agree.

Momma's house really was difficult to locate at the end of a winding red dirt road that zigzagged through ten miles of twisted woods before opening up to a thousand acres of pastureland and thousands of towering oak, elm, and pine trees in the background—definitely not flat and treeless like the western part of Oklahoma. Spavinaw Junction is tucked in between Green Country and the Ozarks, right in the three corners of Oklahoma, Missouri, and Arkansas. I've never wanted to live anywhere else, unless you count the ocean, and as I lay across my sisters' laps I wondered if I would ever again see our lofty pastel blue farmhouse, a century-old structure admittedly in need of a makeover.

I loved how it sat like a giant Easter egg where the bluffs and pasture meet, its two stories trimmed in flaking white paint and shaded by a couple of towering oak trees in the front yard. Anyone looking at our house from the outside would see it as an ideal, albeit a bit sagging, example of Americana, never guessing at the long hidden mysteries its secret spaces and passages harbored, one of them being my very own.

Chapter Two

"I GUESS WE won't make it to the funeral home today." I detected grief in Nanette's voice, and my own sorrow rose up. My heart suddenly felt like a bird, a large annoying crow to be specific, banging at the bars of my chest.

What if I miss Momma's funeral?

The idea should've brought tears to my eyes, but they were dry, despite my sorrow.

How odd.

"What if we have to combine the funerals?" That was Carey's voice. If I had hands that worked I might have reached up and given her blonde, curly head a good shake. "Will two caskets even fit on the church stage?"

Excuse me? A casket?

Mercy, they were pathetic with their complaining.

Carey sniffled. "At least Momma will be glad to see Joy."

"Carey," Nanette scolded. "She's still breathing!"

I couldn't help my thoughts. I remembered those Halloween movies I used to watch with Carey and Nanette in which the poor souls got buried alive and scratched their finger nails off trying to get out.

I'm not dead!

I wished I could holler the words, "I didn't kill myself!" You wouldn't believe how hard I tried to open my eyes.

Nothing. Not even a blink.

I guess I'm really dying, but not from my own hand, just my own stupidity.

My nose tickled from Nanette's tears.

"Momma would hate it knowing that Joy tried to hang herself."

Poor Momma.

I imagined her lying at the funeral home waiting for us, dead and waxen, dressed, I hoped, in her favorite duster robe with the tiny blue flowers that I chose for her. I wished I could get enough air in my lungs to shout.

You've got it all wrong.

Boy, did they have it wrong. As strange as it sounds, I really was simply looking in the chimney for something important before anyone else could stumble upon it, something I'd hidden together with the boy I wanted to marry when we were very young. It was something I should've destroyed decades ago, but kept, like any Talley, in the chimney with Momma's charms. Even though our chimney was so easy to get into that it never could've passed an inspection, getting to what I had hidden inside was still tricky. First, I'd tried to climb up through the fireplace hearth on the second floor, but couldn't reach the place where my boyfriend and I put it decades ago. Finally, I climbed up on the roof thinking I could at least shine the flashlight down and see which old brick we'd crammed it behind.

My name is Joy, not Grace, so like an idiot I dropped my flashlight down the chimney, stumbled, and promptly fell off the roof. I guess it really was a stupid way to look for what seemed to be lost in the chimney, but I was feeling desperate. I was lucky I tied a rope to the chimney for balance, or I might have cracked my head open. And it's a good thing my brothers and sisters showed up when they did, because it wouldn't have been a pretty sight had they shown up a day or two later, me dead and tangled at the end of a rope that oddly resembled a noose, hanging from my momma's chimney.

Anyone else, with the exception of the man who had dumped me for someone else, might wonder why I didn't just leave my secret charm—which wasn't charming at all, I assure you—in the chimney forever; but when that stuck-up lawyer arrived only a few hours after momma died, I knew I couldn't leave it up there anymore.

"LEASE THE TALLEY land?" I asked Mr. Littleton, a skinny, balding lawyer all the way from Tulsa, even though Momma's bank was in Jay, just down the road. "Who would we lease it to?"

"An investor. A farmer. Anyone who will take it," he said. "Someone who might buy it and the house from you if it comes to that."

"But then I couldn't live in it." I glanced at the chimney

and the secret charm seemed to mock me through the bricks.

"Yes," he said, the circles underneath his armpits slowly darkening his yellow shirt. "That's true, but the house will have to come down someday anyway. It cannot stand forever, Mrs. Talley." He spoke like a college-educated man. In most circumstances, I'd have been intimidated, but at the moment, I was too ticked off to be impressed.

"Ms. Talley," I corrected.

"I'm sorry, Ms. Talley." He placed extra emphasis on the Ms., emphasizing my spinster status, as if he knew anything about my love life. Was I that desperate looking? I'd make a point to get my friend Peter to take me out on a date as soon as possible, just to get the town talking about my love life. And Peter's too, for that matter. That would really confuse people, since Peter was a sworn bachelor for life.

Why are single men in their forties bachelors, but women are spinsters?

"Are you a bachelor, Mr. Littleton?"

He cleared his whiney throat. "Yes. But I don't see what that has to do with—"

"Then don't talk to me like I'm just a witless spinster. You and I aren't that different. I'm a bachelor, too. I have a brain."

There was eyebrow raising and throat clearing. "As I was saying, when your mother opened the beauty shop for your sisters, she mortgaged fifty acres of the land, including where the house sits, to help pay for the shop."

I thought of Nanette and Carey, young and wanting their own beauty salon so badly. They called it Momma's Curls, since she was paying.

"Fifty acres isn't much," I said. "We have a thousand."

"Yes, so eventually she mortgaged four hundred and fifty more acres, including the land this house sits on. And then she fell behind on her payments," he continued to explain everything in a tired voice, as if he'd clarified this a hundred times.

"Why didn't she say anything to me?"

"I can't answer that," he said. "But you must understand the house itself has lost its value. It needs significant improvements that, frankly, you aren't going to be able to make on your budget. In fact, it probably needs to be torn down."

You donkey's butt!

He made a show of clearing his throat and sitting up straighter, and for a second I thought—and wished a little bit—that I'd called him that out loud.

"If I might be a bit more personal, Ms. Talley?"

"You aren't already?"

He took off his glasses and rubbed his eyes.

"It would be easier if you sell all thousand acres. You would make a very tidy profit even after you paid off the mortgage." How many men in this part of the county use the word tidy? "I happen to know of some nice places in the country, smaller places that are close to town; perfect for a woman like you."

Perfect for an old maid.

It's true that I was single, but nobody really knew why, except for me. I will give you a hint: It had something to do with what was in the chimney, of course, or why wouldn't I have let well enough alone? Not even my brothers and sisters knew the whole story, and I didn't want them to, either. If the house was sold, someone else might discover more than the name of the one who broke my heart.

In a moment I kind of regretted later, I pulled the plate of chocolate chip cookies from Mr. Littleton's hands and sent the poor man off without an answer. I still remember how disappointed he looked, but I wasn't sure whether it was because he didn't get me to make a deal about the Talley property, or because he didn't get to finish his cookies. My cookies, after all, were famous in Spavinaw Junction, if I do say so myself.

The indignant Mr. Littleton couldn't have known that it wasn't just losing the house I was upset about. The truth of it all tingled along the back of my neck as I ushered Mr. Littleton out the door. I watched him move tersely to his fancy black car and wondered at how he managed to get in, even though he held himself straighter than the stick up his—well, you know.

I had slammed the door behind him and walked over to the fireplace, rested my head against the heavy mantle. Memories of trinkets and old charms taunted me. I'd removed some of them from the mantle when Momma died, because it all made me sad, but I hadn't touched anything inside until that morning. So in a way, it was Mr. Littleton's fault that I had decided to climb into the chimney.

OF COURSE LOOKING back now, I wish I'd not been in such a gosh-darned hurry to get up on the roof, but like all Talleys, I was always pressing my luck. So there I was, flying down the hospital's hallway on a gurney leaving the sniffles of my sisters behind and wishing those girls had just a drop more faith in the possibility I wouldn't die. Thanks to Rory, who mumbled something about bad luck, and River's quiet agreement as they wheeled me away, they now had me worried and bawling in my own head, even though I couldn't actually make any tears.

Momma, I wish I could have one of your teas right about now. Or a magic chocolate. Chocolate was always good medicine.

I hadn't had any of Momma's quieting teas or charmed candies when I felt the gurney move and an unnatural foreboding roll over me like night fog in the hollows near our house, thick and heavy. I got lost in that fog once when I was a little girl. I never even saw Daddy come to me through the murky haze, but I heard him say, "You can breathe now, Joy," just before putting his hands under my sticky armpits and plucking me out of the mist. He knew about my nightmares and that they made me hold my breath when I was scared. I heard Daddy again, there in the hospital.

"Breathe, Joy."

Daddy? I sensed him there, alongside the gurney.

"Breathe."

I'm trying.

I felt awake, as if I should just be able to walk out the swinging doors we'd just rolled through, but my limbs were as lifeless as Nanette's were that time she found Daddy's liquor stash and drank half a bottle of hooch. The lights on the other side of my lids dimmed and I started settling into a sleep that promised to be so deep I couldn't really worry about much else. But then my eyelid was yanked up and a light aimed at my eyeball. A pair of dark eyes peered at me and then my eyelid dropped, but not before I caught a glimpse of a face with a strong jaw and a chiseled cheek.

Gee willikers.

Now, let me tell you one good thing about being single at an age when, let's face it, gravity was not on my side: having time to read as many romance novels as I wanted. The number I've read is my business, but let's just say it was high enough to know that a strong jaw and a chiseled cheek was always attached to a hunk. And the good Lord knows I needed some entertainment after so many years of having been discarded by the only man I'd ever loved.

Momma always said I had an overactive imagination, and maybe almost dying was mixing up my brain signals, but I think the hunky doctor kept me from tumbling into that tunnel I was trying so hard to ignore. Call me shallow, but everyone needs a reason to live.

Chapter Three

NOW, I'VE SEEN enough TV to realize that with the trauma my neck and spine sustained, I probably should've been dead by the time the hunky (based on the strong jaw and chiseled cheek) doctor examined me in the emergency room of the small regional hospital that wasn't exactly known for getting things right—a fact that made me about as comfortable as being wrapped up in a porcupine blanket, if there is such a thing. And I already know that I probably shouldn't have been able to see anything at all, especially romance book heroes, unless I was already on my way up to heaven, and then it should've been the pearly gates. When the doctor lifted my other eye, I saw that he was determined to save me, and that he was a kind soul. I prayed he would see me, see my soul, and know I was in there. The problem was, I couldn't keep that eye open either.

I am so tired.

What with grieving for Momma and planning her funeral, it'd been days since I'd slept at all. Frankly, I needed a nap, but not like this.

Momma.

Had it really only been two days ago when I got home from The Greasy Wheel to find Momma still sitting where I left her that morning beneath the apple tree's magic branches at the edge of the little orchard? It was only the time of day that seemed odd. When I noticed her, she was still in the wooden rocking chair I'd carried out that morning—she refused to sit on anything plastic—with her head bowed down to her chest. Praying?

No. I recognized the same lifeless pose that reminded me of when Daddy died, the way his head had slumped in a simple nod. So, I already knew, even as I started running toward her as she sat in her chair with the breeze tousling her silver curls sprinkled with the white apple blossoms like a tiara, that she was, simply and irreversibly, gone. None of her good luck charms, however magical, could bring her back.

Momma really was gone, and even if all the doctors and nurses in the hospital could wake me out of the stupor I was in, she would still be gone. The truth gathered all the breath I had left and forced it into my throat. The sorrow of it made me want to give up. I didn't know if I could make it without Momma, but when I felt my breath leaving me, I heard my father's voice, the same way I'd heard him through the mist as he'd plucked me up when I was lost.

"Breathe, Joy."

With a petite gasp, I drew it all back into my throat.

LIFE AROUND ME was a series of shadows that passed on the other side of my eyelids. I wasn't sure of the day or time anymore and the pain in my neck throbbed, my head ached, and now a deep burning in my chest tried to pull me out of my dream of Momma. It hurt.

I want Momma.

I heard voices buzzing and a series of loud beeps, but none belonged to Momma. The skin on my head felt too tight, like it might snap, it hurt so much.

So much noise.

The gurney was moving again, this time gliding in slow motion.

"Those idiot Talleys didn't even stabilize her neck during transport."

Are y'all calling my brothers and sisters idiots?

"It'll be a miracle if she doesn't have brain damage."

"If, she comes back at all."

Hey! I'm here, you idiots.

I tried to process their words.

Brain damage?

By all accounts, I'd learn later, I'd been more than a little bit lucky when it came to my fall. I should've been carried into the hospital dead, or at least without all my faculties. I sure shouldn't have been aware of what was going on around me, but I'm here to tell you that I was.

It was like being numb, and even though I tried to lift my hands, I sure couldn't touch anyone back. If so, I might have slapped a couple of them for the way they removed my clothes without even asking me. It was so undignified, and if

I'd had any reflexes, I'd have gagged when they shoved that tube down my throat.

I could hear more of those beeps and other strange noises coming from machines all around me. This all couldn't be good, especially when I needed to help plan Momma's funeral.

And what about my funeral? Who'll plan it?

If I ever—no, when I got out of this situation—I was headed right over to the funeral home to do that plan ahead funeral thing. Just in case.

Wake me up, please.

Another sharp pain in my neck assured me I wasn't dead. I had a deep urge to reach up and rub the pain away.

Wake up. Wake up, my brain screamed to the lazy parts of me, but nothing happened. I continued in that silent screaming and yelling until I finally accepted the cold hard truth.

Nobody could hear me, save for God, and he apparently wasn't listening.

"I wonder how long she can stay like this."

"Don't know."

"Sometimes you have to turn the machine off, don't you?" Was that Carey?

Well, I never.

Silence, except for someone shifting in the chair next to my bed. And the next thing I knew they were making tentative funeral plans. I guess I got my answer.

If I do die, you'll finally get haunted by a ghost, too, Carey. Only my ghost won't be nice, like Daddy's.

Chapter Four

"WE'RE LOSING HER."

Oh no, you aren't. Can't you people hear me?

"Her pulse is dropping."

Please. Don't give up on me.

"She might have lost too much oxygen."

"Is her family still here?"

"Waiting in the lobby. The whole crazy bunch of them."

"Okay, folks." A different voice. One with authority. "This is the ER, not Trapper John, M.D."

There was more poking and prodding at my numb parts, but no more joking around.

Small-time doctors.

"We have a strong pulse, Doc."

"I can see that."

Things were quiet for a long time. I might have been asleep, but the authoritative voice, which I now assumed was the doctor in charge, pulled me back. Was he the one with the strong chiseled jaw? The man who used to love me had a chiseled jaw, too. Long Cherokee hair and caramel skin, but he made his intentions clear when he married someone else.

"My, my. Stubborn woman. She sure is a Talley."

"She's a Talley?"

"Yes," the doctor said. "Her father was famous around here for—"

"—waking up from a heart attack after being medically dead for thirty minutes." The younger man sounded rightly impressed.

"And he was hit by lightning twice when he was a kid. It's the damnedest thing."

"I hear they're all afraid of lightning."

Wouldn't you be, idiot?

"Well, I heard they're all crazy."

For the first time in my life, I was embarrassed of my family. I always liked to think of our family as believing in magic and having faith, but they were talking about us the way I'd heard people talk about hillbillies in Branson.

"Now her pulse is rising too fast."

And then, the same chattering woman shouted from the side of my bed.

"Her eyes! They opened."

They did?

And she was right, so I took the opportunity to peer through the haze. All I could see were a bunch of lights shining in my eyes, so I abruptly, stupidly, shut them. That was a huge mistake. I concentrated very hard on my eyelids, willing the veiny pink shades to lift, begging them, to open again.

"Come on, Joy Talley." It was that bossy nurse with the squeaky voice. "Live."

Clara? My babysitter?

For a moment, I thought I felt them crack just a little, but they sealed themselves tight. And then, just when that nurse had me filled with hope about living, it actually happened.

I felt my heart stop.

I can't describe it very well, and of course not many would believe me, even to this day, but I felt my heart stop, as suddenly as my fall halted with a jerk when I hit the end of that gosh-darned rope. I felt the blood coursing through my body slow and ebb and I knew it, too, was going to stop flowing as abruptly as a river does when the flood gates close.

And all this time, I thought my heart had already stopped when my lover married another girl.

Now, anyone who has a problem with miracles might want to stop listening now, but I heard them, my brothers and sisters, right through the walls of the hospital. It wasn't like in the movies where you leave your body and float around and I wasn't blessed like Daddy was to see heaven. But I died, and I heard them talking about me.

The words of my brothers, sisters, and Reverend Wilson's prayers swirled as loud as the tornado that hopped over our house and slashed its way angrily through the hollows back in 1951. We hadn't had time to get down in the basement, so Daddy herded us all into the large first floor Inglenook hearth of the chimney as dozens of luck charms spilled out of the chimney onto our heads. Momma tried to gather them, but Daddy's voice roared at her.

"To hell with the charms. Get down!"

And then, out of nowhere, I felt something smooth and warm press down on my chest. Death?

No.

Something real: paddles, I guessed, like on TV.

Oh, no. Not those.

The blast rocked my body like an electrocution, or at least what I thought one might be like, but when it relaxed, I started slipping again. My portrait in the stairwell of the Talley house would be young like Daddy's and not that of a wrinkled beloved aunt. I imagined my niece Ruthie saying, "It's a shame all that beauty was wasted. She never even got married." I know that might sound a tad conceited, but it was my dream. And it was true. Someone had thought me beautiful, once, a long time ago.

"Come on, beautiful. Wake up."

Doc must have known some secret about bringing single, forty-something women back from the brink of death. Just call them beautiful and the compliment shoots straight into their broken, dying hearts like cupid's arrow.

Ouch, do you have to do that?

"One more time."

No, please, no more paddles.

I didn't know if I was hallucinating or something else, when I looked up from my hospital bed and saw Daddy standing next to my pillow, a brick in one hand. He lay his free hand on my chest and the pain that reminded me of my nightmares and being sucked into the Spring of Good Luck subsided, but I still couldn't breathe. He lifted his hand to touch my cheek and smiled as he cupped my face. He leaned in close to say something, but I couldn't understand a word. All I could feel and hear was a blast of air. All I can tell you is that the air was there and I inhaled it deep, feeling it rush into my lungs.

Chapter Five

THE ROOM WAS quiet except the whoosh of that fancy breathing machine that I didn't feel like I needed anymore, but they must have had it on to be safe. Thank heavens the paddles were gone, but I could feel the pull of various tubes and things attached to me. My heart sank as I realized I might even have one of those bags sticking out my side.

How undignified that would be.

"Joy."

I heard tapping on the window. In my dream, I opened the window to see my boyfriend, nineteen at the time, tossing pebbles up against my window sill.

"Joy."

The tapping continued until I realized it wasn't pebbles, but rain pitter-pattering on the window pane. I remembered the chimney, the rope, and the hospital. I was still stuck.

"Joy."

It was still my boyfriend's voice that slid into my hospital dream as smoothly as black strap molasses stretching from a spoon in those sweet, rich threads that make a person's mouth water. I'd heard Jimmy's thick, rich molasses voice every Sunday coming from the stage of Hilltop Church as he led the congregation in song; and there's no delicate way to say it, but at times, listening to that voice made my mouth water—like it did now. This was no dream.

So, you came after all, Mayor.

His rich voice hovered in the space between me and wakefulness. I remembered my dream and wondered if he'd been to the chimney since my accident. Maybe he'd come to me because of what he already found in there. But if that were true, then why was he singing to me? Odd occurrences, dreams can be, especially when one is trapped in her body, but I liked the song.

I concentrated on letting the machines fill my lungs, while I allowed his song, something blue and heavy, to wash over me. That same baritone voice encircled my dreams for years, but it hadn't been a dream that our eyes had met every Sunday, once he started leading the singing at church, a gaze held by a memory that couldn't be forgotten, and torn away by the presence of the gold glinting off his wedding band as he lifted his hands to praise God. Every Sunday, it would happen, as our eyes sought each other's and just as quickly end, as if we had never looked at each other at all across the distance of the small church sanctuary. And the distance seemed so wide.

Oh, I know it was a sin, to pine after a man with a ring on his left hand, Spavinaw Junction's mayor and our church worship leader no less, but there was something in both our pasts that tethered our hearts together. Maybe there wasn't love anymore, but there used to be—before he married Fern, because she was pregnant. And even after that, his eyes always found mine each Sunday morning. As much as I hated him, his brief gaze still made my insides churn; and not in an unpleasant way. I've always been a glutton for punishment, so needless to say, I never missed church.

Oh, Lord, save me from that voice.

The low sound of his song swam around my hospital bed, as it did my pew on Sundays. I tried to find his eyes, but mine were glued shut, reminding me that dream or reality, this wasn't church. The soft whirs and whooshes of life-sustaining machines that surrounded me were an odd music to his melody, but gradually they guided me back to the hospital bed in which I lay trapped.

Help me, Jimmy.

I wanted him to see me—I was inside my body.

I'm awake. Don't let them shut me off.

The song washed through my body, reminding me of all we had shared, and then, of how he had walked away, leaving me to deal with the skeleton in the cupboard, so to speak, all by myself.

But then, why would you care, Jimmy?

I tried to discern the words of the sweet song, but the saccharine sound of his voice turned to vinegar as the years of silent rejection engulfed my leaden body in an invisible vice. I tried my hardest to lift a hand, blink an eye, but nothing. A drop of sweat trailed down my temple, but it trickled its way into my hair to hide from anyone who might've seen it as any kind of sign that I might be inside, stressed, worried, and perfectly aware of what was going on around me. I wished I could reach a hand out to Jimmy.

Why are you here?

I was motionless, but not emotionless, and as I fully woke into the present, albeit with eyes tightly shut, the bouquet of antiseptic hospital room met my nostrils. I'd liked the sweet molasses dreams better.

Another whoosh filled my lungs, invigorating me from the inside. I tried to focus on the words of his next song: something not so bluesy that reminded me of the morning sunshine on my face. I strained to open my eyes, to see him, but only my ears were privy to who was in my room.

Do you ever think about it?

My question hung in the air, unheard and unanswered, like it had for years. I'd come to a point once, a long time ago, after he met my eyes in church and then looked away, when I decided he'd moved on, no matter what shared experience drew his eyes to mine on Sunday mornings.

His song found my wondering mind again, so soft and mournful. I let the words flow through my ears and into my heart until they became clear.

Blessed Assurance.

He remembered my favorite hymn, although I wondered if he really felt assurance, or if he was there to make sense of my crawling around on the roof and hanging myself. If anyone knew what I'd been doing around the chimney, it was him.

You know, don't you?

On the day my brothers and sisters found me dangling from that dratted rope, I'd almost been ready to let the sad ending be written. They say the truth will set you free, and maybe that's why I'd climbed up there, to free the truth, even if only for myself, and just look where it got me.

I hadn't figured on falling as part of my plan and I'd only figured a little bit on what he might think of my decision. The current truth was that I didn't know him anymore. Even as tingly as I got when he looked at me, he'd barely looked at me over the years. Only on those sweet Sunday mornings, and the mere fact he'd ignored me and what we shared, the rest of the time—the beautiful and the terrible—had caused me more pain than those few tingles were worth.

I heard a chair screech on the floor and then clunk to a stop next to my bed. The sweet song that had surrounded my hospital bed stopped and silence engulfed the space. Just when I began to think I'd been dreaming again, his voice, un-singing and soft, filled the room.

"Joy."

Darn it.

His voice was molasses. It stretched into me and I felt the back of my nose burn like it always did before tears came. A lump in my chest grew as I remembered what had been done, what we had done to help each other and to hide the truth. We made a promise, foolishly like two teenagers would do. Our desperate efforts seemed a good plan at the time, impulsive and from a place of despair and fear, but logical to us.

I heard a heavy whoosh in the chair and a click of the bedside lamp. I could smell him, oh dear Lord could I—Old Spice aftershave. The room was achingly quiet and the machine that kept me breathing was the only sound in the stillness that stretched on like the years that lay between us, before he'd become the music leader and long before he became the mayor of Spavinaw Junction. It could have been two seconds that passed or it might have been two days. When you're trapped in such a state, it sure is hard to tell.

I focused in on his breathing. It was ragged. So was mine, which surprised me, since the machine was so smooth with its timely, predictable whishes and whooshes. Was I really so excited to see him? I realized I was. Not happy, not sad, but simply excited. A part of me, a big part I admit, felt affirmed that he'd finally come to me; although, he sure had taken his sweet time.

And then, his hand was on mine, squeezing. The gasp trapped in my throat was stolen by the machine.

Oh, that hand!

I could never forget the feel of it. My emotions wouldn't obey. I tried to be cynical and cold, but one moment I was angry at his abandonment of me, and then with only a stroke of my hand I was aching for more touch, and more than making up and being friends. Oh how I longed to squeeze his hand in return, show him I knew he was there, not only so he'd tell my brothers and sisters I was okay, but that I was grateful for his visit.

It was no good. As hard as I tried, my own hand lay in his like a limp fish.

"Joy."

His voice was warm liquid and I wondered if it might bring me out of my body. My heartbeat raced and the incessant beep-beep of the machine echoed it. My breath was still ragged and as a result, I expected the medical staff to come running in at any time.

Without warning, his hand, strong and calloused, left mine and took my heart. Just as suddenly, I felt its warmth, tracing, very gently, along my cheek, over my jawbone and to my collar-bone, where his thumb caressed. I wondered if he could see the flush I felt creep along my skin when I felt his breath across my lips and oh my word, if only I could have puckered up. It might have been a real kiss, a sinful kiss since he still wore his dead wife's wedding band, maybe, but a kiss.

"Sweet Joy." His voice was a soft rumble, and then, in just a feather of a touch, his lips swept mine.

Oh, sweet Jesus.

I felt the warmth of his mouth hover over my cheek for a few seconds and all I could think was that I very badly wanted his lips planted back on my own.

Then again, who did he think he was? I'll tell you who he wasn't! He was no longer the young man who promised me the moon and said informal wedding vows with me in the woods. This was not the man who walked through darkness with me and promised to make everything right again. This was not the man who got baptized beside me in the same waters where we swam together every summer day, and discovered you and me goin' fishing in the dark, years before it would ever become a country song.

I cannot forgive you, if that's what you're after.

I wished he could hear me, this man who'd just stole a kiss from me; this buffoon who left me in the dark with no flashlight to find my way out, figuratively speaking.

I really do hate you, Jimmy Cornsilk.

This was the guy who chose Fern over me, the man who refused to stop wearing a ring even after she died of cancer. I know, I know. That sounds judgmental of me, but you don't know everything yet, and now he thought it was okay to taste my lips while I lay in a hospital bed. Excuse me while I choke on my breathing tube. And if that doesn't make you hate him as much as I do, then you should've been at Fern's funeral when yes, his hollowed brown eyes dared to find mine in the church, while my own sister, Carey, sang *Amazing Grace* over his wife's dead body. Now doesn't that beat all?

I really should hate you, Jimmy.

Of course, I couldn't have stopped the tremors I felt that day at her funeral. Why was he looking at me? Did he blame me for his unhappiness? For the hell he currently found himself in? Or was he blaming me for the out of tune rendition of his favorite hymn wrenching itself from my sister's mouth? I couldn't have stopped her, either. She would sing for anyone who was too nice or desperate to tell her she couldn't carry a tune. That's how things are in small churches. The talent pool is very small.

Naturally, Jimmy's and Fern's daughter, Fernie, twenty-something at the time, had no idea how badly Carey sang or what sordid things lay between Jimmy and I, when she chose music for the funeral. I'm sure she had no idea that her conception was a big bone of contention between her father and I. If she'd been aware, she probably would have banned me, my sister, and my whole darn family from the funeral all together, but all she knew was that she'd lost her beloved mother and that her father couldn't be expected to sing at his own wife's funeral. Carey and I were both once her beloved Sunday School teachers, and so she probably thought the nice thing to do was ask one of us to sing. I'd said no. How could Jimmy have even let her ask?

I do hate you, Jimmy.

Fernie certainly didn't know how much her mother Fern and I disliked each other, all the way up until the last week of her mother's life.

I can't breathe.

And there were his lips, one more time. I wasn't sure if I was dreaming in the hospital again or if his lips were real, but just in case, this time I parted my own and let my breath escape.

Do you feel that?

I don't think he felt it, because after another chaste graze of his lips on my cheek, he put his warm palm on my forehead and brushed back my hair.

Why can't I hate you?

Now that he'd kissed me, if you could call it that, I was done for. Sure, it was only a graze of a kiss and mighty presumptuous on his part, but it was what it was: an indefinable longing of a moment that lay between my hovering consciousness and his pumping heart that warmed mine through his lips.

I couldn't believe the room wasn't a flurry of activity because of my racing pulse, but of course it was only a flurry in my world, somewhere between awake and what—dead? My mind swam back, literally swam—it seemed as I felt a not unpleasant coolness wrap itself around me, through the creek where we used to go together.

At the creek, I had built the confidence to sneak away from my brothers and sisters. The only water I was afraid of was in the Spring of Good Luck, so I wasn't afraid to traipse along the gravel banks and jump into the deep, blue-green water for a dip with hunky Jimmy Cornsilk. It wasn't tropical like the beaches I dreamed of going to someday, but it felt like paradise when I was with him.

"Joy."

Yes?

I heard him whispering beside my hospital bed under his breath, but couldn't make out all his words. Maybe he was praying for me. I was thinking, the good Lord knows I need a good prayer, when he squeezed my hand.

"Joy. I—"

Maybe he was going to say he was sorry. All I wanted, okay, not all, but one thing I'd always longed for from Jimmy was an apology. The following silence was almost too heavy to bear and if I hadn't smelled the cologne that would've sent chills along my arms in a different time and place, I would have thought he left. He was patient, it seemed, and I thought he'd decided not to say anything else.

I was starting to feel faint, wondering when the next whoosh of air might come from the machine, and was close to sliding back into that deep sleep again when he finally spoke.

"Joy. I remember . . . I know why you were up there."

I knew it!

My eyes shot open.

When I saw his beautiful face, his dark eyes flashed, softened, and then he gasped. Tears, real, moist drops that I wasn't sure were my own, filled my eyes just before he disappeared and I felt them run down my temples. My eyes swirled in their sockets, searching, but all I could see were tubes, lights, and the muted ceiling tiles.

Where had he gone?

There was a commotion and more lights shining in my eyes. The cute doctor was there—I don't care if anyone believes me or not—and he smiled, but I hardly cared, since Jimmy had just been there a moment before. The doctor's light was so bright and my lids were so heavy, I strained to keep my lids up. Even the corners of my mouth were heavy.

God knows I tried. I wished I'd had those toothpicks I was always teasing the kids about propping their eye lids open with when they were tired. But no matter, just like the eyes of my sleepy nieces and nephews at bedtime, my eyes eventually shut on their own accord, which by now I knew was not a good thing at all.

Not at all. Who knew when my eyes might open again?

"Her breathing tube is out. The mayor was just visiting her. He said she reached up and tore it away."

I did?

I tried to wiggle my arms, trying to remember moving them. They were as heavy as sandbags.

A plea came from the nurse I had decided was definitely Clara, my childhood babysitter and Momma's friend.

"Joy Talley." She said my name in such a calm, but insistent voice, she sounded like Momma.

Oh Momma. I have something important to tell you about a charm that I should have told you a long, long time ago.

And then, I remembered that Momma was dead.

I SENSED JIMMY had run off, which made me feel like a jilted lover all over again, even though I wasn't his lover anymore.

Not a romantic thing to do, Jimmy.

I heard the scratch of a pencil beside my bed, and the clink of what might have been a clipboard. I smelled lemon drops and heard candy clink against teeth.

"Joy," he said. "When are you coming back to us?"

Ah, Doc. As soon as possible.

I was feeling much better, like I could wake up any day, but how could I tell him? I felt him raise my eyelids and he shined that silly pen light in them. I strained to see him past the glare and in a lucky moment, he switched off the light and peered into my eye. My goodness he really was a looker with brown hair and brown eyes. He looked part Cherokee, like many of the folks in Spavinaw Junction, but he must not have been from my town. For the life of me, I couldn't remember seeing Doc before. He smiled while my eyelid was still up and my heart skipped a beat. His hair looked thick and brown. His eyes were golden and his skin the color of honey, like his voice.

My eyelid dropped.

Oh, Drat.

"You have one hell of a family, Joy." He laughed quietly and I wasn't sure if he meant it as a good thing or not. "Can you believe they tried to talk me into busting you out of here for your mom's funeral?"

It's about time!

"I told them it's very unconventional to take a coma patient out of the hospital, let alone to attend an event. They could get in big trouble."

Do the hospital police have to know?

"I'll tell you one thing," Doc said. "They're very persistent."

Chapter Six

FOR A MINUTE, I thought I'd died and gone to Graceland. I was really ticked off because, as I've always said, I don't like Elvis and didn't want his music at my funeral. It wasn't until I smelled the lavender that I realized I must be at Momma's funeral and not my own.

Y'all busted me out!

I wondered if they'd talked the hospital into letting me out for the funeral, or if they'd just gone ahead and kidnapped me.

"These people are crazy, Clara." Doc's very out of breath voice buzzed around me. "Who does something like this?"

"Like what, kidnapping their comatose sister from the hospital?"

They both chuckled, not sounding alarmed.

"Thank God, we checked in on her, or she'd be here without us."

"I'm getting fired, Clara."

"You'd better not! If they fire you, they'll fire me too." I guessed Clara didn't want to go back to her babysitting days.

Good job, brothers and sisters.

As they discussed how to get me back to the hospital, they poked and prodded, I assume to make sure they wouldn't need a second casket.

"It's too late now, Doc. The funeral's about to start. We might as well go all out and let her stay."

What's happening? Tell me how everything looks.

Nobody heard, so I was relegated to my own ideas about how the funeral my sisters had planned without me was turning out.

"You knew Joy's mom, Clara?"

"Yes. Once upon a time, I knew a lot about Bess Talley that I wished I didn't, but I adored her anyway."

Anyway?

"Full church." Doc's voice confirmed what I would have expected.

"I love all the lavender candles," Clara said. "They smell nice. She would've picked that scent for peace, I think."

My head grew fuzzier as I tried to discern the whispers that rippled over the church.

"One time, Bess made a tea to help me find true love," someone said.

"She had a tea for what ails you. And a chocolate, too."

"She sure did."

Giggles from the back row.

"Remember the tea she made for the principal when Rory got caught kissing girls in the janitor closet?"

A man laughed. "She put hooch in it."

"Lucky for Rory!" another man said. "The principal was so worried about being accused of drunkenness, he forgot all about the punishment."

"For shame," said an older woman, but I thought I heard laughter in her voice.

"Grandma said she was a witch!" That declaration came from a teenage boy and was followed by the sound of a sharp slap and a hiss.

"She loved her family."

"She sure did. Bless her heart."

Yes, God bless Momma.

Sniffles from around the church. Outright crying. A wail here and there, possibly from my sisters. From beside me, someone took my hand. It was large and warm and the scent of Old Spice filled the air.

Jimmy. You came.

Of course he had. He'd probably helped arrange the music. Mayors and music leaders went to all funerals in Spavinaw Junction. It didn't matter who died.

When his hand squeezed mine, I tried to calm my heart palpitations.

"Glad you got here in time, Doc."

"No problem, Mr. Mayor."

"Sometimes her brothers go nuts and do some strange things," he explained and his voice spilled over me. Why would Jimmy be involved at all?

"You mean things like kidnap their sister when she's better off at the hospital?"

"Especially things like that, but they mean well. Like I

said, those boys can be a little nuts sometimes."

"Who you calling nuts?" It was River, the only person able to joke during his own mother's funeral. "The girls were in on it, too. I want that recorded somewhere. I'm proud of 'em."

"I think this is all off the record," Jimmy said.

I heard the clap of their hug, the way men in Spavinaw Junction hugged without touching except for the slap of hands on shoulders. Jimmy offered his condolences to my brothers and sisters, who magically appeared around us.

"Thanks, man." Rory. "And did you take care of the Sheriff? Wouldn't want him trying to arrest us for bringing our sister to a funeral."

In a coma, in a wheelchair.

"Don't worry about him. He won't say a word." With that reassurance, Jimmy was gone and I was left feeling confused about where exactly he fit into anything having to do with me. He'd always been friends with people in my family, but never me; definitely not ever me. He'd kept a very careful distance away from me for more than twenty years.

My heart was swollen. It hurt.

The lavender candles permeated the air and Elvis music filled the church. It almost seemed like Momma might walk in any minute and start singing along. I was surprised, but happy, that the girls remembered how to arrange all of this without my help. I inhaled, thinking it was easier to take large breaths here. Other scents met my nostrils including River's lingering cigarette smoke, Carey's lilac perfume, and

Nanette's favorite honeysuckle lotion. I wanted to wrinkle my nose at Rory who was sweating, a problem he'd always had when he was nervous. I heard my niece Ruthie doing her best to calm several giggling children.

Sweet, Ruthie.

At sixteen, she was always such a help when she wasn't off writing in that diary. I wondered what she had written about this week. Might have made a good story.

I caught a whiff of Aqua Net and couldn't tell if it was on Ruthie or me.

I wonder what I look like.

For all I knew, I could have been sitting in the wheel chair with my tongue lolling out. I didn't remember Carey and Nanette getting me ready, but I was sure they wouldn't have let me out of the hospital without doing something about my hair and makeup. Since I must have slept through the whole ordeal, I guessed at what I might be wearing and hoped it flattered.

Quiet whispers found my ears and I tried to pair familiar voices with the odd mix of fragrances floating about. Besides Aqua Net, lilac, and honeysuckle only one other fragrance really stood out from the others. The scent of lemon drops danced into my nose and I wished I could smile.

I'm glad you're here, Doc.

The scent of lemon drops and a familiar click of candy on teeth made me wish I could smile. It made me think of being a kid. Eating a lemon drop was such an innocent thing to do. If I'd known I might be incapable of eating lemon drops for a whole week, I would have been eating bags and bags of them before my coma.

For a moment, I had a sailing sensation and thought maybe I was swooning over Doc again, but then I realized I was just being pushed in a wheel chair. I heard the wheels squeak on the IV stand as it rolled next to me. I didn't mind the IV too much, but I was sure glad I wasn't using a breathing tube. That was good news, right? I could breathe by myself now, but I still couldn't move or open my eyes, not counting the few times I'd surprised everyone and twitched or blinked back in the hospital.

"Careful, honey," Clara clucked at one of the children.

"I only want to share." It was my niece Hannah, always the helper, at age nine. I felt her patting my shoulder.

"Well, she can't have lemon drops, honey."

Doc must be handing out candy.

A pressure seized my chest for a moment and it took a while before I realized I wasn't trapped, but safely secured to the slightly reclining wheel chair. The chair abruptly lifted and was deposited rather forcefully onto what I expected was the stage where Momma's casket was. I felt the hands of family on me and the faint smell of lemon drops hovering at my back.

"Momma looks good," Carey whispered.

"Why do girls talk about looks during the stupidest times?"

"Cool it, Rory." It was River, taking the lead as always.

"And besides," said Nanette. "Momma does look good."

"I don't want to see her like this." Ruthie sniffled. "I'm

going to sit down."

"Oh, honey," Nanette said. "I fixed her up real nice. She looks just like she's sleeping."

"No," Ruthie choked and I heard her feet pad away from us. Bless her heart. I wished I could help her through this. She had a point, I realized. Maybe it was better to remember Momma alive rather than how she looked in her casket.

Ruthie's footsteps faded and Nanette said, "Momma looks comfortable in her duster."

"That she does." I detected a catch in River's voice and a sniffle in Rory's as he reluctantly agreed.

Carey whispered in my ear. "Joy, we're here, Honey. We're standing by Momma's coffin now."

My heart caught in my throat. I wanted to cry, but of course, my tears only ran on the inside. I tell you what, it was torture to have no outlet, no channel at all to release my sadness as it spun in the center of my chest. I felt like I might fly away right out the steeple of the church if I couldn't cry.

I miss you, Momma. I felt the wheelchair being carried again, presumably down the steps of the stage, and then plunked on the floor of the church. My chair was turned around and I heard the rustling of pantyhose, skirts, and starched pants as everyone shuffled into their pews.

The organ sprang to life and I waited for the whispering to fade, but it kept on. My ears perked up and I heard why people were having a hard time being quiet.

"Would you look at that?"

"Joy Talley. I thought she was in the hospital."

"Why, Bess would turn in her grave."

"Well, she isn't even in the grave yet, so she can't, but it's hard to believe they really took Joy out of the hospital for this."

I recognize your snotty voice, Thelma. Yours too, Mary Sue. I thought you were my friends.

I tried to focus on what was happening with Momma, but the voices riled me up. After all, I did volunteering for Hilltop Church—for free—because I loved Jesus and I loved them. This is the kind of talk that makes people not want to go to church, you busybodies.

"Well you know," said my friend Thelma. "They're Talleys."

And, so we are. And you two are cows.

"Just look at her." I recognized Peter's voice. "Doesn't have any idea where she is. And her hair! Carey needs to get on top of that hairdo. Bless her heart."

Why can't you grab a comb and come over here and fix it for me?

"I do hope she comes out of the coma though," he said. "I miss her strawberry-lemon cake. It's the best."

Okay. At least that was sincere. I do make the best strawberry-lemon cake.

A yank on my arm drew my attention.

Lilacs.

I was pretty sure it was Taryn, who loved to play in Aunt Carey's perfume with her cousin Hannah. She was whispering to me and I strained my ears to hear.

"—looks too tight. Aunt Joy." I felt Taryn's hands under my arms. There were clicks and then she patted my breastbone. "There," she whispered. "Now maybe you can breathe better."

I was suddenly more comfortable. She'd unbuckled the seatbelts on my wheelchair and apparently nobody had noticed.

Well, I'll be darned. Bless you, dear.

"You're going to get in trouble." It sounded like Dawson whispering to her.

"I don't care."

Oh, how I wished I could smile. That child was her mother through and through. It did seem like more air filled my pipes now. I wondered what I looked like. Was my mouth gaping open? Was I pale? If only I could at least smile, so I wouldn't look so bad. I wasn't a beauty queen like Carey had been, Miss Spavinaw Junction herself, but I didn't look half bad when I smiled.

The strains of conversation from Thelma, Mary Sue, and Peter kept drawing my attention. Mary Sue's whisper carried over the others.

"I just love it when she makes that cake. And those lemon tarts are to die for."

"To die for indeed," said Thelma. More chuckles and shushes.

Oh, the nerve of you.

Those three were going to be sorry when I woke up and stopped going to the singles group.

No more strawberry-lemon cake for you!

"We should've asked her for that recipe ages ago," said Mary Sue.

"Nobody has it?" Thelma asked her voice incredulous, as if it were a crime for me to die without leaving the recipe to one of them.

"Of course," said Peter. "I think I could figure out how to make that cake myself."

Thelma and Mary Sue giggled and agreed that he could probably bake just about anything that he wanted to. Mary Sue sounded flirty, which made me laugh inside. If only I could laugh in her face, but I was mostly mad at Peter. He was always my favorite.

You're a snake, Peter. You'll never get my recipe, even when I wake up. And I will wake up.

The organ assaulted my ears. It nearly scared the day-lights out of me and the children both. Nanette and Carey tried to stop the giggling as a short, sad ballad ensued. It reminded me of a haunted house. I wanted no organ music when I died, which I was hopeful would not be soon after all.

"Ladies and gentleman," Reverend Wilson declared with authority and gusto. "It is with deep regret that we gather here today to observe the sad, sad death of one our community's finest citizens, Bess Talley."

My eyes burned with unshed tears as he described Momma as one of the most generous and gracious women he had ever met. When his voice wavered, I thought of his decades-old friendship with my widowed mother, the walks they'd taken, the glasses of herbed iced tea she'd made for him and how he'd drank them with enthusiasm. I thought of the people who'd stopped by the shop to buy her tea concoctions and love potions, saying they were a "touristy" gift for visiting family, but they were always sure to ask her all manner of questions on how to correctly brew the tea, just in case.

Sometimes she'd offer to brew a cup right then and there and then sit and drink it with them. Yes, the kids might have teased us back in high school, and they might tease Ruthie and her brother, Bobby, just a little bit now, but nobody really could've thought Bess Talley an evil witch. She was more of a spreader of goodwill.

"I daresay, everyone loved Bess," Reverend Wilson said, recounting how he'd looked forward to taking her for walks each week, and how some of the girls she'd volunteered to help at The Tulip House for Girls were even at the funeral this day.

Momma, you were so good.

It made my heart ache with sadness.

Soon, my heart sank lower until it seemed to rest like a rock in my belly, causing just the slightest twinge of pain. I could have used some antacid tablets, I thought, and hoped I wouldn't do something embarrassing in my wheelchair, like vomit all over myself.

"But nobody loved her like her own children did."

It's all true. It is. Everyone loved Momma.

I wanted to thank Reverend for being so kind, so I made a mental note. It was the only kind of note I could make just then. "And now, we'll hear one of Bess's most beloved songs."

I braced myself for another Elvis record, knowing it was what Momma wanted for her funeral, but my heart flip-flopped when I heard the rich voice. It wasn't Elvis.

Sweet molasses!

It was my Jimmy, my old lover—I couldn't think of another thing to call him at the moment besides Mayor—and he was singing Elvis' song *In the Garden* at my Momma's funeral. Again, I wondered how he got so involved in my family all of a sudden.

You picked yourself to sing at Momma's funeral?

It aggravated me to no end that my sisters allowed that man to sing. Momma had wanted us to play the Elvis song on the record player. She'd wanted the real Elvis and not someone else singing it, I was sure, even though she'd never really said.

Jimmy's voice immediately shushed the gossiping Peter, Mary Sue, and Thelma, for which I couldn't help but be grateful. To be honest, his voice might have been like a caress over my bruised heart, but I refused to be comforted by the likes of his song. He kissed me in the hospital, when, yesterday? And promptly, ran away! Of course, he'd run away.

Sweet Molasses.

I wished I could take a bigger breath.

This isn't about me. This is about Momma.

I tried to focus on the words and not his rich, resonant voice. Sniffles carried throughout the church, even from Nurse Clara sitting next to me. Carey and Nanette cried and snorted so loudly; Ruthie and Bobby were probably climbing under their pew.

I was sure I felt Jimmy's eyes on me, like on Sunday mornings, even though mine were closed. It made me wish more than ever that I could cry. This was his fault. His fault. Thanks to him, I was alone. Momma was gone to heaven and here he stood on stage butting into my personal life after years—no decades—of ignoring me. What was he trying to do? Rub it in? Absolve his guilt?

We'd once made a pact, after we hid the charm in the chimney, but he broke it.

"IT'S GOING TO be okay," he'd whispered in the attic, as we sat on a quilt just holding each other. I remember looking at the stained glass window and seeing the moon's reflection casting dim, colorful beams around us as we made plans for the future. And for a while, everything was okay, but in a twist that I still found difficult to think about, Jimmy ended up with Fern. He never broke up; he just stopped meeting me, seeing me, or talking to me.

When they got married, he wiped the floor with my heart. He never even explained himself.

The music wrapped around the wheelchair and into my stubborn but very lonely self; its lyrics moving me while the voice that delivered them tugged at the sorrow. Grief for more than just Momma was dredged up from a place where I'd tried to keep it hidden away and the memory of his abandonment weighed heavy on my shoulders. I swear, I slumped down a little in my chair, even though I couldn't move.

I'm pathetic.

I'd wasted over twenty years pining for a married man. And waiting for what? An affair? Friendship? Or just a moment of acknowledgment that he still bore part of the burden of it all with me, so that it wouldn't have been so heavy. For Jimmy, all those stares between the two of us during church might have only been a question: "What did you ever do with that thing we put in the chimney?"

My chest filled with humiliation and fresh grief; sharp pains shot through my stomach. Regret, I figured.

God, please forgive me.

His voice wrapped around my shoulders and I thought about Jimmy's feather of a kiss on my lips in the hospital; but newer, sadder thoughts of life without Momma, no husband or children of my own smothered the alluring feelings his molasses voice usually sent to my heart. The tiniest rumble of anger moved in the pit of my stomach.

Molasses. I should hate the stuff.

A dark feverish cloud spread through my chest. I never liked conflict, but surprisingly, it felt good to really get mad for a change.

How dare you come to my hospital room with a ring still on your finger and put your mouth, as delicious as it was, near my face.

I swear an Oklahoma twister formed inside of me. That's the only thing that could explain what happened next.

How dare you visit me in my heaven-hell of a dream with your kisses, and then dirty up Momma's funeral with your syrupy voice.

You know what the Bible says about hell having no fury like a woman scorned? I think that was a prophetic verse about me.

Your sweet voice tricks me every time I hear it, but not today. Not at my Momma's funeral.

I finally felt the truth deep down in my soul, and for a moment I didn't even notice the wet tear tracing a trail down my cheek.

The nerve of you, Jimmy.

He'd probably only visited me in the hospital to relieve his guilt, the same way Thelma, Mary Sue, and Peter just moments ago tried to pour compliments over their insults to hide their petty motives. And then, I remembered his words to me in the hospital.

"Joy, I know why you were up there." A tear sprung from my other eye and dribbled down to my chin.

My heart thundered and before I knew it I was full-blown crying—on the outside! Fat, embarrassing tears slid down my cheeks at will, and I couldn't wipe them away.

Then I heard Hannah's little voice. "Aunt Joy isn't dead, Mommy. She's crying!"

There was a gasp; an urgent whisper.

"Nanette." It was Carey. "Look!"

"I'm taking her back now." Doc's strong voice sliced through the molasses and into my heart with authority. "This was a terrible idea." Let's get her to the hospital right now, before something happens to her and we all lose our jobs."

The same blood I'd felt pooling when my heart stopped now rushed like Spavinaw Junction Creek after heavy rains through my veins. I felt it tinge my ears red, burning my neck and heating my face in great blotches. And if all the blood rushing around in my ears wasn't enough to make me feel suddenly nauseous, the pinch of the IV and remembering the bag attached to me did it.

I tell you what, I've been hooked up to so many tubes lately, I feel like poor Jenny in *Love Story*. I didn't want to go back in the hospital, no matter how queasy, or weepy, I was starting to feel.

Jimmy's voice wavered, but he kept singing even as the rest of the church's whispers swept over the crowd—like the breeze sweeping through the towering oak trees around the Talley house, their leaves rustling against the truth.

"Auntie Joy." Little Dawson was slapping my leg. I flinched and for once was glad Talley children were such an unruly bunch.

That's it. Wake me up, kids, before Doc takes me back, but be careful where you poke.

The children continued to talk loudly as if a funeral wasn't in procession at all.

"Breathe, Joy."

Daddy? You're here?

"Auntie Joy, wake up!" Now, it was Hannah, whispering too loud and pressing her hand into my stomach that had started to make lots of gurgles and pops.

Not there, sweetie.

There was no way all the little ones knew that when a person is wearing a catheter, it's not a good idea to press their tummies. Thank goodness Nurse Clara told them to stop poking me there.

"You can breathe now, Joy." I turned my head, slightly. I couldn't open my eyes, but I wondered if Daddy was nearby, welcoming Momma to heaven. I wished he would show me.

Hannah patted my arm now and I heard a giggle from Dawson. Someone's thumb raised my eyelid. Dawson's face was almost touching mine, so that I could only see his eyeball. He dropped it and raised the other one. Hannah was peering at me with a smile as their mothers desperately tried to get control. I think Doc and Clara were trying to move the wheelchair, but the children were in the way.

The singing stopped abruptly as the children's voices picked up and I found myself, eyes wide open, looking directly at him.

Jimmy.

Chapter Seven

SALTY TEARS MET my lips and found my tongue. Beside me, Doc and Clara were checking me over, but I was only focused on the stage in front of me.

Yep, I'm awake.

A shallow breath caught in my throat and for a second, I worried I was going back to sleep. I gulped air just as Jimmy dropped the mic to his side, then a few seconds later to the floor. The mic rolled to the edge of the stage where Dawson ran to pick it up. The ornery child spoke into the mic, "Thank you, thank you, very much," and started to sing, but Carey ran to stop him. As all this was happening, my Momma's friend, the poor elderly Reverend Wilson, stood frozen at the side of the stage looking first at Jimmy and then at me with his mouth hanging open. Did the reverend, a man of the cloth, see something moving between me and Jimmy? Did he remember my broken-hearted teenage drama and put two and two together?

Behind Reverend Wilson and Jimmy, there was a mass of daffodils that I briefly wondered over, curious as to how so many of the early flowers could be found in late May.

They were forced in a greenhouse, I supposed, remembering the few that still dotted the grass at the Talley farmhouse, where I'd only just picked one for Momma the morning before she died. I felt gratitude.

You did good, sisters.

Beyond the daffodils, the favorite flower that I shared with Momma, I could see her profile propped on a satin pillow inside the open casket, but my tears for her were mingled with the puzzling emotion I felt about Jimmy. How could he come out of the blue to visit me when I was in a coma?

Maybe you do judge me, Jimmy. And maybe that's easier for you when I can't talk back.

His dark eyes locked on me, wide and searching, and the shock of waking up to his beautiful face weakened my resolve to be mad at him for his years of ignoring me. I felt my knees go weak and was glad to already be sitting down, even if it was in that stupid wheel chair. I tried to conjure the storm again, but couldn't bring myself to hate this man with the silver in his sideburns and the smallest paunch of a belly on his otherwise perfect body.

Oh heavens to Betsy. Why do I always think like this in church?

Each line of crow's feet splaying from the corners of his dark eyes and across tanned, weathered cheeks seemed a record of his own sorrow. The storm in my heart broke up into just a few little dark clouds.

"I remember," he'd said to me in the hospital when he thought I was asleep. His lips had grazed mine, but what had that meant?

People were coughing uncomfortably, whispering about how Jimmy, still standing motionless on the stage had dropped his mic, and about how the Talleys couldn't control their children at their own mother's funeral. With all the havoc, nobody except little Hannah, Reverend Wilson, and Jimmy noticed my eyes open. Jimmy's face didn't change and he didn't say anything, but our eyes locked.

I opened my mouth to say something, but my throat was prickly and dry. I tried to swallow and heard my stomach gurgle. Maybe I was hungry. I wanted to say this to Clara, but I couldn't pry my sleepy eyes away from Jimmy. I wanted to be angry at him, to tell him, to say I didn't care anymore, but my mouth wouldn't cooperate.

Doubt shadowed Jimmy's face, but after a few seconds, he replaced it with a look of resolve. His right hand slowly formed a fist and he brought it up to his chest where he tapped once and then twice before tearing his eyes away from mine and walking off the stage.

I recognized the sign, but what did he mean at that moment? Had anybody else noticed?

Flustered, Reverend Wilson hustled to the front of the stage and tried to get the crowd under control. By then, people had started to notice my open eyes. Strangely, I kept tasting lemon drops, even though my mouth was dry.

"Ladies and gentleman," Reverend Wilson proclaimed. "I believe we've witnessed a miracle in our church today."

A ripple spread through the crowd.

"Joy is awake!" he declared. And after that, the phrase, "Joy is awake!" was repeated through the church, like it was a declaration at the end of a deep and very long sermon.

Doc had the wheelchair in mid-turn just as I stretched my fingers out, reaching my lazy arms as wide as I could.

Stop.

I swallowed. "St-op." Only a whisper. I took a deep breath and said as loudly as I could. "ST-OP."

Doc quit pushing. I leaned forward and sort of rocked myself, until I thought I would be able to stand.

"Joy, no." It was Doc rushing around the chair to stop me, but he noticed the unbuckled belts too late. I felt my body flying through the air and then hit the floor with a thump that almost took my breath away. Thankfully, I hadn't thrown up on myself and it seemed the catheter stayed in place. Still, things inside of my body were starting to churn. My stomach gurgled.

Oh great.

I lay with one side of my face pressed against the floor, drool pooling around my mouth onto the carpet that I knew hadn't been shampooed in six months.

What a way to wake up and show people I'm perfectly sane.

Gasps spread through the room and a few screams from those who were just now realizing I was waking up. There were hallelujahs all around and I swear somebody started speaking in tongues, even though we were Baptists.

As the worried faces and voices of my brothers and sisters filled the space around me, I tried to laugh.

How odd.

Leave it to me to end up looking like the craziest Talley of us all. A guttural sound slipped from my throat and I tried coughing.

Doc spoke to Clara, his voice urgent. "She's choking."

I couldn't breathe. I was terrified to think that after so much work trying to wake up, I'd die from choking. The frantic movements of Doc and Clara were all around me.

"Joy."

Doc was over me, hands on each side of my face. My eyes were open, but I couldn't speak.

"Joy."

Lemon drops.

He reached inside my mouth and with one hooked finger pulled out a lemon drop that we later learned little Dawson had kindly put in my mouth. I had gone without breath too long it seemed, because my eyes and throat closed again.

"—not breathing."

Lemon drops.

Lemon drops were in my mouth again and for a minute I thought I must be falling back into some dream because I'd felt Doc pull the lemon drop out of my mouth.

As a full breath found its way inside my lungs, the fragrance of lemon drops danced into my nose. And that's when I realized, with some embarrassment, Doc's lips were sealed over mine. It wasn't the most romantic way of getting to know him, but it was interesting. I opened my eyes just as he was blowing another breath in. As he pulled away to look at my face, I took several breaths on my own and gave him a small smile.

My voice was scratchy, but I wanted to greet this man who'd saved my life, made me believe I could wake up, and then saved it again. It was more than I could say for Jimmy, who I now refused to look at.

Your eyes are amber, Doc.

"Joy, you're awake." He was out of breath and peering into my eyes, as any doctor would, but I must say, I wasn't unhappy to find his eyes were really as striking as I'd thought back in the hospital.

"I'm Doc."

I smiled wider. "I know."

He looked surprised for a fraction of a second and then leaned in close and whispered. "Welcome back, Joy Talley. I had a feeling you were in there." He smiled, as if we shared a secret the others wouldn't understand, and in some ways, we did. Then, a friendly face of an older woman with tight brown curls leaned in.

"Hello, Joy."

My voice croaked. "Clara."

A memory settled over me as softly as one of my momma's silk handkerchiefs: Clara knitting by the sound of the radio as she watched us kids when Daddy took Momma on trips. She was older, but still had the same sweet face.

Clara and Doc, busy checking me out with his stethoscope, shot each other a brief smile and then one at me. River, Rory, Nanette and Carey were suddenly around me again, saying my name, kissing my cheek. I was so happy to see each of their faces outside of my dream world, but I was distressed about Momma resting in her casket, waiting on us for the time being. My feelings swirled together, but I felt safe when Rory picked me up and deposited me back in the chair, since I wasn't quite strong enough to stand up on my own.

I guessed my spine was fine, but muscles tend to get jiggly after not being used. It had only been a week, but mine weren't that strong to begin with, to be honest, which might be why I'd lost my balance up on Momma's roof. I promised myself I'd get in shape as soon as I could get home and put on a pair of walking shoes.

"Joy, I missed you." Carey's face was in front of mine.

I tried smiling, but then my face scrunched up on its own, filling up with every emotion I'd been holding back for days. I remembered finding Momma dead under the apple tree.

"Momma."

Tears finally washed out my eyes and dripped like rain down my face. Nanette, Carey, and Clara tried to dry them, but there weren't enough tissues that hadn't already been used.

"Time to get you back to the hospital, Joy," Doc said. I didn't want to go back to the hospital, but I wanted something for my tummy. I took a full breath to tell Clara this, and promptly fell forward like a dead duck. My muscles had gone plumb limp lying around and I waited for my face to smash into the floor again, but instead, I fell into Doc, my face buried awkwardly in his shoulder.

For a moment he tried to help me sit upright, but gave up and pulled me into a slight embrace. He patted my back, while I cried and hiccupped like I was hyperventilating, and pretty soon a whole bunch of people in the audience were crying with me.

Our silly tears might have drowned everyone if Doc hadn't gently shushed me until I was breathing normal again. Then, I heard Reverend Wilson shouting.

"Praise be to God!"

Nanette and Carey seemed to be having a contest with Peter, Thelma, and Mary Sue to see who could shout praises the loudest. I'd never heard them shout like that in church on Sunday.

"It's a miracle!" cried Reverend, his arms raised.

Other shouts of praise and waving arms rose up from the crowd.

"Hallelujah!"

A lady in the pew next to us fainted. Some of the same people who'd just been whispering about Momma and witchcraft were now crying and clapping in exaltation. It was all a little much if you asked me.

"We are taking her back," said Doc. I tried to push words through my raw throat that'd had a breathing tube shoved down it for too long, to say I wanted to stay, but my brothers were already blocking his path.

Oh, thank you, brothers.

Rory, my gentle giant of a brother, with Doc's permission, scooped me up and took me to Momma's side. They were all with me, someone pushing the IV stand, and even the kids were there, and, of course, Ruthie, trying to muffle her sniffles. They couldn't seem to stop smiling, despite the fact we were at a funeral.

From my perch in Rory's arms, I gazed down at Momma, her curls soft, her grayish skin brightened a little by her favorite duster with the blue flowers and her thin mouth shaped into the smallest smile.

"I did her hair," Carey said. The boys glared at Carey and some people in the audience tut-tutted, but I couldn't help but smile.

"She looks good. Y'all did real good," I whispered. And they really had.

I stared at Momma for a long time as the Reverend Wilson stepped back to his pulpit and waited. Finally, I was ready to say goodbye to Momma, so I buried my head in the crook of Rory's shoulder, but not before letting my eyes scan the audience to see him once more—Jimmy—watching me.

Are you remembering that day? That night, Jimmy?

Maybe he felt guilty that I'd fallen, and he should have. If not for him, I wouldn't have had to dig through the chimney by myself. Before I could attempt a smile or a glare—I didn't know which to offer him—the good Reverend Wilson's face appeared in front of me, saving me from making a decision right at that moment. He made me want to smile, sometimes when I didn't want to. My sister Carey had the same effect on me.

"Welcome home, Joy!"

I croaked out what was supposed to be, "Glad to be

here," but came out as, "Gad beer."

That's just great, Joy. Now he thinks you want a beer.

Reverend Wilson looked momentarily alarmed, but with a clearing of his throat, he raised his huge, worn Bible and addressed the crowd.

All that attention got my nervous stomach going again. I was starting to think that all the sitting up might've been getting things moving through my system that had become lazy in my coma, what with all those tubes and machines that had been doing all the work.

"This is the strangest funeral I've ever been to!" Reverend smiled and I knew people were smiling back. "And being the old geezer I am, I've been to a whole lot of 'em!"

The crowd chuckled, relieved, I figured, to have a reason to stop whooping and hollering like a bunch of Pentecostals. Not that I have anything against Pentecostals, but after being trapped in my body for so long, I found the excitement exhausting.

"I think Bess would've liked this turn of events." He held his hand out to include me, in all my groggy glory.

"God rest her soul—"

"God rest her," someone in the crowd mumbled.

Out of the corner of my eye, I saw Peter do the Catholic sign of the cross, and I knew he wasn't Catholic at all.

What has gotten into this church?

Whatever it was, I had a feeling it was my fault. The pastor raised his Bible higher over the crowd. I jumped with each staccato of his voice. Reverend had always been kind of like our very own Billy Graham.

"Amen!" Declared someone and a deep chorus of amens went up from the men.

The women were quietly humming, "Mh-hmm." And that's when it happened.

Oh my stars. Not right now. Maybe if I hold my breath—

I closed my eyes, probably looking to the reverend like I was praying.

"Just let those works of darkness blow away in the wind my brothers and sisters!" He bellowed this part at the top of his lungs. "Are y'all with me?"

"Oh God." My scratchy voice was louder than I expected.

"Now, can I get an amen, brothers and sisters?"

More amens.

Reverend paused and I held my breath, hoping with all my might to hold back the whistling sound that trilled up from the seat of my wheelchair.

Oops.

The whistling was quiet at first, but then it sort of whirred through the crowd and then, yes, it really did; it rumbled for a little longer than seemed normal for a lady, which I had absolutely always been.

Oh, heavens.

The church turned deadly silent, unlike my noisy slip of, well, you know. All I can say is that I wanted to disappear, even though my stomach did suddenly feel better. Reverend hadn't said another word.

Say something, please.

The children began to giggle. The reassuring pat on my shoulder from the cute doctor didn't help.

Reverend Wilson looked astonished as he stood with his Bible still outstretched in the air. I smiled, but only because I didn't want to cry. This was worse than falling face first and drooling on the floor. Maybe even worse than falling off the roof, while digging in the chimney. I'd rather be caught streaking through town naked.

"Lord," I whispered, "Please just put me back in my coma."

Reverend Wilson lowered his Bible slowly to his side and sighed—really, really big. He wore a sheepish smile.

"Excuse me, folks!" he exclaimed.

There was a beat of silence. And then laughter surged through the crowd, at which point the Doc spun my wheelchair around and we escaped before it could happen again.

You are a good man, Reverend Wilson.

I waited for the ambulance—or was it just someone's van—to move, but shouts and beating on the door from outside stopped it. Doc swung open the doors and there stood my kidnappers: River, Rory, Carey, and Nanette. They each cast me sympathetic looks and then, burst out laughing. I still wanted to be angry at them for the day they thought about unplugging me, even though they didn't know I knew; but it would have to wait.

Doc winked at me and grabbed a clipboard.

"Do you recognize any of these people?"

"Unfortunately, yes." I pinched my arm until it hurt.

Ouch.

"No chance I'm still in a coma, Doc?"

"No chance."

"Can you put me back in one?"

"Improbable." He gave me a white-toothed smile that I'm sure was meant to be reassuring, and not at all sexy, but I'm telling you it made the whole experience even more awkward than necessary.

Dang.

And that's how I woke up from the most ridiculous of falls, with no mercy and very little dignity left to my name, but I did have a brand-spanking new sense of humor. It's a good thing, too, because the absurdity that invaded my life for the next few months would keep me from doing the one thing I needed to do the most; and it would leave me wondering if the universe was laughing at me, or if I was just the unluckiest Talley who'd ever lived.

Chapter Eight

WAKING UP FROM a coma, since that's what they called it, was sort of like being born again, but without innocence or grace. There were no more beeps or whooshes. The only thing still hooked up to me was the IV. I knew what'd happened and I knew what I needed to do. I wanted so badly to jump out of bed and get on with my life, but my body was lazy and weak. I'm telling you the truth; I didn't plan to ever step foot in that hospital again, not even if my life depended on it, but for the moment, I had no choice. For now, I let myself lay back into the softness of the pillow while my cloudy brain cleared. I didn't dare close my eyes for fear I'd fall back into that lazy-boned stupor.

It hadn't felt like a coma. It'd felt like being trapped in a dream where I could hear everything, but couldn't wake up.

Nobody believed me.

When someone stirred in the chair beside my bed, I turned and stared. I admit my mind was cloudy and I felt sort of confused, until she reached a hand out to me. I grasped it.

"Nanette."

"It's good to see your eyes open, Sis."

"You're real."

"I'm real." Nanette smiled, but when I tried to smile back, my face ached a little.

"Are you in pain?" she asked. "Should I get Doc? A nurse?"

My heart skipped a beat at the mention of Doc and I blushed at the reminder of my secret crush. However immature, it felt good to know someone could make my heart skip, besides the unattainable Jimmy. We could be friends, I'd thought, but of course that was before my unfortunate slip, so to speak. My cheeks flooded with warmth at the humiliation of it all, but what could be done?

"To tell the truth, I would like to get rid of this gosh darn IV. That thing is annoying." I was free of everything, but that one darn tube. Nanette left and returned with a nurse I didn't recognize.

"You feeling okay?" she asked.

"I feel like a limp noodle and my face hurts just a bit, but I'm fine." The nurse made a mark on her clip board, said she couldn't remove the IV yet, and left.

"Sorry," Nanette said. "And your face hurts because you fell on it at Momma's funeral. Do you remember that?"

A small laugh escaped my lips at the memory of my face planted on the church floor.

"Yes. I remember."

Nanette giggled. "Don't be embarrassed. Everyone was so excited to see you wake up they were whooping and hollering like we were at a tent revival instead of a funeral.

You should have seen Thelma! She was crying the loudest."

"I heard her!"

Nanette snorted a laugh. "You did?"

"Yes. And I have news for Thelma and Peter. I heard things they said before I woke up. I'm quitting their group. No more strawberry-lemon cake for them."

She squeezed my hand; I let go before she squeezed it off.

"Joy," she said, and the tone in her voice made my face flush with doubt.

"I did," I said. "I heard lots of stuff."

She looked sad. "Let's talk about it later. You're probably just tired. It's a miracle that you even survived the fall, what with that rope around your neck and—" Her voice trailed off.

"Nanette, that's another thing. I didn't try to kill myself."

"I'm just so happy you're okay. You were lucky."

"Speaking of luck—" I reached for a small length of twine she was holding in her lap. It had beads braided into it and I recognized it as the kind of charm that Momma would've put inside the chimney. "What's this doing here?"

"Ruthie found this charm in the hearth when we checked on the house. A bird nest or something fell out of the chimney and this was in it." I joined her soft laughter. "Momma's silly hidden charms."

I took a deep breath, gathering confidence from the warmth and safety of her smile.

"Speaking of things that are hidden, Sis. I have something I need help with."

"Anything. What do you need? A magic carpet?"

"I did something a long time ago, Nanette."

She gave me a blank look, crinkled her eyebrows.

"Joy, we both know that Carey and I were the wild ones."

I bit my lip.

"What'd you do?" She teased. "Kiss Jimmy under the magic apple tree?"

I gave her the look that only sisters understand.

She giggled. "Wouldn't Fern Cornsilk have been mad if she'd known about that one?"

"Never mind."

"Come on, Joy. Carey and I never really believed you and Jimmy were just friends when we were all kids."

"That has nothing to do with what I'm trying to tell you." My voice, still not used to being used, cracked a little. This brought a look of compassion from Nanette.

"Okay, Sis. What is it?"

"I've lost something and I wondered if you'd help me find it."

She shook her head, still smiling. I could tell she thought I was loopy, and maybe I was.

"There's something I need to get out of the chimney. A charm. That's what I was doing on the roof. Did Ruthie happen to find a flashlight, too? I dropped it down the chimney."

Her eyes grew wide and for a minute I thought we were tracking, but then she frowned. She squeezed my hand and reached out to touch my cheek.

"What were you looking for? I thought you didn't really believe in that luck stuff anymore."

"I don't," I said.

"Good," she said, patting my hand in the same way she would one of our nieces when telling them why they couldn't go see a particular movie, because they had to be grownups first.

"Because there are some people who would think, well, they think—"

"That I'm nuts."

Her smile looked guilty. Some of the happiness I felt about waking up whooshed right out like the air in a punctured inner tube just before you sink into the swirling creek.

Frustrated, I sat up and swung my legs over the side of the bed.

Nanette had her hands on my shoulders trying to get me to sit down. I gently shrugged her off. I was tired of being in bed. I was tired of being asleep. I felt like I'd been asleep for decades, and in a way I had.

I reached down and pulled out the IV. I didn't let on how much it hurt.

Nanette shrieked and grabbed for a paper towel, which she pressed down on my arm to soak up the blood beading on the inside of my wrist.

"Nanette, I want to go home. Now."

Shaking her head, but not arguing, she dug around in her bottomless purse and pulled out a Band-Aid and placed it where the IV tube had been.

I stood up, straight as a soldier, and reached back to make sure I was still wearing my panties. It wouldn't do to be mooning the poor staff in the hallways with a rump that not at all resembled the nice firm bikini-clad bottom from my younger years. I pulled the back of my hospital gown together and walked out of the room where I almost bumped into Ruthie, who stood in front of me holding a Styrofoam cup of coffee and a glazed donut.

"Thank you, my dear." She wore a sheepish smile that told me she'd been eavesdropping. I let go of my gown and took one in each hand.

Nanette, who was part giggling now and part complaining, ran up behind us with her purse in one hand and my pink terry bathrobe draped over the other.

The donut melted in my mouth and tasted like holy manna from heaven. I was suddenly ravenous. I hadn't really eaten in a whole week and one donut didn't seem like enough.

"This is good, Ruthie," I said through a mouthful. "Run and get Aunt Joy another for the ride home."

"Do you think eating that much so soon is a good idea?" asked Nanette. "All that sugar's liable to come right back up."

"Oh, Mom," said Ruthie. "She'll be fine."

The girl was having trouble keeping her grin back. It sure was good to see my niece smiling. She was even prettier than I'd remembered when I was in my coma.

"Well, what are you waiting for?" I asked.

Shyly, she reached out and hugged me very gingerly, so as not to spill my coffee.

"Welcome back, Aunt Joy. I missed you." And with that she ran off and came back with a whole box of glazed donuts that I had a sneaking suspicion might have come from the nurse's break room. I made a mental note to send a dozen, or maybe even a cake, over to the other nurses to replace the box, but in the meantime we had to sneak past the nurses counter. We walked out shoulder to shoulder, me between my niece and sister, as quickly as we could.

Nanette sat behind the steering wheel and started laughing.

"What's so funny?" asked Ruthie.

"This," said Nanette. "This wonderful crazy day."

"Well, we are Talleys," I reminded her.

We all three sat there saying nothing and looking out the window at the overcast sky. The sun had disappeared behind the clouds, but I didn't care. I felt buoyed by the fact I was finally again in control of my body, as much as any cursed human can be.

"Do you want to go straight home," Nanette asked. "Or do you want to see the boys and Carey first?"

"Let's go to Carey's house first."

"Should I run back in and let her know you're coming? She'll have a fit that I didn't call."

"Then they'll catch us, Mom," Ruthie said.

I smiled; feeling a bit wicked after eating so many donuts in such a short period of time. I'd just been so happy to taste real food again. Like Ruthie's innocent beauty, food was even better than I'd remembered during my coma.

Nanette had to repeat herself before I could focus on her instead of the donuts.

"Joy. Do you want me to call Carey and tell her we're coming?"

"No need," I said. "Let's surprise her."

"Aunt Joy, you're my favorite," Ruthie said. "But please don't tell Aunt Carey. I don't want to hurt her feelings."

Oh, shoot.

I wondered if this was a good time to confess to Ruthie that I'd found her diary—and read it—when I'd been going through some of Momma's stuff just before I climbed up to the chimney, but that sweet look on her face made me wait. In fact, I wouldn't tell her at all I decided, feeling smug to know I was the favorite, even if my having been in a coma might have been the reason for Ruthie's announcement.

Sighing, I smiled at Ruthie, promising myself not to read her diary again.

I'm sure going to miss seeing into that girl's heart.

Chapter Nine

AFTER WE PARKED in Carey's driveway, I stepped out of the car, my robe catching in the breeze. I didn't even care if anyone saw my hospital gown. Nanette gave Carey a wobbly smile as Carey appeared on her front porch wearing a light peach sweater. That was Sis, Carey, always pretty and sweet-looking, wearing a sweater even in the summer. Three of my little nieces, Sydney, McKenna, and Jovie clung to her blue-jeaned knees, while she gripped the porch railing for balance.

"Aunt Joy!" The girls ran and wrapped their arms around me. I smothered them with kisses.

"Aunt Joy, why are you in your jammies?"

"You didn't call me, Nanette." Carey jammed her fists into her hips. She was so skinny I wondered if it hurt. "You were supposed to call the rest of us before—"

She paused then, and stared at me, a smile finally playing across her face, before she stepped quickly down the steps to embrace me in a gentle hug. Her eyes were glossy with tears. I knew Carey didn't mean any harm with her bossiness, but it annoyed me.

"What are you still doing in your robe, silly?"

"It was a quick escape from the hospital," I said. "I didn't have time to get dressed."

"So you weren't supposed to leave?" Carey asked, shooting Nanette a look. "Well, at least you're warm. And I'm so glad you're okay, Sis." She clung again, until I gently pushed her away.

"I do still need to breathe."

Carey made a big deal out of helping me up the steps, through the screened door that slapped shut behind us, past the living room littered with toys, and into the big kitchen with the large, green Formica table. Glasses of iced tea were handed out, unsweetened. I added two heaping teaspoons of sugar to mine.

"If you keep looking at me like that, Carey, your eyebrows are going to stick up forever."

I noticed how poor Ruthie looked down at the shiny table top, hiding a smile, I was sure. Carey blinked, but to her credit, she didn't fly off the handle.

"I thought you liked your tea without sugar," she said.

"Yes, well, when a girl has been without sugar for a week, she learns to appreciate it more."

Ruthie and I exchanged a laugh. Carey and Nanette exchanged disapproving looks.

"Don't rush things, Joy." Carey sounded like she was talking to a disobedient child instead of to me. "It can't be good to have so much sugar after being on an IV for a week."

And you need an IV full of the stuff.

"Too late," Nanette said. "She's had a bunch of donuts since leaving the hospital."

"Only four." I lied. Ruthie stifled another giggle. Nanette even laughed that time. Carey, while obviously thrilled that I was no longer in a coma, was a sourpuss for the remainder of the visit. She insisted I put regular clothes on and wouldn't let the children climb all over me, even though that was exactly what I wanted.

"I want to go to The Greasy Wheel. I need to see my brothers, and check on how much of a mess they've made of the books."

"I'll come along," Carey said, herding the kids into her brown and gold station wagon.

"I'll ride with Aunt Joy and Mom," Ruthie said.

As we drove down Main Street, I leaned out the window, waving at everyone I saw. I wish I could've seen Carey's face back there in her station wagon, but when I glanced back, it was hidden by her cat-eye sunglasses. Everyone waved back, of course, because that's the kind of town we live in, so I shouldn't have been surprised when the mayor stepped out of the diner and raised his big, dark hand, and then he made a fist and tapped his chest twice.

I ducked down in the seat, hoping neither Nanette nor Ruthie noticed how short of breath I was all of a sudden. I was relieved when Carey honked behind us. I swiveled to see her laughing and waving us along.

"Mom, Aunt Carey thinks we're not going fast enough," Ruthie said.

"And she's right." I waved out the back window, the

upper part of my arm flapping like a bird. I used to be insecure about that, but hey, now I'm just glad to be alive. What's a little flappy skin?

"Let's get going!"

Ruthie and I rolled our windows down, letting in the breeze.

"Wahoo!" My sisters probably thought I was nuts, but Ruthie popped her head out her window beside me and did the same thing. I don't have words to explain how much I love that girl. Almost like a daughter to me, she made me feel okay that I never had any kids of my own.

"Joy!"

"Aunt Carey's going to be mad," Ruthie yelled.

"That's what I'm hoping for."

I think I annoyed Nanette with my non-stop talking during the entire fifteen minute drive. I had forgotten how stunning the scenery was between Spavinaw Junction and Momma's house and it kept reminding me of things from our childhood.

I pointed out landmarks to Ruthie as we passed by.

"That's the place where Nanette changed her first flat tire."

"There's where your Aunt Carey had her first kiss."

"Oh, isn't that where Daddy always took us fishing, Sis?"

And because Nanette didn't seem to be listening, "And that's where we used to go swimming in our underwear when we skipped school."

"Mom! You swam in your underwear?"

Nanette flicked her hand as if it were nothing at all. "The only boys around were my little brothers."

"All except for that one time."

Nanette gave me a playful slap on the shoulder. "And that one time was the last time. River made sure of it."

"Remember how cute he was, trying to defend our honor?" Nanette smiled despite herself. We laughed, our giggles bouncing out the window with the rocking of the car along the red dirt road. When thunder rumbled and rain started to sprinkle outside, we had to roll up our window, so instead we cranked up the radio and sang country songs slightly off key.

Once at The Greasy Wheel, the girls wrinkled their noses at the smells of oil and whatever other scents made up the odor of automotive parts and broken cars. It reminded me that I had things to do to keep the boys organized and I couldn't help starting a mental list. River and Rory, who'd already given me loads of bear hugs that Carey claimed were bound to squeeze the life out of my frail body, once and for all, were already back to assessing a motor. They looked like two James Deans side by side, only not as young. River even had a pack of cigarettes rolled up in his grease-stained white T-shirt sleeve and one of the cigarettes hanging off his lip. I am not kidding. Sometimes I think my brothers stepped off a movie screen from the fifties.

I couldn't have been more relieved when we finally got home and I shocked Carey and Nanette by getting down on my knees and kissing the floor.

"Eww! Get up." Carey tugged on my elbow and for a

second there I thought she would spit wipe my mouth. I got the giggles after that. You know the kind you get when you're a kid and you're so tired that everything is hilarious?

"Okay, Sis. You're hitting the hay." Nanette took my other elbow and my sisters helped me up the stairs, one on either side, and we left a giggling Ruthie downstairs to sweep the floor.

"I've been sleeping for days," I said.

"Just a little rest," Carey said.

I lay on top of the pink and green quilt Momma had made for me, with the door opened, listening to their idle chatter carrying up from downstairs. The one thing that struck me about their conversation, was how much they talked about my "condition."

Great. They're going to treat me like I'm an old tea cup when I want to go outside and run and shout—as soon as my legs get their strength back.

The other thing I kept hearing them mention was Daddy's ghost.

"And you believe her?" Carey asked.

"I don't see why not," Nanette said. "Everyone else thinks they've seen him."

"Well, I haven't seen him," Carey said. "I think you all are nuts." But I knew she didn't. It was no secret that Daddy never appearing to Carey was one of her biggest hurts.

"She probably imagined it," Nanette said, probably to appease her.

"That and a lot of other things," Carey said, "according

to some of the nurses at the hospital."

I was glad when they finally decided to leave, after telling Ruthie she could stay.

"Call us, if you think Joy needs anything," Carey said.

"Clean up the house for her, too," Nanette said. "Especially get rid of all this dust. That monster of an old chimney makes the whole house dirty."

"It needs a chimney sweep," Carey said.

I heard a throat clear and some uncomfortable silence, in which I could only hear the grandfather clock ticking. I didn't know why Carey even said that. She knew nobody would ever let her clear the charms from the chimney.

After a few seconds passed, the sounds of bustling started up again.

"I can at least sweep out the hearth," Ruthie said.

I listened to the muffled voices, planning to hop out of bed and help Ruthie with the housework as soon as my sisters were gone, but I fell asleep before I heard the door click.

Ruthie's Diary: KEEP OUT!!!!!

Dear Diary:

I can't believe we broke Aunt Joy out of the hospital today! Anyway, I overheard my mom and Aunt Joy talking about this charm thingy that Aunt Joy lost a long time ago and you will never believe this, but I think I know exactly where it is. It's not in the chimney, but in a box, hidden in a secret compartment in the hearth.

Anyway, all you do is push real hard and the heavy iron plate that says Talley twists around and it's filled with what I like to call Talley Treasure, even though it's not worth anything, according to Grandma. It's just a bunch of old charms that only Grandma believed in, some pictures, a big old Bible that says Talley on it, and this weird wooden plaque that says "Talley Luck is Well-Treasured in this Home." I don't know why nobody else knows about the secret compartment, or why Grandma didn't tell Aunt Joy she found her charm and put it in there, but I never told anyone because she told me not to. What makes me think the box is Aunt Joy's were Grandma's words when she showed it to me: "This one's important, Ruthie," she said in this cute voice that made me think of Thelma from Scooby Doo. "Don't open it. She'll come looking for it someday and want to get rid of it, but she needs to be the one."

Well, I think she came looking, Grandma Bess

Ruthie

Chapter Ten

"RIVER, WHERE'S RUTHIE?" I was bleary-eyed from my long nap and having been woken up by a sound that I first mistook for a train. "I have no idea, but I'm gonna spank her bottom when we find her."

The sound grew louder, whining like bent metal in a movie racecar pileup. The crackling radio announcer urged us to head for cover, now.

"I bet she's in the attic. Ruthie!"

River lumbered up the stairs in front of me. The kids had this playroom attached to the attic, the same one we had all played in as kids. It was full of what the kids always called secret hiding places with its shelves of old knick-knacks, built-ins, and a closet connecting to the attic. Ruthie liked to read up there, and, as I knew, write in her diary. I reached the attic just as River swung open one of the low so-called secret doors that led into a storage area. It was where we hid when we were kids, and unbeknownst to Ruthie, where we knew she hid too. She tumbled out, landing at River's dusty boots, her diary landing on the floor beside her. She hastily grabbed it.

"What's that sound?"

The house shook. River scooped her up and set her on her wobbly feet.

"Tornado," I explained, spinning around to run back downstairs.

"Come, now. Basement!" It was the safest place, with its maze of rooms and more hidden spaces. River caught up and grabbed my hand. Ruthie and I followed like ragdolls, flopping around the corner and jerking to a stop at the door to the basement. River fumbled with a skeleton key that he grabbed from a nail behind a picture frame. It wasn't safe down there, and we never let the kids explore. Most people didn't even have full basements in Spavinaw Junction, due to flooding risks, but the Talleys who built our house didn't care about that. They wanted the basement anyway.

Ruthie froze. The girl wasn't budging.

"Quick!"

Later, Ruthie would say I resembled a scarecrow in the wind the way I was flapping my arms around trying to get her to go through the door. Outside, the twister roared.

"River!"

He urged; well, honestly, shoved us into the stairwell. I tripped before finding the spiraling stairs beneath my feet. I grabbed the wall for balance, feeling the bricks of the fireplace beneath my hand. Ruthie landed in a heap on top of me. Her arms found mine and we clung. It was so dark, I didn't even know where to go, but River grabbed my elbow, pulling us deeper into the damp-smelling basement. Eventually, we stopped.

There was a click and dim light stretched around us from a single bulb. River let go of a little chain that dangled in the center of the room and we were in a space about the size of my sewing room. Shelves overflowed with papers and books, old couches swelled with an assortment of pillows and tattered quilts, and yellowed sheets covered furniture I identified by shape and size, all except for a few shapes that gave me more shivers. I hadn't been in there in a while and I was filled with a sense of nostalgia that made me dizzy. I had snuck down there with Jimmy to hide from Momma, but that didn't change the creepy factor.

"We'll be fine back here." River gently pushed Ruthie toward an old straight back chair, his hands on either side of her shoulders. He ordered her to sit, and then tried helping me over to an old couch. I slapped at him.

"Do I look like a child, River?"

"Sort of," he smirked. "You shrunk in that coma."

"Aunt Joy, he's just teasing. Are you okay?"

"I'm fine, honey."

But I didn't feel fine at all. I looked at Ruthie, my young twin only her with brown hair, and knew I probably looked as bad as her. She looked like she'd seen a ghost, a possibility one shouldn't quickly dismiss when it comes to the Talleys. I motioned her to move to the couch and squeezed her to my side, as much to calm my shaky breath as hers. I hated tornadoes.

"Sorry." River cast me a sympathetic look. He placed a kiss on the top of my head and one on top of Ruthie's.

"It's okay," I said. "I'm glad you showed up when you

did."

"Don't be afraid." River sat opposite of us, in an old rocking chair. "No tornado has ever hit the house, but we have to be safe, just in case."

Ruthie nodded. "Where's Mom?"

"Home."

I tried to ease the tension. "Makes me feel sort of like Dorothy!"

River stood and paced. "Man, I hope it goes around us."

"Is it big?" Ruthie asked.

He nodded, stretched his arms wide and swirled them in a circle. "It was cutting across the pasture a couple of miles off, headed this way. The lightning lit it up or I might not have seen. Course, we heard it. You didn't hear it?"

"No. I was too busy I guess." She studied her lap, and for a minute she reminded me of the time she lied to me about who got into the chocolate, even though it was smeared all over her little kindergartner face. I knew she must have been writing in her diary—probably something about a boy.

"I just thought it was a train whistle," Ruthie said.

River fumbled in a drawer and produced a couple of modern looking flashlights that worked. "Momma always had me keep a few supplies down here, just in case."

It was quieter in the basement, which was deeper than most basements. We were silent for a long time, alone with our thoughts, as they say. I stared toward a bookshelf that I knew was a door, another strange thing about our home. Since both Momma and Daddy were gone, I didn't know if we would ever know the complete history of our house, but at least they had shared a little. Now I understood why people say they wish they'd listened to their relatives more before they passed. Momma had so many silly stories. We mostly just humored her. We seldom really listened.

"This house is so weird," Ruthie said. "Have you all ever thought about having someone write an article about it for a magazine?"

"That's not really a Talley thing to do," River said.

"Well, don't you ever wonder why they built it like this?" Ruthie asked.

River shrugged. "Us kids were always kind of embarrassed about it—and all those charms. Didn't want to be made fun of, I reckon."

"There were rumors that outlaws stayed here," I said. This made Ruthie's eyes light up. I was glad for the chance to distract her from the roaring above the house. "There are even rumors that some Talleys were on the wrong side of the law back in the day, but those might have just been stories."

The outlaw story was one that Daddy used to tell, partly to thrill us, partly because some of it was true. He said that when the Talleys built the house, they incorporated enough space downstairs that a person, or whole family, could actually hide for an indefinite period of time. There was even access to a well if one had to hide down there for a long time, and if anyone was brave enough to trust the building skills of the Talleys, who designed this place, a fireplace with its own flue that shared a chimney with the one directly above. Of course, considering the amount of missing mortar in the unlined chimney and the fact the crown on top was missing, you can see why none of us were brave enough to use the fireplaces anymore.

"Momma didn't agree with the outlaw story," I said. "She said the secret rooms and passages downstairs, the spaces in the walls, were accessible due to a fear the Talleys had of being accused of witchcraft."

"Which part do you believe?" she asked.

"I don't know. I like both."

"How come I've never heard those stories?"

"Oh, maybe because, like River said. Us kids were embarrassed when people mentioned it. You know how it is. Parents can be so embarrassing."

She laughed. The talking to distract her seemed to be working.

"By the way, what were you doing, Ruthie, that kept you from realizing there was a tornado out there?"

"I . . . I was . . . just . . ."

There was a huge crash that shook the very foundations of the house. And believe me, I would know, because we were sitting on them. The lights went out.

River grabbed and pulled me into a corner while pulling Ruthie with his free arm. We ducked while dust fell from the ceiling and various things crashed around us in the dark shadows of the basement. The three of us crouched there for a few minutes until the vibrating was gone. Then, everything was quiet again, as if nothing had happened. River clicked his flashlight on. I did the same.

"What was that?" Ruthie and I spoke in unison.

"You girls stay here. I'll be right back."

"Uncle River, no!" Poor Ruthie was scared again.

"It's going to be okay," I told her, but I didn't have the heart to tell her that after what I'd been through lately, I didn't have confidence in everything being okay.

We sat there in the corner, holding hands and unable to see anything beyond the glow of my flashlight, the only sounds were water trickling from somewhere and a scritch-scratch from the next room. According to the minute hand on Ruthie's unicorn-faced wrist watch, it had only been four minutes. The scritch-scratching grew louder.

"Okay, Ruthie. What would Nancy Drew do?"

"Investigate," she said.

Grabbing Ruthie's hand, I pulled her with me a few steps. My knees felt tight.

Scritch-scratch.

A few more.

"River?" My voice bounced back.

Scritch-scratch.

A few more steps and then the scratching grew frantic.

"What is that?" I cocked my head toward the sound. A screech penetrated the room as a ball of fur flew towards us, smacking me in the chest and sticking to my shirt.

"Ouch!" Ignoring the pain, I laughed, digging my fingers into the ball and holding it out, my shirt still sticking to it.

"Lucky!"

I passed him to Ruthie, who hugged him tight, until he

wriggled away and darted through another door.

"Lucky, come back." Ruthie followed.

"Ruthie, wait!" I hurried after her. Heavens knew what could be waiting.

Together we followed Lucky into a hallway. We hesitated outside the orb cast on the floor by our lone flashlight, wondering what unknown horrors lay outside the light's boundaries.

"Where's Uncle River?"

I swung the flashlight beam around, searching the corners and walls until I shined the light on a large hole in the ceiling. I angled the light down until I saw Lucky, his eyes sparkling in the flashlight beam, perched atop a pile of bricks. Ruthie moved to pick him up.

"There you are, you silly kitty."

I grabbed her arm.

"Wait," I said. "We don't know if it's safe to barge over there."

Lucky disappeared up through the hole in the ceiling. That's when I noticed the dust hanging in the room around us, the particles glowing in the light.

"Oh my gosh!"

I turned to Ruthie, who was as frozen as the mannequins on display at JC Penney. Not that we had JC Penney in Spavinaw Junction, but I liked to take Ruthie there when we went over the Oklahoma state line to shop in Siloam Springs, Arkansas. My eyes traveled back to the hole in the ceiling, just as a brick fell through it. The chimney had collapsed into the basement, while the house stood still. It seemed a miracle.

Goosebumps raised along my forearms.

We ducked as a shower of dust that billowed into the air around us and then hung there, luminous.

"River?" I coughed out, the dust thick in the back of my throat, but the only response was my voice echoing off the brick walls around us. I moved forward, stepping gingerly toward the pile.

What if River was in that pile?

"Aunt Joy, wait." But I'd already stopped at the edge of the rubble.

"Joy?" River's voice carried to us from somewhere in the basement. Thank God.

"River?"

"Stay right there," he said. "I'm coming."

I surveyed the pile in front of me, calmer now that I knew River was okay.

"Look at all this stuff," Ruthie said.

"Oh. My. Holy. Word. Momma would be so upset."

Before us mixed in the heap of mess before us was not only a pile of bricks, but in the pockets between the bricks and strewn on the floor around us were oodles and oodles of Talley luck charms, undoubtedly placed in the chimney by our dead ancestors: knotted ropes, tiny wooden carvings, little books splayed open, their spines split, blue and green colored stones, animal bones, feathers, and all sorts of talismen attached to lengths of cracked, rotting leather. I think my heart skipped about eleven beats. I don't know if it's medically possible, but I swear, my heart stopped beating and then, I panicked.

"My charm." Jimmy and I had made the charm to protect us. Now, it was in this mixed up rubble somewhere.

"Aunt Joy?" Ruthie lay her hand on my forearm. "You okay?"

"I'm fine." And I was; just surprised. It's not that I thought that silly charm could really keep someone out of jail, although come to think of it, maybe it had.

I didn't turn away from the pile as River ran in, his feet padding heavily behind us and sliding to a stop, not unlike Fred in Scooby Doo, his flashlight beam sweeping around the room.

"Holy cow."

He let out a long whistle and moved closer to the crumbled chimney.

"Now I'll never find it." I hadn't meant to say it out loud.

"Find what?" River.

I shook my head. "Never mind. Can we get out of here now?" I just wanted to get away.

Chapter Eleven

IT WAS UNBELIEVABLE how the chimney had collapsed, almost as if it was on purpose.

In the daylight that streamed through the main floor windows, I gazed up at the rip in the ceiling and stepped closer to the gaping hole in the floor, pressing against the arm Rory put in front of me.

"Careful."

The dust had settled and the debris cleared, exposing the gaping hole where the fireplace used to be like a wound in the middle of the house. My stomach swirled a little. I didn't know if I was relieved to know the charm would be hidden for good, or disappointed. Somehow, always having it hidden in the chimney within arm's reach had been comforting. It was as if I had control over the decision. Now, nobody did.

"It's such a shame," I said. "So many years of keepsakes placed in here by so many people."

"We're calling Momma's charms keepsakes now?" Rory asked. "I'm glad they're gone. They probably weren't even lucky."

"Are you sure?" River teased. "Why didn't the tornado take out the whole house instead of spreading those charms all over the place? They're everywhere. I even saw some of them hanging on the roof of the barn."

"Strange," Rory agreed. The boys shook their heads in unison. I swear, sometimes they are just like twins.

"I've seen some tornado damage in these here parts," River said. "But never seen it shove a chimney down into the ground and leave the house still standing. Usually, it's the other way around—a chimney without a house." He indicated the holes in the living room floor and ceiling. "Know how much that's all gonna cost?"

I frowned. "More than we have, that's for sure. Blasted luck charms. See? Not lucky at all."

Reaching for a board sticking out of the bit of rubble that was left, I held up an ancient looking wooden sign.

"Where'd this come from?" I'd never seen it before, and I'd done my share of exploring the things propped on the lower shelves of the chimney.

"Must've been way up in the chimney," River said.

"Talley Luck is Well-Treasured in this Home." Rory raised his eyebrows as he read.

I ran my hand over its carved surface. It looked ancient. "I wonder why Momma never hung this up."

"Probably didn't know about it."

"Or because it was ugly."

"We'll save it; put it on the mantle of the new chimney," Rory said. "It's like that word. Iconic?"

"Ironic, you dingle-berry." River punched Rory's arm.

I smiled. "It'll be our little joke."

Ruthie, always helpful, began collecting the papers and clutter, but I grabbed her hand and pulled her to my side.

"Let's wait until the Uncles say it's safe to walk around here. Let's sit in the kitchen."

Ruthie smiled, the stack of papers and pages in her hands momentarily forgotten. I reached out for them and set them on a dusty side table. We sat opposite the wide kitchen window at Momma's heavy, painted farm table. I ran my hand across the paint that had been rubbed away over the years, glad the tornado had not taken it, too, or the grandfather clock, or any of the things that were really Momma.

Just the charms that only she cared about.

I was about to survey the damage in the orchard.

"Jimmy." There he stood in the doorway, right in front of me. I could smell his Old Spice cologne and the morning's coffee still on his breath. Those darn butterflies stirred inside my chest. How could I feel like this just after a near disaster? I touched my hair. It felt chalky. I must have looked like a mess.

"The town's fine, but we're going house to house out this way to check on people. Phones are out."

"Oh." That was right. He was the mayor. He was just doing his job, not stopping by to check on me—or the charm.

"Are you okay?" he asked.

I nodded that I was. Told him who was in the house and promised to have River call as soon as the phones were up.

"Thanks, Mr. Mayor." I wondered if I sounded sarcastic like I hoped. I reached for the doorknob, but before I could pull it shut, his eyes fell on the mess in our living room. Without being invited in, he stepped around me into the house. His troubled gaze rested on the hole in the floor and up to the ceiling.

I didn't explain; didn't have to.

"Any more damage?"

No, Jimmy. I never found it.

"River's checking it out. Rory's helping."

"Let me know. I'm happy to help when they get ready to rebuild it. Until River has the house inspected, you and Ruthie probably shouldn't be inside the house."

He stood there.

"Oh, you mean, now?"

He nodded. I called for Ruthie and we inched out on the porch; we sat in the rocking chairs, avoiding the swing, which would have caused way too much movement for my taste at the moment. When we were settled, Jimmy nodded and then disappeared into his big black truck as if I was just any citizen of Spavinaw Junction, who had just survived a tornado.

I suddenly felt exhausted and for a minute I regretted pulling my IV out and sneaking out of the hospital.

River walked out on the porch and I told him the town was fine. "Do you think everyone at the hospital was okay? I forgot to ask Jimmy." I thought of Doc and Clara, and all those who had watched out for me during my coma.

"I'm sure they are, or he would have said."

Gravel crunched. Two cars pulled into the drive as Jimmy's truck drove out.

"Mom!" Ruthie cried, and her teenage self morphed into a little girl as she ran to meet them. Car doors burst open and out piled Nanette, Carey, Rory's wife Faith, and all their kids, which basically would fill up that little school in Little House on the Prairie.

I held my arms open, while the kids piled over me and my siblings made over me, telling me how happy they were we were all okay, how nobody could have guessed my homecoming would be like this.

Chapter Twelve

IT TURNS OUT that River was right about Doc and Clara being fine.

"How'd you manage to get out of the house?" Donna asked when I stopped at her store, aptly named Miss Donna's after her mother, and now her. She handed me a can of the new Diet Coca-Cola. "Carey makes it sound like you are still too fragile to leave."

"The boys sent me to get something at The Greasy Wheel. I decided to take a detour and escape." The bell dinged.

"Joy Talley," Doc said. "I didn't expect to see you here." My breath caught in my throat. His eyes traveled over my yellow sundress dress and back up to my face.

"You look—so different than when I saw you last."

I smiled, hoping my face wasn't as red as I suspected. I could have told him he looked different, too, all dressed down in his Levi's.

"I hope that's a good thing."

He shook his head. "Yeah. It's a good thing. Not that you looked bad last time I saw you. It's just that now . . ."

"Now, I'm not wearing a hospital gown."

"Where you headed?" he asked. "Can I walk with you?"

Next thing I knew, we were walking toward the parking lot at the edge of town, which isn't a very long walk, unless you've recently been immobile for an entire week. Doc slowed his steps for me and I was surprised at how easy he was to talk to, once you got past the heart throb part of him.

"Hey, uh." He ran a hand along the back of his head, like he was considering if he should say something. "You wanna, maybe, meet me for a cup of coffee some time? Maybe a Coke?"

"Is that allowed?"

"Why not?" he asked. "I'd like to talk to you more."

"I mean, because you were my doctor."

"True," he said, like this was a big dilemma. "Of course, I was your doctor in the ER. Now you go to someone else, right?"

"Dr. Duncan."

"Right," he said, a smile tugging at the corner of his lips.

So, when he asked, I gave Doc my home phone number, which I don't think I'd ever given to anyone. Certainly not to Jimmy. Of course, Jimmy already knew it, but he had never called, now, had he?

WHEN I THOUGHT about it later, I decided that Doc was just being nice. Why else would he want to have coffee with me? I didn't know how long you were supposed to wait on a phone call from a man before giving up, so after one day, I forgot about it. Besides, I had things to do.

You might think that after being in a coma for only a week, a person might be too exhausted to do anything at all, but then you don't know me. I started my engine back up the day after the tornado, taking the little kids fishing at Spavinaw Junction Creek, scrubbing the dust off the floors, planting summer flowers, and pruning away the dead branches left in the tornado's wake in the orchard. I was so glad the trees had not been destroyed. The orchard, if you could call it that since it was so small, had always been special to Momma, and to our whole family, all the way back to great and great-great grandparents I'd never even met.

While we kids didn't like repeating Momma's stories, she never let us forget that our special, if not actually remarkable, history wasn't limited to the house with its creepy chimney. Outside, the fruit trees sprawled along the north side of the house encircling our ancient magic apple tree that, magic or not, I'd always imagined concealed more Talley secrets and love affairs from days gone by. Jimmy had kissed me beneath that apple tree.

When Momma thought Jimmy was too wild for me, he would hide in the tree and I'd climb up to meet him. We even joked that since it was magical, it would hide us from her. And maybe it had. Who knows? Sometimes Momma had even cut the branches in full bloom and sold them at Miss Donna's store in town. People bought them for good luck. Those kinds of things, the tree, the teas, the chocolate—those were the good things. We might not have thought they really worked, but they didn't embarrass us. Who doesn't need that kind of magic in their lives?

We weren't sure how old that tree was, but the stories passed down told that it was there when our people first built the house—like Lucky the first, second, or third, we didn't know—and surprised everyone by living for so many decades. Its branches were easy to scale with its numerous arms reaching out like an old grandmother welcoming us to her bosom. Which is exactly why, if I'd been planning to die, I would've definitely used the magic apple tree to hang myself, or even jumped off one of its branches into the orchard well, ancient itself by any account and unused.

Who knew how deep that well really was? Daddy always said it tapped into the spring water from above and we had proof that the well opened into a honeycomb of caves. Some geologists once asked if they could explore them, but when one of the men drowned and they liked to never have gotten him out of the crevice he was wedged in, nobody asked to explore it again. If I'd have jumped in there to kill myself, maybe I would've disappeared into its bowels forever like in my nightmares—but never mind that.

"The point is," I told Bobby and Ruthie, "Is that I didn't try to kill myself, no matter what people say. So whatever you hear, don't believe it."

"We know that, Aunt Joy." Ruthie's face turned pink. "But I don't know what the aunts and uncles think."

"Yes, you do," Bobby said. He smiled, looking for all the world like a teenage version of my dad. "They think you're nuts."

"Bobby!" Ruthie said. She slapped at him.

"Now, you two; stop that!"

Nuts? Carey, you are such a drama queen!

"I didn't mean to be rude, Aunt Joy," Bobby said. "But, I heard them talking and they think that rope cut off your blood flow to your brain. That's why you had all those dreams and thought you heard everyone talking during your coma."

"But Doc said her brain is fine," Ruthie said. "All those specialists from Tulsa looked at her."

"It's crazy Aunt Carey you have to worry about. She's the one who really thinks you've gone off your rocker."

"It's okay," I said. "Aunt Carey is just stressed, and sometimes when she gets mad she says things she doesn't mean."

What could I expect from Carey anyway? She was our very own queen of crazy. Oftentimes, the only person who could calm down her excitable nature was Reverend Wilson. He had a calming effect on everyone, but it seemed to go right to Carey's core faster than with the rest of us. Thank God for him, because not even Momma could calm her down when she makes a fuss. I wondered what Carey would think if she could have heard Momma all the times she'd told me, "Don't mind her, Joy. She's nuts."

Momma.

I thought about when I'd settled her into the chair the morning before she died. She asked me to pick one of the daffodils, late blooming that spring. Later, I would think the daffodils came late, just so that one could bloom on that day. They were her favorite flower, and mine too, so I'd plucked one from a sunshine-dappled spot in the orchard and held it out for inspection. She took it and gave me a contemplative smile. I'll always wonder what she was thinking about, but I hadn't asked. I'd smiled back, making sure she had her blue, crocheted lap quilt and her walking stick, in case Reverend Wilson dropped by to take her for a walk, and planted a kiss on her forehead. A kiss goodbye, it turned out.

Chapter Thirteen

ONE OF THE things I missed most, when I was in my coma, was cake. Strawberry-lemon, of course—chocolate, carrot, you name it, I wanted it. So, during the weeks after my coma, I cooked up a storm. Baking was my thing. And we're not just talking cupcakes, although I made my share of those. We're talking oodles of five-layer cakes with fresh flowers on top, French-looking pastries with Momma's secret frosting, and even donuts, which Miss Donna's shop bought to sell at her place in town every Monday morning at 5:30 am. One day, when Ruthie and I were right in the middle of baking a devil's food chocolate cake, I heard a dog yapping.

But we don't have a dog.

We rushed out to the front porch to see Jimmy—looking hunky in his boots and Wranglers as usual, which was beside the point, but true—with the most adorable puppy I'd ever seen.

"What made you think we needed a puppy?" I asked the mayor quietly after Ruthie took the dog into the orchard to play. What I was really thinking, was why would *he* bring *me* a puppy?

How am I going to keep from falling back in love with you, Jimmy?

But of course, I already was. He made it so hard to be angry. We still had the past to deal with, but sometimes I wondered. Did we have to deal with it at all? Was it possible that the past could just stay buried in the rubble of the tornado?

"He needed a home. You needed a friend. So, I checked with your brothers and they said to bring him out."

He was standing close enough that his sleeve brushed my bare arm, sending a shiver up behind my neck. I reached back and rubbed, a habit that I'd developed since the accident.

The mayor had turned to leave.

"Jimmy." He turned back expectantly. "Um, do you have time for some iced tea?"

Was that a sparkle in his eyes?

I felt stiff and unsure as we walked up the porch steps, and even more awkward as we sipped our tea in silence, watching the kids play with the new puppy. Bobby had come out of the house and was helping Ruthie name it.

"What are we going to call him," Ruthie asked.

"Mutt. Let's call him Mutt," Bobby suggested. "Come here, Mutt!" And wouldn't you know it, the little mutt ran straight to him. But Ruthie was right. We couldn't call him Mutt.

"Come here little fella," Bobby said, but the puppy ran past and stopped to pee on the fresh dirt where we'd planted a daffodil bulb. They laughed as he ran to the next and peed there too.

"Let's call him Daffy," Ruthie said.

"Why?" Bobby gave her the 'you're crazy' look.

"Short for Daffodil. Since he keeps peeing on them."

I sighed, thinking that Daffy was more entertaining than his giver, who sat beside me, stiff and quiet for a while, before handing me his empty glass, nodding, and climbing into his truck.

Sometimes, when I was mad at Jimmy for his aloofness, I found myself wondering how Doc was doing. I thought about going to the hospital to see him when I drove past one day, but realized that was ridiculous and weird. He hadn't called. Still, I thought of him sometimes. How could I not? He had saved my life.

IN THE MIDDLE of all the gardening and cooking, I had to constantly clean up after Daffy, as well as after River and Rory, who were busy every day spreading mortar and stacking bricks to rebuild the chimney. Everyone agreed that we still wanted an Inglenook hearth, because of its openness, and the boys agreed to build a few shelves inside to honor the past, but in the future, we wouldn't hide charms inside the chimney. This one would meet building codes and be fully functional.

All of the ancient charms had been hauled away to the dump in buckets, or swept into a corner to sift through later. I rummaged through that mess several times dusting a few special things off and wrapping them in tissue to be stored away, but of course, I came up empty-handed when it came to what I really was looking for. It appeared that it really was gone.

There was a knock one afternoon and I looked up to see Jimmy at the door.

I attempted to smooth the frizzy strands of hair sticking out of my pony tail. Why did he always show up without warning?

He stood in the doorway for a moment, then touched my shoulder before moving past to talk to my brothers. I wondered if he had any idea how just a touch on my shoulder like that made me feel.

"Thanks," I heard the boys telling him. "We're good, but thanks for the offer."

"There's some tea in the fridge though. Joy won't you pour him a glass?"

I wasn't sure what my brothers were up to, but all I could do was pour him his glass of tea and invite him to sit out on the porch like before.

Out on the swing, we sat side by side, our thighs touching because Jimmy's frame was so big he took up over half the swing. The heat from his leg touching mine made my hands shake, causing the ice to clink against the sides of my glass.

Oh, heavens.

There are so many things I wanted to say, but I wanted him to speak first. I felt like he had a lot to explain and I refused to make it easy on him.

Why are you here?

I didn't know if he was there as the mayor, the music leader from church, or just Jimmy. And if he was there as Jimmy, which Jimmy was it? My old lover? Or the widower who wouldn't take off his wedding ring? And he wouldn't talk!

Maybe he's waiting to see if I found the charm.

I reached for his empty glass, but instead, he took mine and set them both on the floor of the porch. Then he took my trembling hands in his, rubbed them until they stopped shaking. When he pulled me to my feet, my knees went all wobbly, but he very gently wrapped his arm around my waist. I did not dare look up, but I couldn't bring myself to pull away when he placed his hand on my cheek. I closed my eyes and let him pull me gently to his chest.

Oh, Lordy.

If he had tried to kiss me just then, I wouldn't have stopped it. I half-hoped he would, half wouldn't. I longed to feel his lips on mine, to feel the warmth I used to know so well, and yet I was still pretty mad at him for marrying Fern. When he leaned down and kissed the top of my head, I felt like a child who had just been offered a cookie and then someone stole it from me.

What was I thinking? That he would really kiss me?

I wriggled from his arms and moved to pick up the empty drinking glasses. I refused to turn around, but when he leaned down and kissed the top of my head one last time, I had to fight the urge to spin around and throw my arms around his neck. His lips pressed into my hair, lingered, and

I tried to remember what kind of shampoo I'd used that morning. Lilac-scented?

It's too bad he doesn't have any idea what flavor of lip gloss I was wearing.

I leaned back into his chest for the briefest moment before he let go of my shoulders. I listened to his boots clop down the steps before he slammed the car door and started the engine.

Ruthie's Diary

Dear Diary,

It has been hard to keep up with Aunt Joy since she woke up. She's exhausting me—a teenaged girl! It's like she's a teenager again, too, but I'm not complaining. Aunt Joy is my favorite aunt and she's going to be happy when I let her know about the box. Thank goodness it was in the attic with this diary and not in the chimney, although I can tell she thinks it was destroyed in the Tornado. I can't hardly wait to tell her, but I decided I can't give it to her yet.

I don't agree with my mom and Aunt Carey that Aunt Joy went a little nuts while she was in her coma. Why is it such a big deal that she claims to have heard us while she was in the hospital? And I certainly can't figure out why her claims to have seen our Grandpa are a bad thing. All the brothers and sisters have seen his ghost except Aunt Carey, and it's never been a bad thing before now. But if Mom and Aunt Carey are right and Aunt Joy really is unstable, I don't want to stress her out. Aunt Carey says I'm a teenager and that she can't expect me to understand (rolling my eyes to the heavens here), but that Aunt Joy's fragile and we aren't supposed to give her any bad news or trouble. So the question is, would my giving her the box from the chimney be good news or bad?

Ruthie

Chapter Fourteen

I KNEW RUTHIE was hiding in the tree the day the mayor took me into his arms. I hated for her to see. Not that we were doing anything wrong, of course, but I knew Ruthie and that her mind would be filled with all kinds of romantic notions. Her favorite book was *The Outsiders*, but I knew she liked it mostly because she imagined the boys were attractive. What she read most were romance novels, like I always had, and still do. My favorites were set on the beach, which is where I had always wanted to take my honeymoon.

I knew all about the stacks of novels Ruthie hid in the same place as her diary. I'm guessing she thought if she hid them at the farmhouse, her mom wouldn't find out. And she was right. I kept mine stuck beneath the mattresses and the bed frame when I was a kid, since Momma thought they were bad, but Ruthie was more creative. Of course, it was impossible to beat Aunt Joy at her own game. I never told on Ruthie, because who can blame her for wanting to be in love? And more importantly, wanting someone to love her back. I understood that feeling all too well.

When Jimmy had kissed the top of my head, I grew

weak in the knees wishing he might love me back the way I'd always hoped, but then I found my dignity. Who did he think he was touching me after all that time? As if jilting me all those years ago for reasons I wouldn't want Ruthie to know about wasn't enough, he had been a widower for five years. To me, that spoke as loud as the cheerleaders screaming at homecoming. The looks of regret I thought I'd seen on his young face as he sat beside his pregnant teen girlfriend, Fern, must have been fake. Or else, I misread the gesture. If he hadn't spoken to me before now, even after Fern had been gone for five years, God Bless her soul, then he had loved her. Funny, how I never thought of that before my coma. I was so stuck in the past, in my hurt and longing for all I'd lost, I never grew up on the inside. Now, things were in reverse. I felt like a teenager again, but where Jimmy was concerned, I was finally a woman. I had to let go of the past, no matter how much his touch made me tremble.

"Aunt Joy?"

I looked up to see Ruthie standing in front of me at the bottom of the porch steps. I hadn't even noticed her, since I'd been lost in thought, as I had a cup of morning joe.

"Ruthie. Where'd you come from?"

"I walked from The Greasy Wheel. Mom's there."

"All that way?" I remembered those days when I was a kid. Momma hadn't thought girls needed to drive, but we had anyway.

Ruthie followed me inside the house and to the kitchen table. What I didn't say out loud was that I knew Ruthie was bored and she needed something to do. She had no idea

I saw her spying on me and the Mayor multiple times, which meant she was bored. Maybe if she had some errands to run, she might not be so inclined to being sneaky. I chuckled to myself. I remember spying a few times myself when I was a kid, such as when I saw Nanette kissing a boy under the magic apple tree. It wasn't my fault I was sitting up in its branches. Ruthie had discovered my same hiding spot.

"I'm teaching you how to drive."

"You're teaching me to drive?"

"Yep, as soon as your uncles get the old Chevy started."

I knew she wanted to drive the cherry red car that had been sitting in the driveway for too long, but she was too afraid to ask. She was a fast learner and once she had her license, she drove it back and forth to town for all sorts of trivial things that I needed, like salt, lemons, and rutabaga, a vegetable I threw in just to see if she was listening.

I sure loved that girl, but she was at my side every single moment, and while I enjoyed her company, I didn't think it was good for her to hang out with a spinster like me. She should have been off finding herself a boyfriend. Long before Jimmy jilted me, I at least had a romance. Even if mine ended up a tragedy, every girl should at least get to experience the sweet part. Ruthie needed that.

Truth be told, I needed that. A second go around would have been nice.

NOT LONG AFTER Ruthie had gotten her license, I sent her off to town for a made up errand, I think it was shampoo that time, and I started pruning the magic apple tree. It seemed to be blooming late this year, and I was grateful. I thought it would be fun to decorate the kitchen with the branches, plus it needed pruning anyway. If there was one thing I wanted to do for Momma, it was to take care of the tree she loved to sit under, and that held so much meaning.

After I'd cut several branches, I climbed down from my ladder and plunged the branches into a galvanized bucket of water.

Maybe I could sell these branches at Miss Donna's, like Momma used to. Or, at the beauty shop.

When I was about twelve, I asked Momma if the apple tree was really good luck.

"Yes. It is a tree with a special kind of magic."

"What kind of magic does it have?"

"Love magic," Momma said.

The idea of finding love beneath the apple tree's branches had made the butterflies inside my adolescent self quicken their flutters. Much like they did the afternoon that Jimmy had pulled me into the safety of his arms. That was the moment I'd realized Ruthie was hiding in the apple tree. I'd heard her sharp intake of breath, sounded like a little squeal, when he kissed the top of my head. Ruthie was a romantic, but she didn't know the whole story. If she had, she might have known that I hadn't really been in the arms of a man who was good for me. But she could never know why my feelings for Jimmy were so complex. She was too innocent, too fresh. I wanted her to stay that way.

On the other hand, I thought, as I snipped another branch. It fell to the ground, making a swishing sound as it hit the soft grass. I hadn't felt innocent when Jimmy had pulled me into his arms, any more than when I pined away after him every Sunday morning as his beautiful voice rushed through me, accompanied by the sounds of the piano, as he plucked out tunes that stirred my soul in a way that probably wasn't appropriate for church. You see, people think I'm one of those spinsters who doesn't mind being a spinster and never has had a romantic thought. Well, that's just ridiculous.

Dear Lord, if people knew the things I thought about in church.

"I need to get out. Meet someone." Daffy ran over to my ladder and sat on his haunches. "Someone besides you, Daffy Duck."

I heard gravel crunch a few miles away. I knew it would be Ruthie back from her errand. She was supposed to bring me a Diet Coke from Miss Donna's, and so I waited for her to come to me in the orchard, too busy snipping branches to turn around.

"Hi!"

That was not Ruthie's voice. I looked back.

Doc had his hands out, ready to catch me if I fell, which I promptly did. I shrieked, and he helped me gain my balance keeping his hands on my shoulders, even after I stopped wobbling. I noted they weren't rough and calloused liked Jimmy's, but capable like he knew how to take care of a woman.

Oh brother.

I'd definitely been reading too many romance novels, but what can I say? That's how his hands were.

"Hi, Doc!" Why am I shouting?

Then, I remembered the scarf I had tied around my head. My hands flew to my hair, then to my face, and finally to smooth over my denim jeans, which were entirely too snug to be wearing around visitors. Especially good-looking ones like Doc. Carey would never approve. If she were me, she would have excused herself to go change. But, she wasn't me.

"I followed Ruthie out here. Ran into her in town and she said she would show me the way."

"Were you trying to scare me?" I couldn't help but respond to his grin with a smile of my own.

"No. Just teasing," he said, his beautiful mouth turned up in an apologetic smile. My heart fluttered.

"Oh, heavens," I said, and then realized I said it out loud.

"You okay? You sound a little out of breath, Joy."

Good heavens, I love how you say my name.

"Yes. A little out of breath, but I'm fine."

"You sure?"

"Trust me, Doc. It's not what you think." If only he knew!

He gave me a long look that swept me into a wind tunnel in which I heard nothing, even though I saw his lips moving.

Kiss me.

The thought made me blush like a teenage girl.

Good heavens. Act your age, Joy.

He was looking at me, those golden brown eyes bright with good things—happiness. I wanted to be part of that. I'd spent too many years without good things when it came to the men.

"Joy?"

I blinked. "Yes, Doc?"

"I was saying that actually, it's not Doc. It's Kyle Christie."

I nodded, still not believing that Doc was standing right there in my Momma's orchard.

"You came here just to see me?"

"Yes."

"You didn't call, and since you don't live in Spavinaw Junction, I figured I wouldn't see you again, since I don't plan on falling off anymore roofs." This made him laugh.

"Nurse Clara likes to pretend to be mom. I like to let her, so I come here occasionally. I was in Miss Donna's that day to pick up dessert for dinner at her house. I bought cake. And I did call."

"What kind of cake?"

"Rum."

"Hmmm. Did you like it?"

"Best ever."

I smiled. "That's good, because I made it. Miss Donna's has been selling some of my cakes."

He shook his head. "I am not surprised, Joy. It fits."

"Fits what?"

"Your personality. Of course, I'd never seen your personality, until I talked to you that day in Miss Donna's. That's why I had to get your number."

"I never received a call. Are you sure you called?"

"Yes. I talked to your sister, Carey. Said she would give you a message."

Well, that little heifer.

"I hope you don't mind that I came all this way unannounced, but the message was that I'd be in town today to see Clara. I thought you might be expecting me. Besides, I wanted to see how you were."

So, maybe you *are* here as a doctor.

"Well, Doc, I'm fine. No headaches. My back doesn't hurt much. Just a few nightmares, but I've always had those."

I heard a cough and remembered Ruthie was still standing by her car. I should have given that girl a longer errand.

"Ruthie, could you get the Doc some iced tea and cake? What'll it be, Doc. Carrot? Or Twinkie?

"Twinkie cake?" He looked doubtful.

"You'll love it."

"Twinkie it is."

He peered down at me, raising his hands back to my shoulders.

"I'm really glad you're okay," he said. "And I'm glad I ran into you at Miss Donna's. It was great to meet you in real life." He winked.

A giggle escaped my lips. "That's right. I wasn't easy to

get to know when I was asleep in my coma. I was definitely lacking in personality."

"You were just a patient on my list, but you were so beloved by everyone who filed in to visit you that I remember thinking that I hoped you made it, because lots of people were waiting for you to wake up."

"Is real life Joy what you expected?" I asked.

"No. I didn't expect to see the waking Joy in real life again, but I definitely didn't know you were so adorable and witty. Of course, I should have, after the funeral."

Oh heavens.

"I wish you would just forget about that, but Doc, I do want to tell you something."

He squeezed my shoulders. "What's that?"

"I am so grateful for you. You literally saved me." I dared to reach a hand up, place my hand over one of his. In response he, stepped closer.

He smiled, and those same butterflies that still go crazy when I see Jimmy, fluttered around in my chest at that moment. As butterflies went, they had no loyalty to any man. Maybe they were just excited for someone new.

I could stand up all by myself now, so he really didn't need to hold me anymore, but I certainly didn't mind. I had forgotten how to play this game. Did I need to lean closer, or did I wait for him? And did he even want to kiss me or am I just crazy?

A series of loud yips interrupted us before I could decide what Doc was thinking.

"Joy," he said, suddenly the doc again. "What do you

think you were doing up on a ladder?"

I felt my cheeks go warm and knew I was blushing like a teenager on prom night.

"Oh, fiddlesticks!" It was all I could think to say. Good looking or not, lemon drop breath and everything, I didn't like people bossing me around.

"Fiddlesticks?"

"Why is everyone trying to tell me what to do?"

He was standing very, very close. Close enough he might have been able to smell the honeysuckle perfume I'd dabbed on my neck that morning.

"I was just telling Ruthie. I've had plenty of rest. I slept for a week, Doc."

"Kyle."

I shook my head, stepped back. His hands fell away, breaking the romantic tension.

"Listen, Doc. I have lots to do. What are you doing here?"

He suddenly didn't look so confident. I couldn't read what he was thinking. "Joy. I didn't come as your doctor. I'm not your doctor anymore. Dr. Duncan is your doctor."

He stepped closer, although there wasn't much room left between us.

"Then why are you here?" I was breathless again, but I think he might have realized it wasn't because I was dizzy or over exerted.

He reached down and curled his hand around mine.

Now, I might really pass out.

"I thought . . . Maybe I misread your feelings, but I

thought . . ."

I held my breath, trying to remember if there had been a look, a gesture or something, that would've told me he was attracted to me. He was just my ER doctor for Pete's sake. I hadn't thought he was as attracted to me as I was him.

Of course, there was the other day in Miss Donna's. Could that have been something more than just Doc being nice?

I couldn't ask him of course.

"I'd like to get to know you, Joy. That's why I asked you to coffee."

It occurred to me that Doc was younger than me. Maybe by a whole decade. But we were both over thirty, so surely that was okay.

I studied his face, his side burns free of the grey that he might have in ten years. Going out with a man like Doc would make Carey go off like a train whistle.

"Okay," I said.

He smiled. Nodded. Looked me up and down, which lit all my fires, of course.

"You look very nice," he said quietly. "Very pretty out of your hospital clothes."

At first I was mortified, but then when I saw in his face that he hadn't meant it that way, I laughed so loud that Ruthie peeked out the screen door for a second to check on me. Oh, it felt good to laugh! I hadn't laughed like that in a long time.

"My, aren't you charming, Doc. You know just what to say to a middle-aged, single woman to make her wake up from a coma, but you can't think of something appropriate to say now that I'm awake."

He blinked and took a small step back. His hands slid down to grasp mine and he held them gently.

Oh, my goodness. I did feel like a teenager again, just the same as when I'd first seen Jimmy in the hallways of Spavinaw Junction High.

Only, I'm not a teenager. I'm a grown woman. And this definitely isn't Jimmy.

Doc tilted his head, smiling, but clearly not comprehending.

"I heard you in the hospital. You said, 'Come on, beautiful. Wake up.' Or something like that." I smiled. I turned to walk toward the house and he caught up, fell into step beside me.

"I said that?" He looked bemused.

"Doc, I heard lots of things—I had visions and feelings and—nobody believes me, except for your nurse, Clara. And Ruthie."

He tilted his head, like he wanted to hear more, so I jabbered on. What's the worst that could happen?

He might think I'm off my rocker, too. And maybe he already does.

"My brothers and sisters think I'm three gallons of crazy in a two-gallon bucket, but I swear, Doc, it's like I told you back in the hospital. I heard people talking the whole time in my coma."

He took my hand, the touch of his fingers sending shivers across my palm, and folded it against his chest. "My diagnosis of the situation, even though I'm not your doctor anymore, is that you should give them some time."

Not my doctor?

He cleared his throat, smiled that sexy smile that I imagine all my favorite romance novel heroes had.

"Is your name really Ned?"

"Kyle," he corrected. "Actually, just Doc is fine if you insist, but—"

"Doc," I said. "But you aren't my doctor anymore."

"Correct. I'm not your doctor, which, again, is why I'm here."

The way that he looked at me just then, like I was the sweetest thing since strawberry jam, set the butterflies to fluttering around again.

He leaned in a little, and wouldn't you know, that's exactly when his dad-gummed doctor's beeper went off, squawking like a duck, spoiling the whole moment.

No wonder he is still single.

Chapter Fifteen

WHEN I WALKED into the kitchen, my arms laden with the apple branches, Ruthie rushed to take them from me.

"I have them, but thanks, honey."

"Where's the doc?" She set the branches in the sink and I smiled at how she took a moment to bury her perky little nose in the apple-blossom scent that wafted through the kitchen.

"His beeper went off."

"Do all doctors carry those?"

"I don't know," I said. "I think so."

I lowered myself in the chair and let Ruthie pour me a tall glass of mint iced tea and fix me some lemon cake. I wouldn't have admitted it to my sisters, but at that moment I was worn out, and not from the work, but from all the pitter-patters Doc had caused me.

"You need to rest," Ruthie said. "I'm supposed to be taking care of you."

"For now, let me finish my tea." But before I could take a sip, the screen door banged open and Bobby charged in, ball cap on, Nanette trailing right behind him.

"Just look at you in those cowboy boots and ratty blue jeans. And what happened to your shirt?" Bobby glanced down at the black Hank Williams, Jr. t-shirt with the sleeves torn out of it. "What is wrong with the kids' styles these days?" I teased.

"Just like his uncles," Nanette said. "Thank goodness Ruthie has you and Carey to copy."

"No, no. Ruthie dresses much better than her aunts." Ruthie was too busy staring out the window to hear me. I knew that look. It was called "smitten" in my romance novels. Her cheeks turned pink as apples when the screen door burst open and Bobby's best friend, Carl, breezed in. He was dressed almost like Bobby with a Motley Crüe t-shirt on, except unlike our Bobby, he stamped the dirt off his feet and politely took off his ball cap and hung it on a hook by the door. Ruthie's cheeks flooded with color, as she stared down at her legs clad in denim shorts.

"Brain! How you been?" His smile was easy as he greeted all of us, but his eyes never left Ruthie's. Bobby noticed too.

"Hey, man." Bobby clapped him on the shoulder. "Come out back. There's something I want to show you." Carl looked disappointed as he said goodbye to Ruthie.

I sent Ruthie a smile when the screen door slapped shut. Her eyes begged me not to say anything, but of course there was no need. Nanette just started jabbering about Bobby like something gigantic hadn't just happened in Ruthie's love life. My heart ached a little for Ruthie. It wasn't her fault that Bobby's wild streak took most of Nanette's time.

"I'm worried about Bobby," Nanette said. "Did I tell you he was caught smoking pot while you were in your coma?"

Ruthie's eyes bugged out in alarm. "Mom," she said under her breath.

Nanette patted her arm. "It's okay. She needs to know this so she can keep an eye on your brother when he's here."

Now, that was odd.

Nanette and I didn't usually keep big secrets from each other. I didn't know what Ruthie was worried about.

"That boy is taking the same path as our brothers," I said. "And they turned out fine."

"Well, I wish he would take a different path. I don't remember them ever getting arrested for pot, even if they did smoke it."

"My uncles smoked pot?"

We both glanced at Ruthie, surprised she didn't know.

"What I want to know is, who sold him the pot in the first place? I swear if I find out, I'll shoot him. I have a gun in my purse, you know."

"Nanette!"

"Mom!"

I couldn't believe Nanette would ever even step on someone's little piggy toe, let alone shoot them.

"You shouldn't just carry it in your purse. That's dangerous."

"Okay, maybe I'll just shoot his foot or something."

"Maybe just punch him?" Ruthie suggested.

"Or pinch him? Really hard?" I asked.

"Sure," she said. "But whoever it is will be sorry. Mark my word."

"Never mind all that," I said. "Bobby's going to be fine. He just needs some direction. Heaven knows, the boys were worse than him."

"I think Bobby needs a distraction," Nanette said. "And so I'm giving him one. He's staying with you and Ruthie all week. I know you can use help while you are recovering."

Another teen to baby sit. Lord almighty.

She slipped her arm around Ruthie. "I figure that between the two of them helping, you won't over-extend yourself."

I sighed. "I'm not over-extending myself, am I, Ruthie?"

"No. She's been, um, resting." It was partly true.

"You haven't been digging through those charms in the basement again. Has she Ruthie?"

Yes, I had, but I wasn't saying anything. Not much was left that the boys hadn't hauled away with all the debris, but I'd sifted through what was left and so far, no lost charm.

"There was never anything in that mess that I need anymore." I lied. "Just forget what we talked about in the hospital. It was silly to begin with."

"Sis, I've been meaning to ask. Is that really what you were, you know . . . ?" She cast a glance at me.

How'd Nanette finally get so smart? "What made you think of that?"

"Well, Fernie came in the shop the other day. I swear, as soon as I saw her, she looked more like her dearly departed snotty mother than herself."

"Nanette. Don't be disrespectful of the departed."

"Sorry," she said. "So, when she came into Momma's Curls, she was the only customer. I thought it was a good time to just grill her a little about her dad's love life, why he never takes off that wedding ring."

"You didn't!"

"Of course I did."

"What did you find out?" I hurried to pour three glasses of iced tea, gesturing for them to sit. Nanette noted the three glasses, looked at Ruthie, and I knew she was going to tell that poor girl to skedaddle.

"It's okay," I said. "Let her stay. She's practically a woman." Maybe including her in these little chats would keep her from being so bored and feeling left out since her best friend was spending the summer at her dad's.

"So, what did Fernie say?" It felt good to gossip with my sister again. It was one of the more trivial things I'd missed in my coma.

Nanette could get anyone to talk about anything. Hers was the chair to avoid if you didn't want to spill what was troubling you. She always came across as if she really cared, and she did, but she also liked to gossip with me and Carey—but only a little, so when you made her promise not to tell, she always crossed her fingers behind her, one for me and one for Carey, whom she kept no secret from—ever.

"Well," she said. "It was weird, to tell the truth. She claimed that before her momma died, she told Fernie that her father used to love someone else, someone that he'd never really gotten over." Nannette smiled. "She made me promise not to tell. She claimed it was you."

I felt my face flood, and it wasn't sweet like under the magic apple tree with Doc. It was more like I felt the time Momma made me drink a shot of pepper sauce to ward off the flu, it had turned out to be a terrible idea, as was this conversation.

"That's what she claimed, but I told her it was ridiculous, because you were barely friends with her dad for the past twenty-five years. Am I right?"

"And?" Ruthie asked. She was obviously feeling grown up being part of the conversation.

"She claims that you and Jimmy have a secret together that you've never told anyone, even though she didn't know what it was."

"And why was she telling you? Besides the fact that you nearly hypnotized her to divulge her secrets like you do all your clients."

"Because, she wants me to help figure out what is going on between you and Jimmy. She likes you. Thinks you and her dad need to make up or something."

Make up?

"I didn't know we were fighting."

Nanette gave me a pointed look.

I glanced back at Ruthie. "What do you think of all this, sweetie?"

"Me?"

I smiled, happy I wasn't the one in the hot seat anymore. Besides, this would be good practice for her if she wanted to be a grown up.

She cleared her throat, looking adorable, like a little girl wearing a tiara crooked on her head and gloves that were too big. "I think Fernie is weird."

Her mother and I laughed. "Well put," I said.

"But I do think she's right about one thing. The mayor likes you. And it does look like you two are in a fight, or like you can't decide whether to kiss him, or hit him."

"Ruthie." I was unable to hold in more laughter. She was one smart cookie.

Out of nowhere it seemed, the screen door slammed and Carey breezed into the kitchen, tossing her oversized black faux crocodile purse on the kitchen counter.

"Now, where do you keep the chocolate these days? This has been a horrible afternoon and I need something, quick."

Nanette grinned. That's how the women in this family are. When rough times come, we stop everything and ask for chocolate.

"What's got you in a blither?" Nanette asked.

She plopped into a chair beside us. "Well, let's see. I've had to watch other kids in addition to my own." She gave Nanette and Ruthie a pointed look, reminding me that Nanette hadn't been doing much babysitting because of her assignment to help me out. "Plus, the twins nearly killed each other in the bathtub, Dawson tried to tie Mason to a tree, and Marie pooped on the floor. Anyone having a worse day?"

No answer needed, I decided, and walked over to the closet. Poor Carey. She loved kids and kept having them, even when the doctor said she was past her child-bearing years. She was a great mom, but sometimes being forty made it just a little harder. I pulled on a barely noticeable knob. A small cabinet door that only the Talley women knew about swung open to reveal a jar filled with all manner of chocolates meant to heal all manner of problems. Some of them were made by Momma, but one of the things I'd done since I'd been home was take a whole day to teach Ruthie some of the old recipes I knew.

I held out a piece of chocolate for Carey, who wasted no time popping it into her mouth. We all watched, letting her appreciate her moment. Then Nanette held out her hands to accept her chocolate. She sighed. "Some things about being a Talley are good." She popped the chocolate in her mouth and I swear her whole face changed from worried to happy.

"I agree. Momma's recipes might be the best part of being a Talley, isn't that right, Ruthie?"

Ruthie's face brightened. "Let me show you what Aunt Joy taught me." She pointed out the chocolates in the jar and which recipe we used to make them and what the recipe was for. Nanette looked duly impressed.

"For instance, the dark peanut clusters promote silliness, something I'm sure Grandma Bess made up, but I've always liked."

Nanette and I giggled in Carey's direction. Carey looked at us, deadpan.

Ruthie handed her a Sassafras Heart, which made us all smile. We all knew they were to heal a broken heart.

Carey didn't say anything, but her eyes glistened. The truth about Carey was that she had been hurt more than the rest of us, and that's probably why she was so unbending at times. Not that I don't get tired of her peacock-walk attitude, but at least knowing there is a reason makes it bearable.

The only sound for several long seconds was the crinkle of the cellophane as we unwrapped our candy.

"So," Nanette said, obviously not ready to drop the subject. "Why do you think Fernie would say something like that, Joy?"

"Say something like what?" Carey asked.

Nanette took the moment to fill Carey in.

"I thought we were supposed to take it easy on Aunt Joy," Ruthie said, but nobody was listening, except for me, of course.

"What?" I put my hand on Ruthie's arm. She leaned over and whispered in my ear.

"You know, to protect you. No arguing in front of you. No bad news."

I raised my eyebrows. "Oh, really?"

Ruthie nodded.

"Well, I think she's nuts," Carey said.

"Like me?" I asked.

"No. That's not what I meant. Don't put words in my mouth."

"Well, Joy," Nanette asked, serious now. "What really went on between you and the mayor?"

They were all staring at me.

Ruthie spoke, before I could think of something to say. "I'm sure it was a long time ago before the mayor was married. It's not like Aunt Joy wanted to jump his bones when he was married."

Carey almost choked on her candy. I wondered if it would still work on her attitude.

Nanette glared at her daughter. "Jump his bones, young lady? Isn't there a nicer way to say what you just said?"

That girl was definitely growing up too fast and was way too smart to be a Talley. She didn't have the story straight, but she had obviously been piecing something together.

Carey clucked her tongue. "Are you sure about that, Ruthie?"

Ruthie's face turned red. They all looked at me for confirmation, but I had a feeling the look on my face said more than I was willing to admit just then.

She looked away. "I'm sorry, Aunt Joy. I know you don't want anyone to know you like Jimmy, but it's plain to see you do."

I blinked, popped a chocolate into my mouth, waiting for the barrage of questions, but instead they each popped another chocolate in their mouth.

"Mmm!" Carey squeaked.

"Mmmm." Nanette said.

"Mmmmm." Ruthie said, stretching it out like the chocolate was a secret.

"Mmm-Mmm." I said, thinking we sounded like we were doing some strange meditation together.

Eventually, Ruthie was the one to break the heavenly

spell in our mouths.

"I'm going upstairs to read," she said. We waved goodbye to her as we each reached for more chocolate.

"So, Joy," Carey said. "You and Jim did used to be friends, right?" She looked pointedly at me.

I felt my pale cheeks go splotchy. That's the problem with being a red-head. When you blush, there is no hiding it.

"None of your business."

"Well," Carey huffed, and just like that we were thirteen again. "You don't have to be such a heifer about it."

"Did you just call me a cow?" I stood. For what, I wasn't sure, but it made me feel meaner.

"No," Carey said. "I called you a heifer."

"Oh forget it," I said, tired of being upset at my sister. "What do you really want me to tell you, girls?"

"Ruthie's right," Nanette said. "This has something to do with Jimmy, right? And I know that whatever you wanted in the chimney had to have been lost when the tornado destroyed it."

I shrugged. I didn't know if I was ready to tell them when I'd just started to get used to the idea that since it was destroyed, I could drop the whole thing.

"Please, Sis." I felt as sad as an old fence as the truth rose up around me. They could never handle it. I barely could. "Just forget about it. It doesn't matter anymore."

Carey reached across the table and tried to take my hand, but I pulled it away. "We won't judge you—if you ever want to tell us. If there's something worrying you, we just want to help."

"You won't judge, Carey?" I laughed out loud in her face. She looked shocked.

"Well, I never . . ."

"You always judge. I've been sick of it for years."

Her face turned so red that I worried she might be the one to have a mental breakdown right then and there.

"Joy," Nanette scolded. "Don't be so mean."

"And you," I said. "I'm tired of you talking the big talk when Carey and the boys aren't around, and then just caving in whenever they're around. Stick up for yourself. For me!"

"Joy, I—"

"And trust me. It's gone," I said. "It doesn't matter. I don't want to find it anymore. I should have never tried to get it out of the chimney. Before then, it didn't bother anyone but me and Jimmy probably never thought about it, but now everyone wants to know about it and it's nobody's business. Will you please forget about it?"

We all reached for chocolate.

"Okay," Nanette said. "I'll forget about it, but only if you'll give Jimmy a chance. Ruthie said she saw him kiss you."

Were they not listening to me? Jimmy and I were not a thing.

"On top of the head. It meant nothing." I lied, although it wasn't a full lie. I really didn't know what it had meant, if anything.

Nanette shrugged. "It would be nice to see you with

someone, Sis. I know you don't think you need a man, but . . ."

"What makes you think that?"

She shrugged. "I don't know. It's just that you never go on dates, Joy. And you're the prettiest out of all us girls."

I laughed out loud at that. "You don't have to butter me up, Nanette."

"It's true," Carey said, looking serious.

"Spoken like Miss Spavinaw Junction herself."

Carey shot me a withering look.

"Okay," I said. The secret was partly out anyway. Maybe if I appeased their curiosity about Jimmy, they would stop asking more questions. As long as they didn't know the whole truth, it was okay.

"Yes, there used to be something with Jimmy, but it was a long time ago before Fern. We were barely out of high school. Momma didn't approve. I'm surprised you didn't hear her harping about it. But, it doesn't matter anymore."

"I knew it," Carey said, her eyes twinkling with mischief. "All that time you claimed the two of you were friends, you were dating."

"No," I said, then revised my answer. "Yes, but trust me. There's nothing there now. He's been a widow for five years and that stupid kiss on my head was the closest we've been in decades. Besides, he's a jerk."

"Jimmy's a jerk? Of course he is not a jerk!"

"Joy, he is the mayor! And the music leader at Church!" She said it like he was God himself.

"Trust me," I said. "He is not who you think he is."

"Are you saying there's really something wrong with Jimmy?" Nanette asked. "Lots of women are pining after him, you know."

They would never believe me if I told them.

My mind swirled back to a Jimmy standing in cut-offs by the creek, water drops dripping from his long, dark wavy hair and trailing down his naked chest. He was waving me toward him, trying to get me to jump off the bluff opposite the bank. When I was afraid, he waded out into the water and caught me, and we'd kissed and he'd promised we'd be together as long as he lived.

He lied.

"No, but there's something wrong with me," I said. "Thinking about a married man."

Nanette laughed. "Sounds human to me. And he's not a married man."

"It was a sin to have the hots for him when he was married," Carey said.

Nanette shot her a dirty look. "Thanks for that, Sis."

"But it's not a sin now, since he's not married," Carey finished.

"What about Doc?" Nanette chimed in. Carey's eyebrows poked straight up like exclamation marks, I swear. I popped another chocolate.

"He's got to be ten years younger than Joy. Why, that would be a scandal!"

I huffed. "Did Ruthie tell you about him, too?"

Nanette smiled. "She's a hopeless romantic, Joy. She reads all these romance novels that she hides under her bed at home. I bet she hides them here, too, and thinks I don't know. She even talks about taking her honeymoon to the beach someday, just like you used to dream of."

"Life isn't a romance novel." I knew that for sure.

"Of course not," Nanette said. "But there's nothing wrong with being happy. Ruthie wants you to be happy. We all do."

"But people will talk."

"So?"

"So," I said, happy to shift their attention from Jimmy. "Doc's a hunk."

"Isn't he a hunk, Carey?" Nanette gently shoved Carey's shoulder.

"Okay, so he's a hunk, but that's speaking as a married woman."

"Me, too," Nanette said. "My Chad's pretty good-looking himself, but now, Doc." She waggled her eyebrows, making me wonder if it were really possible to go out with Doc and not scandalize the community. I looked at Carey. Could she really handle my being the center of the town gossip—again? I highly doubted it.

Hmmm.

This would give people lots to talk about. It could be a scandal, and we haven't had a good scandal in a while.

Ruthie's Diary

Dear Diary

Aunt Joy and I have been driving the cherry red Chevy all over the countryside, we've watched every old movie on the TV, read all the books we could find in the house, including a ton of teen romance novels from Aunt Joy's high school days that she finally admitted she had. Now that our romance habit is out in the open, we have even more to talk about. We go to the library every few days and check out arm loads of romance novels.

It has been forever since I've been up here to write in my diary, but when Aunt Joy, Aunt Carey, and Mom got into that discussion about the mayor, it made me realize that Aunt Joy might be ready for me to give her what she lost. Aunt Joy seems fine to me.

But before I give it to her, I have to confess here in my diary: I looked inside.

Ruthie

Chapter Sixteen

ONCE WHEN IT was hotter out than Tabasco, Ruthie and I nearly got caught running around in our bathing suits, which we'd put on just to cool off. I guess it's better than being caught in your birthday suit, but not much. So, when both the mayor and the doc drove up at the same time and I was sitting with Ruthie on the upstairs balcony in my black and red hibiscus print bathing suit and drinking iced tea, I almost broke my toe trying to get back in the house, before they could see me and my floppy places up close.

"That was close!" I hopped around the room while I pulled on my favorite old pair of jeans. "I wonder what they're doing here. At the same time!"

As I dressed, Ruthie peeked through the curtain.

"Don't know," Ruthie said. "But they look kind of surprised to see each other."

I couldn't imagine what either one was doing there on a Thursday afternoon, and at the same time.

"They're shaking hands," Ruthie said.

Jimmy hadn't shown up to the house in a few days,

although at church I'd noticed his eyes kept sliding to the empty spot where I usually sat. He had no idea that after being the center of attention at Momma's funeral, I'd started sitting in the empty church balcony, right behind the curtain where nobody could see me. I liked hiding there not only during church, but also when the choir was practicing, or when Jimmy thought he was alone and sat at the piano singing all my favorite hymns.

"Doc's walking up on the porch now." Ruthie's bottom was sticking into the room and her head all the way through the curtains.

"Get back. They're going to see you, honey."

"The mayor's just standing by his car. He's watching the Doc."

I doubted Jimmy was jealous of Doc, but if he'd still loved me, he should've been. Any woman in town, even the young ones like Fernie, would have been glad to be visited by Doc, whether they were sick or not. I can't deny that my heart went all a flutter on the day he came out to the house and told me he was no longer my doctor.

"He wants to be your boyfriend. They both do."

This caused a myriad of feelings in me, from giggles to denial, before I chided her about delving into my non-existent love life.

Naturally, Ruthie takes after all of the Talleys, and we've never been the kind of people to let sleeping dogs lie, as some British guy named Chaucer once said it was best to do. That's because our father, Leroy Talley, was born and he eventually switched that old saying to, "Never let a sleeping dog lie. If he bites ya', it's because you weren't ready."

I had a feeling I was probably about to get bitten, when Ruthie snapped the curtains together and giggled a laugh that took me back to another time, same place. I still remembered peering out my window and sneaking a wave at a much younger Jimmy. He was standing, looking just like he had in my hospital vision, his wavy dark locks pulled back in a ponytail, his sinewy arms relaxed, and hands in his pockets staring up at me. Afterward, I'd snapped the curtains together, slipped down the kitchen stairs, and out into the kitchen garden where he'd been waiting for me behind the leaning brown-eyed-susans, their heads spying as we talked, and then up in the apple tree, where we kissed until Momma found me missing, and hollered until I came inside.

It's too bad you weren't waiting in the garden when I needed you to be there, Jimmy.

"I think the mayor saw me! He just looked up and waved at the window." Ruthie giggled and rolled onto my bed. I loved that girl with her head full of princess fantasies and Prince-Charming dreams.

She didn't know about the dark side of love. She didn't know what it was that I'd lost, for good I guessed, in the chimney, and why it mattered. And while she had questioned me at length, she didn't know how Jimmy was connected to that loss. Of course, Ruthie couldn't understand how Jimmy being widowed and burdened with secrets made his interest in me nothing more than friendship, and a very fragile friendship, at that—even if being near him still made my head spin like a top, especially when he kissed it.

That left Doc, you'd think, but while I don't mind admitting that Doc's eyes did set my skin on fire, something always doused it before it could really get burning. I don't know what it was about him, but just when I'd start to see him as more than just Doc, images of Jimmy swimming in the creek, drying my tears in the attic, and kissing me in the woods messed up the whole romantic scene. It's all a crying shame, to be honest.

"An impossible situation," I said aloud.

"Not impossible! You just have to decide who you like, Aunt Joy."

I couldn't help but smile at that pretty girl, in spite of my inner worries, and give her narrow shoulders a hug.

"We should be talking about who you like, honey."

"Nobody." But her cheeks reddened.

Shielding my eyes from the sun with my hand, I surveyed the driveway. Jimmy was still standing by his truck, staring up at the balcony, which oddly, my momma said used to be called a widow's walk. Maybe, I thought, we should rename it an old-maid's walk. Jimmy, a real widower, I reminded myself, raised his hand, and I responded in kind. It was instinctive, a replay of the past. He did the little double fist on his chest, just like when we were young, and climbed back into his truck. My heart flip-flopped, just like back then.

What do you want, Jimmy? Why do you come and never say what you're thinking?

There was that one time when he took me in his arms

on the front porch, but when I turned away, he went. That's not what I'd wanted him to do. I'd wanted him to apologize, to explain, to let me know he was on my side, and that he hadn't forgotten.

"Where's he going?" Ruthie complained as he revved his engine and drove away.

We both stared after his truck even after it disappeared into the hills, Janis Joplin's voice singing "Take another little piece of my heart, now baby," rolling through my mind, until a knock on the downstairs door traveled up to my bedroom, drawing me out of my reverie long enough for Ruthie to tug on my arm. She rushed me down to where the other potential suitor she'd picked out for her dear old Auntie, stood on the front porch.

"Ruthie, slow down. He's not going anywhere."

"Sorry, Aunt Joy," she whispered. "He might. The mayor just did."

HE MUST HAVE been younger than Jimmy by a good ten years, which made him younger than me, but why would I complain?

"How are you?" Doc asked.

"Feeling better. I don't sleep well, though. It's like I slept too long in that coma. And I have weird dreams."

He looked at me with a funny grin on his face. "Well, I didn't mean in a medical way, but—"

"Oh. I'm sorry." I laughed at myself, feeling embarrassed.

"Hey, no problem. What dreams?"

"You would think they're strange."

"Try me."

"Sometimes I have a nightmare I haven't had since I was a kid, in which I fall into the Spring of Good Luck out behind our house, can't breathe, and drown. I also dream a lot of something I lost decades ago and will never find. Plus, and here's the kicker, I wake up at night and think I see Dad, who is dead." I laughed. "He says, 'Breathe' like he did in the hospital."

He pressed his lip together then clicked his tongue. "Sounds normal."

I laughed. "You see? Carey is right. I'm nuts, Doc. Do you agree?" I smiled the best flirting smile I knew how, and I didn't really know how to flirt, but was rewarded with kind eyes and a soft smile.

He reached for my hand and I let him hold it, enjoying the tingles that danced up my wrist, to my elbow, and around the back of my neck. How many times had Jimmy sat on this porch since I woke up from my coma and never held my hand, let alone carried on a conversation the way Doc was now? "No. I think you've been through a lot. And, I think you just need to find a new purpose for your life."

"A purpose?"

"Yep. Something besides taking care of your family." I must have looked offended because he hurried to explain. "It's just that you spend a lot of time taking care of your family. Maybe you would enjoy doing something different, or taking care of people in a different way."

So we launched into a conversation of possibilities and I promised him I'd make a list and decide on something soon.

"Thanks, Doc."

"What for?"

"For talking with me."

He squeezed my hand, and he might as well have been squeezing my whole body.

"I like talking to you, Joy."

The only time Jimmy and I had shared more than a couple of words since my coma was on the day of the tornado. That didn't go well at all, which to be fair, might've been the reason he only ever sat with me and didn't talk, but I didn't think that was a good excuse. What did he expect? That after all those years of ignoring his rejection of me, we'd shake hands and be best friends?

"Joy?" I stepped out of my thoughts and back to the porch swing where I sat.

"Sorry, Doc."

"You were saying that at night, you worry about something you lost a long time ago. This is something real, right? Not just a dream?"

"Right," I said, but a tiny part of me wasn't so sure anymore. "It used to be real. Now I really sound like a loon."

"Is it something I can help you find?" His eyes were kind, just as I remembered them being in the hospital when he shined that little light into mine.

"It's gone."

"Hmm. So you don't want to find it."

I shook my head. "Not anymore."

"Excuse me, Aunt Joy?"

Doc and I both swiveled to see Ruthie standing in the doorway. I wondered how long she had been listening.

"I made a cake."

"What kind?" We both asked in unison.

"Lemon-blueberry," she said. "I wanted to try something different."

"In that case," Doc said, "We must eat cake."

He held his hand out, and I took it, thinking of how when I was a girl, cake had fixed so many things.

Chapter Seventeen

I THINK RECLINING around in a coma makes one take a closer look at life. I did so and found mine to be very dull. All my years of not moving on from something that happened years ago is what had turned me into the town spinster.

"I think I need a new purpose."

"A purpose?" Carey asked.

"What does that even mean?" Nanette asked.

"What I'm saying is, I want to do something to help someone else. When I was in my coma, I thought a lot about my life, and . . ."

"Oh brother," Carey whined. She looked at Nanette, and spoke as if I couldn't hear. "She's going to talk about her secret life inside her coma now. Do we have to hear about that again?" Nanette rolled her eyes in their sockets, but I couldn't tell if it was for Carey's benefit or mine.

I ignored them both and held up a letter I'd received in the mail just that morning. It was almost as if it was meant to be my new purpose.

"This letter came for Momma today."

"A little bit late for letters to Momma," Carey said.

"I'm sure her name was just part of a list of volunteers. It's from The Tulip House for Girls," I said. "They are looking for people to form fund raising committees in the region. They're in danger of closing."

"That would be a shame if they closed," Nanette said. "They've helped a lot of troubled girls over the years. Momma loved helping them. That's really what she did with all that money she made from the apple tree branches."

I paused. "Really? I didn't know that."

Something about the idea of Momma using her Magic Tree to help troubled girls made me smile. Surely, I could be as creative as Momma. Maybe we could sell the chocolates and teas, too. Or maybe have a big supper and charge people.

"It's too much work for you right now, Joy."

"Oh shove off, Carey. I'm tired of you talking about my delicate state. It's been more than a month now since I woke up."

"Who'll be on your committee, besides us?" Nanette asked.

Carey frowned, but she didn't argue about Nanette automatically assuming she would be on it, too.

I hated to do it, but I smiled and said, "Let's start with Peter, Mary Sue, and Thelma."

"I advise against this," Carey said. "You need to take it easy."

I called Tulip House as soon as the girls left.

I clutched the yellow phone receiver in my fist and

stuttered out the words, "Can I do something to help the girls living at The Tulip House for Girls?"

Nobody would ever call me a stutterer, I don't think, but sometimes, when my confidence is low, like in that moment, I wish I had some Chapstick. All the moisture goes out of my lips and I trip over my words or can't even remember them. Thankfully, the lady on the phone at Tulip House didn't even notice, or pretended not to, and when she said they really needed my help, I covered the mouth piece and danced and whooped around the kitchen.

Out of the clear blue Oklahoma sky, my world got bigger. I'd never realized how little it was before. Tiny as one of those little Christmas towns in a snow globe is what it'd always been, but I never even knew it, until I picked that phone up and volunteered to help people I didn't even know.

Now, I'm not saying that it was a bad calling to take care of people I loved, but after being trapped in my body for a week, I wanted to do even bigger things, like some of the women I read about in the paper. I was inspired by women like Margaret Thatcher and also Nancy Reagan, who looks just like a housewife when you see her on TV. A well-dressed housewife, but a housewife just the same, only that lady has a brass neck. Even after her husband was almost assassinated, Nancy was expanding her world, teaching kids to say no to drugs, and replacing the White House china, for heaven's sake.

My china is made up of twenty different patterns, but like Nancy's husband, heaven obviously thought it was best for me to stay alive when I could've easily died, and I'm not going to waste my time. Don't get me wrong. I don't think my future is as important as the President's and Nancy's, of course, but I did survive hanging from the roof. That counts for something.

THE TULIP HOUSE for Girls is sort of a halfway home for young girls, who are either pregnant or have experienced some kind of trauma. Another reason I chose it was that I understood what it was like to have been a young woman, still a girl really, and go through something terrible. I will never forget how difficult it was just to put one foot in front of the other when my world fell apart at such a tender age, and going through it alone was worse. If I'd been brave enough to call their anonymous hotline back then, maybe I never would've been up on that roof and Carey might not have been telling everyone who would listen, "Be patient with my sister. We think she might be just slightly mentally ill. It's temporary."

Since nothing remains a mystery for long in Spavinaw Junction—unless it was hidden in the Talley chimney—I got on the horn right away. Before I could blink, I had a list of ideas and my gang of helpers. Thelma, of course, was one of my volunteers. Her, Peter, and Mary Sue had started coming around again and Thelma said she loved the idea, but found an opportunity as we met at Carey's house for a planning meeting, to give me her all-important advice. According to Thelma, I should've "sought counsel" from

Reverend Wilson before I ever started, to get his take on the whole thing, of course.

"Why would I do that, Thelma?"

"Because, honey." I hated when she called me honey, like I was her sister or true friend. "We all know you're delicate right now. Peter and I talked about it this morning."

Oh you did, did you? I could just wring that Peter's neck.

"Even Mary Sue agrees," she said.

"About what?"

"That you don't want to overexert yourself," Thelma finished.

Well, I didn't call the reverend, but I guess Thelma did, because a few mornings later, when I was still dressed in my pink-flowered satin pjs, my hair standing at all different angles, and my freckles exposed in all their glory, minus the Maybelline, I heard Reverend Wilson's ratta-tat-tat on my door. It just happened to be a morning after one of my particularly sleepless nights, during which I'd had three nightmares, baked two dozen snicker doodles, and scribbled a list of eleven things I might do in order to raise money for The Tulip House for Girls.

Reverend didn't seem to mind my appearance as he sat looking over my list, his gnarled hands resting lightly on the cane that lay across his knees. He must have been one of those people who developed arthritis early because he'd had those hands, with varying degrees of twistedness, for as long as I could remember. Of course, I didn't care about his hands. Nobody did. He was a good man, the same humble soul who'd taken responsibility for the . . . um . . . bodily noise I'd made at my Momma's funeral in front of the whole church, the entire community, in fact. Why would he care what I looked like without makeup, or even notice my cheeks flushing red at the memory of that day?

"These are good ideas, Joy." Reverend Wilson smiled, which wasn't what I was expecting at all. "I especially like the one about the barbecue supper here at the Talley house. Raise your prices on the meal by a dollar. I bet people will pay it for a good cause."

"You mean you didn't come over here to tell me I'm too 'delicate' to be working so hard at raising money for The Tulip House for Girls?"

"Of course not. I have a special place in my heart for that home. Your Momma did a lot of work there, as you know, and so have I. And you've never been delicate, now, have you?"

I smiled, knowing instantly he meant this as a compliment.

"Course," he said. "I didn't come here to talk about Tulip House, but I did come to check on you." He handed back my list, and the way he stared into my eyes made me touch the swollen tissue beneath. It wasn't only lack of sleep that bothered me that morning. I hoped he couldn't see any traces of the tears. I'd awoken not an hour earlier to racking sobs, from a nightmare about Jimmy that was really not scary, only sad. Dreadfully heartrending.

"Nothing's wrong, Reverend." I shrugged my shoulders,

letting the lie roll right off. "I just can't sleep." He nodded, as if he'd expected me to say exactly that, and I knew he didn't believe me.

"Prayer might help," he said. I smiled in response, a reaction I forced, not able to find enough energy to explain to a preacher that my prayers weren't working anymore. I'd been hiding in the balcony on Sunday mornings listening to sermons, and taking in Jimmy's songs, but while my former young lover's voice still moved me the way it always had, the meanings of the words didn't sink in like they used to.

Reverend and I sat quietly in the living room, him on his usual settee in the corner and me in a chair where Momma used to sit when she was still with us. I squirmed in my seat, my hands on my knees, like a nervous un-praying child, listening to the slow tick-tocking of the grandfather-sized grandfather clock.

Tick-tock! Tick-tock! Tick-Tock!

Finally, I couldn't take it anymore. The tick-tock sounded like a series of gunshots in the quiet of the big living room. I'd never thought of Momma's house—my house—as eerie before, but the sheer size of the living room made it feel cavernous and the tick-tock echoed through it, reminding me of a haunted mansion straight out of *Tales from the Crypt*. I jumped up, opened the little door of the clock, and stopped the pendulum.

Reverend looked amused. "Did somebody die?"

He leaned forward and placed his elbows on his bony knees. His ancient looking jacket reminded me of a mortician's.

"It's the old way," he said when I scrunched my face in question. "To stop the clock on the exact second that somebody dies. I figured with Bess's superstitions, you would get the joke."

I glanced over at the clock. Seven-thirty-eight. Who stops in at somebody's house this early in the morning?

I feel dead when I wake up from my nightmares.

"I feel dead, sometimes," I blurted. Since he didn't looked shocked, I continued. "Dead or in some kind of trance. And then, other days I have insurmountable energy, like a . . . a . . . hummingbird."

He nodded his head like I'd said the most normal thing in the world.

"So it's typical?" I asked. If so, then I was going ahead and picking out my own casket.

"Typical to feel like a hummingbird?" He asked.

I knew he was only teasing, but I sighed just the same. How could I expect anyone to understand why I'd been on the roof? All the things that'd happened in the hospital? The stuff that'd been crisscrossing my dreams and thoughts since I'd been home?

A part of me, inexplicably, wished Jimmy had come to check on me, instead of Reverend Wilson, but of course, this was a weekday and Jimmy would be working. And then there were his previous visits when we sat two feet apart and I didn't talk to him at all, even though I'd felt his eyes on me each time, studying, stirring my emotions into a raging storm just beneath my freckled pale skin. There was no way I was giving him the satisfaction of talking to him as if we'd never kissed, never planned to get married, never gone through the horrible thing that made us hide our secret in the chimney, and especially as if he'd never abandoned me for Fern. I reminded myself I should not feel guilty at all for being attracted to Doc. But at the moment, I didn't want Doc. I wanted Jimmy. He was the only one who'd understand everything I was thinking. He would believe me.

Jimmy. Come back to me.

"You were in a coma," Reverend Wilson was saying, and I blinked three times before remembering what we were talking about. "You were as close to death as anyone I know has ever been, except for your father, of course"

"Reverend, can I tell you something?"

"Tell me anything, Joy."

I moved to sit beside him and realized the old love seat was the most uncomfortable seat in the house. No wonder Momma had always ordered us to sit there when we were about to receive a talking-to.

"It's really going to sound strange. Course, Carey thinks I have mental problems anyway, you know."

He nodded, but didn't laugh along with me.

Oh, Reverend. Maybe you think I'm 'mental' too.

"Just spit it out, Joy." The map of wrinkles under his eyes seemed deep with experience. I would have bet my favorite Emmylou Harris record that he'd heard a lot of people's secrets. I wouldn't doubt if he had a wrinkle for each secret he carried, and he had a lot of wrinkles.

"Reverend . . ."

"Yes." He said it like an agreement and his glassy eyes

were the sincerest as I've ever seen. For a second there, I remembered him looking at Momma just this way. I'd come in from the garden and they were at the kitchen table, his hand resting over hers on the table top. To me, it had looked sweet, like something two elderly friends would do, but now, I remembered that they'd been sitting together like that ever since Daddy's funeral. Now that I thought about it, they weren't old back then.

"What is it, Joy? You can tell me." I wanted to ruminate more on the hand-holding between Momma and Reverend Wilson, but he was staring at me, waiting to hear my secret. That's what I'd give him, but, I decided, only one.

"Reverend . . . my dad came to me when my heart stopped in my coma. It was Daddy who blew the breath back in me."

He sat there, looking at me like I was a stranger.

"I heard everything. I knew what was going on. I heard my brothers and sisters fighting," I said. For a moment I saw the clouds part in his eyes and I knew he understood what I was saying, but then the fog rolled over him.

Disbelief.

"I heard you praying for me. You said, 'Lord, please help Bess's daughter. Keep Joy with us.'"

My whisper was quiet, but it hit Reverend Wilson like a rock in the forehead. His eyes widened as he stared at the grandfather clock, at Momma's black and white photo on the wall, at his feet, and then at me.

"You were in bed, Joy. I know this because I was at the hospital. River called me and I drove right over and sat in the lobby. I prayed for you the whole time."

"Yes, I know," I said, as quiet as the breeze blowing the kitchen curtains. "Daddy was there. He was real. I don't care what you say."

There. I've said it.

Since he couldn't seem to respond, I continued. "And the other thing is, that I'm in love with Jimmy Cornsilk."

He raised his watery eyes to mine, and I could see he wasn't surprised.

"Even when Fern was alive."

He looked at me, like he was expecting more.

"But now, after my coma, I've realized what a fool I've been. How much time I've wasted. I'm going to move on."

At that, he just smiled.

I've really done it now. Bring on the straight jacket, or at least doom me to hell.

But he didn't. I waited on egg shells for him to say something. Time passed, despite my stopping the ticking of the grandfather clock, and Reverend Wilson just kept shaking his head, widening his eyes like he had something in them he wanted to get out, and rubbing his temples. I was pretty sure I knew what he was thinking, but as so often happens when I think I know all about someone, he opened his mouth, and I found out I was wrong.

Chapter Eighteen

EVEN THOUGH I hadn't even made breakfast for Ruthie and Bobby who had stayed over—again—I had an itch to get out of the house. Thanks to Reverend Wilson's visit, I felt energized, so I left Ruthie and Bobby a note and drove to Momma's Curls.

"Joy!" Nanette set her comb down, leaving Thelma in her chair with half-combed hair and rushed to me.

When Carey saw me, she did the same thing, so maybe, I thought, they were moving on from their ridiculous worries about my brain.

"Look at you!" Carey immediately started messing with my hair while Nanette took my chin in her hand and peered at my eyebrows. "I hope you are here to let us work on you, Sis. You look awful."

"Carey," Nanette said.

"It's okay. She's right." I walked to the empty chair next to Thelma and sat down. "I still like it long, but it needs a trim."

"And let's face it," Thelma said. "A color."

"I do not," I said. Thelma was always sticking her nose

in where it didn't belong. I looked to my sisters for back up.

"We don't color red-heads, Thelma." Nanette went back to combing Thelma's hair, leaving me to Carey.

Carey picked at my hair like I had head-lice. "Red hair fades with age, but yours looks like it's highlighted. I wouldn't mess up your hair for anything."

I sighed, relieved.

"But you need to start using some mousse, Sis. Do something about that frizz."

"I can't be at tomorrow's Tulip House meeting," Thelma said.

Praises!

"I'm sorry to hear that, Thelma. You'll sure be missed."

Carey winked at me. She only got along with Thelma when she needed backing up on something nobody else agreed with.

"Peter said he'll make the cupcakes, since I can't." Thelma said this like Peter's cupcakes were atrocious, so this would be a grave injustice.

"I'm sure we'll manage."

Nanette, always looking to keep her customers happy, finished combing Thelma's hair and began to fluff it up.

"I'm sure going to miss your cupcakes, Thelma. Don't you tell anyone, but his cupcakes are like eating a dried up sponge."

Thelma laughed, even though she was Peter's self-proclaimed best friend. "I sure won't tell him you said that, Nanette, but it's true."

Backstabber.

I huffed, while Carey sent me a warning look, smiled, and handed me a Diet Coke. For the next few hours I let them work their magic. By the time I left, I'd been washed, scrunched, buffed, moisturized and my toenails and fingernails were painted the lightest pink. I hated nail polish, but I had to admit, it made me feel put together. Even Thelma complimented me in her own grumpy way.

"You do look a lot better than you did a few hours ago." She leaned back in her chair while Nanette filed at her toenails, which I didn't mention to her looked like they were yellowed and several months overdue for a trim.

"Now, you go home and rest," Carey said.

"Sure thing." I gave her what I hoped was a convincing smile.

"Promise?" Nanette said.

"Of course."

"Besides," Carey said in my ear. "You need to look good for you-know-who, when he shows up to see you." She whispered it so that Thelma wouldn't hear.

"I thought you didn't approve of Doc," I whispered.

"I don't." She whispered back. "But since when do you ever listen to me? At least you ought to look good if you're going to act frivolous and carefree."

I kissed her cheek.

I was wrong about you, Carey.

But I wondered what Carey would think if she knew I'd heard her leading the conversation about switching me off when I was in a coma.

I'll try to forgive her.

I walked out to the car I now shared with Ruthie and admired the cleaning job she, Bobby, and Carl had given it the day before, amidst spray hoses and flying sponges.

To be a kid again.

I started driving toward home, thinking about what I'd make them for lunch, when I made a U-turn.

CAREY WOULD BURN my bacon if she knew I wasn't going home yet, but what she didn't know wouldn't hurt her. I promised myself I wouldn't be long. I just needed a moment that didn't involve the kids or my sisters and brothers. To throw my sisters off, I parked a block away from the church and took the alley behind the stores. A few people raised their eyebrows at seeing me, but just as quickly they smiled and said hello. I swear most of them gave me one of those smiles that said, "You're secret's safe with me." Carey's reputation to be just a tiny bit controlling is widely known. It wouldn't surprise me at all, not at all, if she'd told everyone in town to call if they happened to see me out of my cage.

Piano music floated out the church window: hard notes followed by gentle plucking that quickened my steps. I climbed the little hill and pulled out my key to the church. When you volunteer there as much as I have, you get your own key, so I went in through the side, took a back staircase, and sat in the balcony shadows where I could barely see between the curtains. I didn't really need to see. I only needed to hear. Listening to Jimmy play always made me happy. Even when we were young, he had played for me, usually the guitar that he kept in his pick-up truck, and on a few occasions, had written some songs just for me.

As he began to sing *In the Sweet By and By*, I wondered if he ever thought about when we were young, before everything went wrong.

Those were the best times.

Blessed assurance . . .

I listened to his voice soar from the auditorium into the balcony and the thought I still couldn't get out of my head niggled at my conscience. We were standing on the front porch of Momma's house only a few days earlier, both adults, Jimmy's graying sideburns crinkling as he gave me a sad smile. He pulled me close and I melted, utterly dissolved, in his arms. But then he had kissed the top of my head again. Not what I had in mind.

Why do you bother to hold me, Jimmy? Are you just being a friend?

But, a friend loveth at all times.

The thought spun through my head till I was dizzy, reminding me that he hadn't loved me at all times. I couldn't trust Jimmy. So then, why had I felt safe for just a moment in his hold when I should've been feeling betrayed? And why had my skin sizzled when he touched my face and then ached when I heard his heart beating, as he pulled me into his chest.

Friends don't make each other feel that way.

Of course, Doc made me feel that way, too, but it was different. And with all the touching and hand-holding, Doc hadn't kissed me yet. Maybe when he said he wanted to get to know me, he didn't mean it like that after all.

How am I to know? It's not like I've been practicing.

As the music of Jimmy's voice caressed my cheek in the balcony, a glimmer of hope sputtered deep inside my chest. I replayed his arms encircling me, his breath in my hair, his kiss on top of my head, and the beating, no, thundering of his heart in my ear as I pressed my cheek to his broad chest. Maybe, I dared to imagine, Jimmy knew we couldn't ever be just friends. Maybe he wanted more than a kiss to the top of my head, but I hadn't done anything to let him know. The glimmer sparked just as Jimmy sang the last note of his song, reminding me of his lips brushing mine in the hospital. I tell you what, I might be naïve, but I'm not stupid. I know what electricity is.

I WOKE UP later, my cheek on the rough seat of the pew, to the feeling of someone's hand brushing the hair back from my forehead.

Momma?

I stretched and found myself looking into the dark lashed eyes of the one I'd dreamed of waking up to my whole life. That electricity I told you about jolted through me and in trying to sit up too quickly, I saw stars. Course, the stars might've been caused by the proximity of Jimmy's face to my own.

Lord help me.

"Sh-sh. Lay back down."

"Jimmy?"

He nodded, still smoothing my hair away from my eyes. He was seated on the floor facing me. His long legs stretched beneath the pews and he leaned his broad back against the pew in front of me.

"Joy, what are you doing here?" He took my hand in his, traced his fingers along my jaw line.

Oh Lord, help me. I want to kiss this man.

I blinked, noted the warmth sliding from my hand up to my neck, and tried to decide if maybe I was back in my coma having a dream about Jimmy, my lover, or if we really were together in the balcony of the church. I inhaled, and sure enough, his Old Spice cologne filled my senses. I touched his cheek, just to be sure, and electricity shot up my shoulder.

"I was just listening to you play piano." My voice was scratchy from sleep.

"I finished hours ago. Your family is worried sick. They think you ran away, maybe found another roof to jump off of." He chuckled, but I was too tired to laugh with him.

"I don't care," I said, my eyes sleepy, but never leaving his. I wanted to be away from everyone, to be alone, but I'd be lying if I said it bothered me that Jimmy had interrupted my solitude.

"Especially, your niece. She said you missed your date with Kyle Christie."

My heart fluttered.

"I feel like a jerk. Poor Ruthie."

Poor Doc. I would call him tomorrow.

"It wasn't a date," I said. "But he was coming over to see me."

Jimmy had nothing to say to this.

"I should go call one of my sisters."

He put his hand on my arm. "Stay. Rest. I'll get Nanette a message."

I thought that maybe Ruthie and Nanette might understand, so I lay my head back down and let my eyes close. It occurred to me that this had been the longest conversation Jimmy and I'd had in years.

It was some time before Jimmy returned. I was sitting up in my pew, staring through the now open balcony curtains into the darkened church. He lowered himself into the corner of my pew, so close that tingles started from the tips of my toes and worked their way up through my torso. The truth was, I loved a man who had a lot of explaining to do, and so far he hadn't even begun to set things right, although his thigh pressing into mine as we sat in the pew beside each other might weaken my resolve.

He was there beside me, his breathing filling my ears in the silence of the church. Didn't his proximity mean something, even if we were still so far apart? I didn't know, but I was content to sit beside him all night long.

Okay, I wasn't really content. In fact, I was really quite agitated with all the butterflies and electrical currents exploding from his shoulder over to mine. What can I say? At least now, he was not a married man. And I'm not saying I'm glad Fern was passed away. I'd go without Jimmy my whole life if Fern could still be alive and Fernie and her brothers still have a mother. But truth is, she wasn't alive, and all I'm saying is that the situation was what it was.

I still didn't know how Jimmy felt about me. He was wearing his wedding band after five years of widowhood, and I, of course, had both loved and detested him for a couple of decades, but mostly loved. My heart was still his, because he'd never bothered to give it back, and the good Lord had never seen fit to answer my prayer to forget him if he couldn't be mine. Momma used to say that the ways of heaven are a mystery, and that much I would agree with.

I don't know what you're doing, Lord, but thank you for this sweet moment.

Sitting by Jimmy alone in the church still steeped in the joy of his music was more than I could've expected. As far as I was concerned, we could've sat there, just like that, side by side, our shoulders barely touching for the rest of my life, and it would have been enough for me, but after a while, he shifted and put his arm around me.

Oh.

I was wrong. I wanted more.

I sat very still, feeling the warmth from his arm against my shoulders, and it made me think of the time in the water when he cradled me and walked me into the creek, the cold water rushing around us. I remember how the water carried the ugliness of that day away in its current, and how my Jimmy's arm around my shoulders had warmed me later in his truck on the way home.

A tear for the past trailed down my cheek.

Jimmy was so close, his heat burned through me. I inhaled a shaky breath, trying to force the old sadness away, but a lone sob held in for decades escaped.

Great. So much for keeping my feelings to myself.

I heard Jimmy's intake of breath, felt his arm stiffen behind me, and—maybe it was just because we were in a church, but I wondered where God had been that day, and why he'd let Jimmy leave me.

It's a fair question, God.

I held back the next sob and it came out anyway, as a yelp. Yes, I was a sight, let me tell you. Snorting and heaving, trying to hold back a raging river of years and years and years of rejection, empty hope, and unanswered prayer. I waited for Jimmy to get up and walk away like he had before, but an amazing thing happened.

"You don't have to leave," he said. "You can stay here."

"In the church?"

"I'll drive you home when you're ready. Or—we can just stay up here."

He didn't have to tell me twice. I didn't want to go home. This was the most peace I'd had since I got home from the hospital. And he was there.

After a while, Jimmy's arm relaxed behind me. His breath grew even. He said nothing at all, but gently, tentatively, as if he thought I might be the one to run away from him, he pulled me closer. The idea that he might care if I was the one who ran away was like fresh rain washing the countryside clean. Gently, I leaned against him, testing the way his shirt felt on my cheek, how his scent permeated the air around me, and the way his heart pounded a rhythm that calmed me and steadied my breathing.

Jimmy.

I almost whispered it out loud. His breath caressed my cheek. My heart fluttered.

I want you back.

I couldn't say it aloud, but I raised my palm and pressed it against Jimmy's heart. When I raised my face, his lips caught mine in the lightest feather of a kiss, just like in the hospital, only this time I wasn't frozen in a coma. This time I didn't miss my chance. I reached around his neck and the longing of too many years parted my lips in a moan that echoed through the balcony. It was a forbidden kiss, I suppose, since we were alone in the church balcony, sprawled out on a pew in the dark and my beloved's ring finger encircled by a symbol of a marriage to his late wife, but obviously Jimmy wasn't worried about that. His arms wrapped around me and when he pulled me closer, I would have given him anything he wanted, but he only took one very long kiss. And it was a kiss to stop the earth from spinning.

In the moonlight coming through the balcony window, I saw that his eyes were closed, leaving me to believe that maybe he'd been asleep during the whole kiss. But he'd said my name. And then as if to confirm my thoughts, he said it again. I sighed.

This would happen, I whispered, not even bothering to keep my thoughts in my head since Jimmy was asleep. "We finally kiss, Jimmy, and you're asleep."

I didn't know whether to be happy or sad, which was so

often how it was being around that man. As he shifted, he tightened his arm on me, and so I gave in, at least for the night, and snuggled up to Jimmy, imagining what it would be like to fall asleep like that every night.

I smiled to myself, my last thought being that I couldn't wait to tell Carey that I slept with Jimmy Cornsilk.

Chapter Nineteen

As I CLOSED the church doors behind me and took the sidewalk over to Miss Donna's shop, I felt threads of hope stretching behind me and knew Jimmy and I were still connected. Just how that would look in the coming weeks, I had no idea, but I did know that the feeling of unsettled business that I'd always had wasn't just my overactive imagination.

In Miss Donna's, Donna herself greeted me with a smile and poured a cup of coffee.

"You're up early this morning, Joy."

I thanked her for the coffee and she set the whole pot beside me before excusing herself for a few minutes. I sat at the café counter and sipped my coffee as the tinkle of the bell signaled a few early morning travelers coming in for Honeybuns and Orange Juice. When she came back, I'd refilled my own cup and helped myself to donuts I knew Ruthie had delivered to her the day before.

"You know," Donna said. "These donuts are usually fresher."

I washed the donut down with the coffee, gave her a

guilty smile. "I'm sorry to show up before you're open. I haven't been home."

She smiled, as if she'd known. "It's okay. But you should know that your family was in here looking for you last night. How you doing?"

"Good," I assured her. "Just been spending time with an old friend."

"Anyone in particular?" I knew she wasn't prying and I appreciated her for caring enough to ask.

"Someone I thought I'd lost."

"So . . . You didn't lose him? Or her? Is this a romantic thing?"

"Him," I admitted with a smile. "And I don't know."

"Still friends?" she asked.

I nodded yes and she came around and sat beside me at the counter, while we sipped coffee together. That's what I'd always loved about Donna, even when we were still in high school. She asked questions, but she didn't really expect you to answer unless you wanted to.

"Do you think men and women can be just friends, Donna?"

She snorted. "I used to say no, but sure. Sometimes, at our age, it's best to be just friends."

"Our age?" I chided her. "You may think you're old, Donna, but I, for one, don't think I am."

"Forties," she said.

"We're the same age," I reminded. "But I think I know what you mean."

"I guess I've always thought that friends are forever, so

friends might be best. Love on the other hand, isn't always for that long."

I sipped the last of my coffee and set the cup down with a sigh, the click on the counter echoing along with the clink of spoons and plates. The diner side had opened up and the two girls who worked for Donna were busy running about in their turquoise aprons and pink waitress dresses.

"I wish we could have both, love and friendship, don't you, Donna?"

"Sure," she said. "A girl can hope. I mean, look at you. We thought we lost you, honey. And now here we are having coffee and talking about our man problems."

"You're a good friend."

"I'm glad you're alive, Joy. And glad you got past Carey and out of that prison." I thought about defending Carey, but Donna was no fool.

"She probably doesn't know I'm still out." We both laughed.

Outside, everywhere I turned, someone greeted me with a hello.

"Glad to see you, Joy." Mrs. Reed, the Kindergarten teacher on her way to school.

"Hello, Miss Joy!" A former Sunday school student.

"Happy you're okay, Joy." Officer Gray, not to be confused with the mean old sheriff.

"Joy!" Jack, the old town landscaper. "Glad you woke up, honey."

"Joy!" A gentle hug and a kiss on the cheek from Peter, my favorite gossip, who loves my strawberry-lemon cake and one of the newest members of the Tulip House for Girls fundraising committee. "Joy, I'm glad to see you out and about. I need to get that strawberry-lemon cake recipe." I smiled. "Thelma was going through withdrawals while you were in the hospital."

"It's a secret." I teased. "And I saw her yesterday. She was fine."

"Oh," he said. "Then, you haven't heard. I thought your sisters would tell you."

"I haven't exactly seen them since yesterday," I said.

I leaned closer, sensing something was wrong.

"What's up, Peter? Is everything okay?"

"Thelma had a stroke, right out of the blue, yesterday after she left Momma's Curls."

"Oh, no," I said, and meant it. "Poor Thelma." That's when I noticed how pale Peter was, how dark the circles under his eyes.

"Of course, all strokes happen out of the blue, but it was just so much more surprising that it happened to Thelma. But she can talk slowly, and the doctors said that besides needing a wheelchair for a while, she'll be okay. They say if she works hard, she'll regain her usual speech, maybe be able to walk with a cane." My heart swelled with emotion. Thelma, in a wheelchair. Not able to talk at her usual speed. Thelma loved to talk.

I gave Peter a small smile. "I'm glad she's going to be okay. And you're a good friend, Peter. Glad she has you." I really was glad. I didn't like Thelma sometimes, but I did love her. I'd known her for as long as I'd known Peter and

Donna. We'd all been good friends in high school, but Thelma had held onto the teenage pettiness a lot longer than the rest of us. Still, she didn't deserve to be stuck in a wheel chair.

"I'll tell her you said that. Thank the good Lord above she'll still be able to talk."

Indeed.

"Someday I'll get that strawberry-lemon recipe from you, but obviously she won't be at the meeting today."

"No problem. Ruthie and I'll take care of the cupcakes."

He patted me on the shoulder as he walked away, and some of my grudge against him loosened. Peter used to be one of my best friends, my junior prom date, and he was so kind to Thelma, even though she had always been a bit difficult. Maybe I'd been too hard on him, just because he acted ridiculous at Momma's funeral.

After doing a little shopping in the handful of stores, I headed back to my car. As I stepped into my cherry red Chevy, for a minute I was overcome by the love in Spavinaw Junction and had to pull the tissue out of my pocket.

Poor Thelma.

I was thinking about how I was always so preoccupied with Talley stuff that I never really stopped to think that much about all my friends. And there were quite a few of them, I guessed, judging by all the people who'd wished me well. So, why hadn't any of them besides the reverend been out to see me yet?

A loud knock at my window liked to have made me jump out of my seat. It was Carey, shaking her finger at me through the glass, and then I remembered. Carey kept everyone away, except Jimmy. Even the meals that people from church made for me were delivered through Carey. It made me sad that she didn't even realize that it would have raised my spirits to have more visitors from town.

I rolled down the window.

"Where in the tarnation have you been?" She planted her hands on her hips. "We have all been worried sick about you. Who in the world stays out all night without calling someone?"

"Hi, Sis. I was thinking we need to have a party." I really hadn't, but as soon as it rolled of my tongue, I couldn't believe we'd never invited the residents of Spavinaw Junction to a party at the big Talley house.

Carey started wagging her finger again, but stopped when I spouted out my idea.

"What did you say?"

"I said, let's have a party out at the Talley house."

Her jaw dropped. "Absolutely not. You know we don't have parties for the community at our house. Even if you were ready for more company, and you aren't, there's too much at stake."

"Not anymore," I said. "We have a new chimney and it's free of charms. Nothing embarrassing to hide."

She opened her mouth to protest, but I stopped her short. Gone was the sweet Carey from the beauty shop the day before. So much for my hope that she was on my side.

"Bring those Whoopie pies you make so well, Carey." I rolled up the window, but then rolled it back down again.

"And while you're at it, make some of those with that poor husband of yours. Maybe it'll loosen you up a little."

With that, I backed away, window down, careful not to run over my sister's toes as she stumbled along side of me shouting something about how she didn't need to make Whoopie pies with her husband.

"What's so great about Whoopie pies?" she shouted. "And why would my husband and I want to make them together? I want to bring something else!" I saw her stamp her foot in the rearview mirror. "I don't even like Whoopie pies!"

By the time she let me out of the parking lot, a little crowd of older women were giggling and pointing in front of the church. My sister stood with her back to them, arms crossed and looking huffy as the meaning of my joke set in.

Chapter Twenty

THE NEXT MORNING I did some more visiting around town, enjoying my newfound freedom, but when I got back at lunchtime, everyone was at my house sitting at the kitchen table.

"Where have you been, Joy?" Nanette asked.

At first I was just so surprised at Nanette's tone that I stood there, but then I realized she was serious.

"What am I? A teenager? How long have you all been here?"

"Long enough to know that you aren't resting like you should be. And we know you didn't come home the other night, like Jimmy told Nanette you would."

It was pretty clear to me that Carey hadn't bothered to enlist her husband's help in making Whoopie pies, as I'd suggested. That girl was wound tighter than a top, as she now stood in front of the newly built fireplace wagging her finger at me.

"Are you crazy? What's this really about? I'm a grown woman. I can come home late if I want to." I didn't think now was a good time to tease her with the joke I'd thought of about sleeping with Jimmy.

"It's not *my* mental state that's in question," Carey said.

"Are you calling me crazy?"

"I didn't actually say crazy."

"You didn't have to!"

Carey arched her eyebrows and shot a look toward Nanette, who cast reluctant eyes at Rory, who shot a disheartening glance at River, who sadly looked at me. But nobody else was brave enough to say anything yet. After several beats of my angry heart, Carey, naturally, was the one to unleash their terrible idea into the room and it rose up before me like the Howler Momma thought she'd exercised from our woods.

"What's this about?" A sense of foreboding encircled me like a spell.

"Joy?" She said it like a question, her voice soft and sickly reassuring. "We all," she nervously motioned towards the others, and I knew I was outnumbered this time. "We four agree that it would help if you saw a psychologist."

"How ridiculous. I'm not doing that. You go do that."

"What?"

"You think I need to go see a psychologist, because I stayed out all night? What's wrong with you?"

"Well," Carey said. "It's not just about that night. You have to admit. It's out of character for you. Just like lots of things, like your stories about your coma, and—and—"

"Like dying and coming back to life? And what, hearing what people say?"

"Yes."

"Hearing people say things like, you all saying you should unplug me in the hospital, if I didn't get better? And planning my funeral?"

Carey walked slowly to the table. Sat. The looks on the others' faces were priceless.

"How did you know about that?" She looked around the room. "Who told her?"

"Nobody told me, Carey. I heard you say it."

"But that was in the hospital, when you were—"

I didn't say anything, just stared at her as the truth registered.

"Oh gosh," River said. "We were never going to do that Joy." Everyone joined River's protests, except Carey, who sat completely still.

For a second or two, I thought I'd reached her, but when she stood up to her full five-foot-two inches, five-foot-six when you had the height of her Aqua Net hair, I knew the moment had passed and she was back to being the self-righteous bossy Carey.

"But you tried to kill yourself, Joy. Don't you think at least talking to a psychologist would help?"

"Carey," I said. "Have I made any comments since I woke up about ending my life?"

"No, but that doesn't mean you haven't thought of it."

"What is wrong with you? Have you been watching *The Donahue Show* again?"

She didn't say anything. My brothers and sisters stared at her.

"Oh my God. You have. What was it, an episode on

depression or suicide? Both?"

Carey shook her head. "It just sounded like your situation."

"Right," River said. "Because everything about Joy's situation is so common."

I laughed. Couldn't help it. "Well, this is ridiculous." I plopped down in a chair. "And I'll have all of you know once and for all that I didn't try to kill myself."

Blank stares. They still thought that part was true.

"Listen, y'all. I think it's time everyone stopped judging. You know I'm not crazy any more than you're crazy."

"I never said crazy, Joy." Carey stared at the table. "I wasn't suggesting the looney bin, only a psychologist."

"Well, I'm not talking to one. I don't need it. I think this tornado and the chimney, the charms being dislodged, has all made us a little batty."

"I agree." Nanette.

"And what we need is cake," I said. I walked to the fridge and took out a five layer, three-berry cake with cream cheese frosting that I have to admit looked just like a cloud on top.

"Cake can't solve everything," Carey said.

"Why not?" My brothers echoed me.

Carey didn't answer, just plunged a fork in her cake without saying anything.

"What about Momma? Should she have seen a psychologist?"

"Of course not." Rory.

"Well, maybe." River.

"That's not nice!" Nanette.

"Momma making calming teas and chocolates isn't the same as throwing yourself off the roof." Carey looked tired and unsure of herself.

"So you *are* saying I'm nuts?"

"Not exactly nuts, but not normal, not lately."

"Carey, honey." I struggled to be calm. "What makes me abnormal? That I believe in miracles? That my heart stopped and started again? That something happened back in that coma that I can't explain?" I paused, thinking about the miracles I had seen lately. "Or that the chimney took what I was looking for and made it disappear?"

Oh my word. It's gone.

I smiled, in spite of the anger that'd been rising in my chest just moments ago.

The tornado saved me.

"Joy," Nanette said. "Are you ok?"

Miracles.

I looked up, still smiling.

"Miracles," I said.

River shrugged. "What are you talking about now, Joy?"

"All of it. Miracles. Isn't that what our family has always believed in? Well, I don't need to see a psychologist just because I believe in miracles."

River stood up and announced he was going to the shop. "I have work to do." Rory followed.

Nanette stood to go next. "Come on, Carey. We have to open the beauty shop." To my surprise, Carey followed Nanette, then paused.

"The mayor said you were coming home after we couldn't find you. Where did you go anyway?"

My straws were all gone.

"Not that it's any of your business, but, I was sleeping with Jimmy Cornsilk all night . . . in the church balcony." It gave me a huge amount of satisfaction to get her goat, and technically I wasn't lying.

"You slept with someone?" Nanette sounded interested.

"With Jimmy?" Carey made it sound like I'd danced with the devil.

"Yes," I said. "Imagine that. Me! Having a life, Carey."

Nanette grabbed my arm. "Is he a good kisser?

"Nanette!" Now, Carey wagged her finger at Nanette.

"Yes, he's a great kisser."

"So what about Doc? You're seeing them both?"

The question caught me unawares. I wasn't sure, but she took my silence as a yes.

"That makes you a slut."

The insult slapped me stupid, so I slapped her back, but for real, just like we were on a soap opera, and I didn't feel bad about it. She rubbed her cheek, but to her credit didn't retaliate. She just looked sad, which took all the glory out of it for me. How does she do that?

The screen door slapped shut and we all looked to see who it was.

"That will be enough of this." The words echoed through the house like the voice of God, and I guess they sort of were. It was Reverend Wilson. "Now, Joy. We have a meeting. Can I give you a ride?"

I didn't know what meeting he was talking about, but I wasn't about to say no.

"What do you think your Momma would've thought about this, girls?"

Carey shrugged, tears pooling in her eyes. One thing I knew for sure was that Reverend Wilson's opinion mattered as much to Carey as God's.

"I'm sorry." She bowed her head. "I was just trying to help."

"Reverend, what meeting do we have?"

"No meeting," He said, his head bobbing along with the car as we bounced down the gravel road a little faster than I would expect for a preacher. "I just stopped by for some more cake, and it sounded like you needed an escape."

"Thank you. It got a little out of hand."

"Joy?"

"Yes?"

"Did you and Jim really, um, spend the evening in the balcony?" I felt my face turn red as a beet, but I couldn't lie.

"Yes," I said. "But it wasn't like that. I just wanted Carey to know I don't have to follow her rules."

Am I really talking about this with a preacher? Oh my word.

"We kissed, but we didn't . . . well, we wouldn't have . . . not there. I'm so sorry if it sounded like that's what happened." I wished I'd never said it out loud now. "Please don't fire him. He's a good man. It's complicated, but . . ."

"Why would I fire him?"

I shrugged. How humiliating.

"I'm not going to fire that boy."

I looked over to see him smiling. Smiling! Can you imagine a reverend smiling when he found out two people spent the evening together in the church?

"In fact, I'm going to give Jimmy a pat on the back, and say, 'It's about time.'"

Chapter Twenty-one

AFTER THE PSYCHOLOGIST discussion I started taking more of my life into my own hands, instead of being at the mercy of the meddling ones of my sisters and brothers. Some might say that a small-town, old maid like me would be lucky to have one option after so many years of being by myself, but it turned out, I had a choice. Not long after, I sat at my kitchen table with Doc. He'd stopped by early in the evening just to check on me. He did that a lot, and I honestly looked forward to his visits.

We'd talked for hours as usual, and now it was midnight. We were talking about The Tulip House for Girls and about how my grumpy friend Thelma sat in her wheel chair and slowly talked the mayor into giving one hundred dollars of his own money.

"Lots of folks are stepping into help," I said. "The mayor has been especially helpful." Since the night we spent in the church, Jimmy hadn't said another word about the kiss. It hurt me a little, but I tried to believe it was for the best. Maybe he really had been asleep and couldn't remember it, but obviously, Jimmy didn't want to face that past with me, and he certainly didn't want a future with me as more than a friend.

"Like everyone else," Doc said. "He probably cares about seeing you succeed. Cornsilk's been talking about The Tulip House for Girls to everyone, urging people to give their own money to help you out."

That he would enlist others to support Tulip House was a surprise. My heart warmed to think he cared that much, at least for the cause.

"In fact, Cornsilk talks about you a lot around town." I saw the question in Doc's eyes, but refused to answer.

News to me.

"Is that so?"

"It's so," Doc said. "In fact, he was just bragging at coffee this morning about your lasagna. Said you served it at one of your fundraisers a few days ago. I'm sorry I wasn't there to help you this time, Joy."

"It's okay." I thought it was sweet for him to think he needed to be at something so common as a lasagna supper, just to be supportive. "You were busy saving lives, no doubt." I reached out and squeezed his arm. "Much to Carey's and Thelma's surprise, we made three hundred dollars. You did miss some darn good lasagna."

"So, Cornsilk also mentioned you two went to school together." Now that comment was out of the ordinary. Why were we still talking about Jimmy? I studied his face. He didn't seem to be prying, just making conversation, but I wondered.

"The mayor was older than me, but yes, we were friends

once upon a time."

Once upon a fairytale. One with a very sad ending.

Since the fairytale kiss in the church balcony, I'd seen a lot more of Jimmy, but he was careful to keep his distance. He probably couldn't remember the kiss, and if he did, he might've decided it was a mistake. For all I know, I'm a bad kisser. It's not like I have anything to compare it to, after all. I looked at Doc, wondering what it would be like to kiss him.

"Pretty good friends, according to him," Doc said. I blushed at the thought of explaining just how close. "Were you two an item?"

I blinked. I'd had this crush on Doc ever since he'd first peeked into my eyes during my coma. I'd enjoyed Ruthie's romantic ideas about his "liking" me, but since he'd never made any kind of move on me, I'd come to the realization that Doc and I were only friends, and it was okay with me, because not only was he a little young as far as our age difference, but I could use a friend like Doc more than I needed a boyfriend. I had already decided that if he wanted to be friends, then I'd take it, but seeing the worried look in his eyes as he plied me with questions about Jimmy, I wondered if I was wrong.

Could Doc like me?

"We were friends a long time ago," I said. "He's a widow now, with grown kids. You know how it is. You can be friends with boys in school, but when they grow up, you change to being friends with their wives, or not at all. His wife and I were never close." I would have never been close with the woman who got pregnant with my boyfriend's baby.

He chuckled. "I have to admit that, God rest her soul, I was never crazy about Fern either. I knew her when we were kids."

"You knew Fern?"

"Her and Cornsilk both." Well, that was a surprise.

"Cornsilk's mom and my parents were friends. My mom was always trying to help her since Cornsilk's dad was a first class jerk before he left, but I guess you knew that part, since you were friends. You knew about his dad's disappearance."

"I did," I said, hoping he didn't notice the shudder that moved through my body at the mention of Jimmy's dad.

"Fern was way ahead of me in school, but I remember that she dropped out when she was in 11th grade," he explained. "Because she was—"

"Pregnant."

Doc's eyes formed that question again, and then a realization. "And then she married Cornsilk."

"Yep." I scooted away from Doc.

"The whole thing about his marrying Fern never made sense to me," Doc said. I wanted him to stop talking, but I also wanted to hear about it from his perspective. "Cornsilk had always had this secret girlfriend that he wouldn't tell any of us about. Said she was younger than him and he was just waiting for her to get out of high school, so they could get married."

I found a spot on the table to stare at, hoping the sound

of my heart beating wasn't as loud in the kitchen as it was in my ears. I never knew Jimmy told anyone about a mystery girlfriend. Was that me?

"Maybe Fern was the mystery girl."

"No," Doc said. "The mystery girl was a pale princess. 'Sweet as honey and more beautiful than roses.' We made fun of him for it, of course, but I think we all secretly wanted this mystery girl for ourselves."

It *was* me.

That did it. My heart burst open. I looked at Doc. He'd noticed, and I saw the full realization of the situation spread across his face.

"You're her, aren't you?" I turned my chin away, so that Doc couldn't see, but he's no dummy. He placed his hand over mine, but I pulled it away, stood to refill the coffee, my eyes misting over at the revelation of all I'd really lost back then. Doc would never understand that it was more than losing a boyfriend. I lost everything. And in some ways, so had Jimmy.

"Why didn't you tell me you used to date the mayor, Joy?"

I composed myself and stirred a spoon of sugar into my coffee before looking at Doc.

"He never told me Fern was pregnant," I said. "I found out when Reverend Wilson announced it at church."

"What an idiot," Doc said. "How could anyone do something like that . . . to you?"

I didn't correct him, didn't defend Jimmy. I remembered how days and days would pass before I would hear from him, and eventually, I stopped hearing from him at all.

"From what I remember," Doc said, "Cornsilk was wild and Fern was looking to be wild, too. That's when she got pregnant with Jimmy's baby and well, you know the rest."

"They had two more kids and were married for over twenty-five years," I said.

Doc reached across the table and took my hand.

"Wow. I never guessed you were the one he was so in love with, the pale princess." He smiled. "I always wondered why, if she were so great, he would get together with Fern. Now, I really think he was stupid."

I made my face go blank. "It was a long time ago."

"But he visits you. I guess you've made up and are friends now, right?" He looked hopeful and I knew that he didn't just want to be my friend. If I'd known that fact a couple of hours sooner, I might have donned Momma's old wedding dress and rode away with him on his motorcycle. Now sad memories of Jimmy clouded my mind. Darn it, fate.

"Yes. We're friends now." I feigned a yawn. "It's almost 1:00 am."

"I should go."

I grasped his hand. "Thanks."

Doc's amber eyes captured mine. Everything he'd told me about Jimmy made my heart ache. His fingers were warm around my own, safe.

"Joy," he whispered. "I would never hurt you that way."

For a minute I thought of Jimmy's kiss in the church balcony, but listening to Doc talk about Jimmy and Fern, I knew I was stupid to have ever put too much meaning on that one kiss. He'd given her his last name, a house, and children. He'd led a whole entire life without me. How stupid, and wrong, was I to hang on to him?

Doc ran his thumb across the top of my hand, sending pulses through my lonely, aching body.

You've been such an idiot, Joy.

"Do you still want me to leave, Joy?"

"No," I breathed, nervous about his touch, knowing it was my grief that made me cling to his hands, but not wanting to let go either. I could use a friend.

What would it be like to kiss Doc?

I could use more than just a friend, and it was obvious from the way he was looking at me that Doc didn't want to be just friends.

"Let me wash these dishes," I said, gathering up the saucers and coffee cups we'd just used.

"Let me help."

He came around the table and stood in my way, hooking his thumbs in his belt loops. I set the plates I'd been holding in the sink, and then turned to lean back on it, facing him. He looked so comfortable in his caramel skin, his amber eyes studying my face, a lot like Jimmy had when he was younger.

Don't think about Jimmy!

Doc smiled encouragement. I couldn't help but appreciate how his thick hair curled down to where I knew a thin braid was tucked into the button down shirt he'd worn to work. He'd unbuttoned it at some point in the evening and

I could now see how the white cotton t-shirt he wore underneath stretched across his chest. He was a bit too young for me, but obviously nobody had told him that.

"Joy," he was saying. I blinked, letting his image register in reality again. "You in there?"

"Sometimes I'm not sure," I teased. "Since I woke up from my coma, I don't always know where dreams and reality meet anymore."

"Let me show you, reality, Joy." He placed his hands on the counter on either side of me. I could feel his eyes on mine, but was too jittery to meet them. We weren't two teenagers sneaking down to the creek. There were no brothers and sisters to hide from, no Momma to answer to. No late wife whose memory could steal his mind away. No golden band on his wedding finger. But I'm in love with the last man I made out with.

I kept my eyes fixed on his t-shirt while he slid his arm softly around my shoulders.

"Doc?"

His voice was low and even. "Please, would you stop calling me Doc?"

I forgot what I'd been about to say.

"Why?" My heart pounded like the bass drum at a Friday night Spavinaw Junction football game.

He tipped my chin and like a silly school girl, images of movie kisses scrolled through my mind.

"It makes it hard to kiss you when you call me Doc. Doctors kissing patients is inappropriate."

"True," I whispered. "And illegal."

"So say my name."

I took a shaky breath and let it out slowly. What would Jimmy think, if he could see me now?

I worried about it for a second, but then remembered that Jimmy hadn't made a move since the church balcony. Doc, on the other hand, had been waiting silently all these minutes, caressing my arms and tracing my jaw with his fingertips, while I'd been pondering, deciding, allowing my heart to reach from one old memory into a new moment, pounding its way toward Doc.

Doc's hands were on my shoulders now, squeezing them gently, his thumbs encouraging, massaging the fatigue away. He slid one hand behind my neck and kneaded my spine where it had ached since my accident with the rope.

"Relax, Joy."

I closed my eyes, tilted my head back, letting Doc's hand massage the dull pain of my neck that had never quite gone away since my fall from the roof, while his other hand left my shoulder to gently cup my chin. I noticed, to my delight, that his breath was as shaky as mine, but doubted he was the least bit nervous like me.

"Kyle."

His name came out like a gasp and he captured it with a kiss that wasn't slow and sweet like in so many of my romance novels, but heavy from waiting. I wrapped my arms around his waist, marveling at the feeling of muscle and bone hot against me.

So this is what it's like to kiss a younger, but very grown, man.

He mumbled in my ear. "Joy, you are—" he pulled me closer and buried his chin in my hair and growled. "Incredible." He captured my lips. "That kiss," he said between pecks, "was worth waiting for, I guess."

Emboldened I ran my hands up his arms. "I had no idea what I was missing these last few decades."

He pulled back. "Decades?"

Not the right thing to say?

My face flooded with warmth. "Maybe I shouldn't have said that."

He gently cupped my face in his hands. "Are you serious? You haven't kissed a man in that many years?"

"Once." I omitted the fact that it had happened recently and the fact that it had been Jimmy. "And of course there was Peter, on prom night, but you probably can tell. He's on my team, not yours."

He chuckled. "Never mind about his team, how can it be that you haven't been kissed properly for so many years?" He smoothed my hair back from my face and the way he looked into my eyes made me want to cry. "You are so beautiful. You should be kissed every day."

"It's not as if anyone has been banging down my door asking me to dinner." Although even as I said it, a list of dinner invitations from men at church and around the area scrolled through my mind. I blinked, realizing how my pining after Jimmy had kept me blinded to other chances at happiness, and maybe even love.

He planted another kiss on my mouth. "I'm not complaining." He whispered between kisses. "In fact, I think it's sexy."

Sexy?

The thought thrilled me.

"If I'd known, I would have held back a little." He gently brushed the hair back from my face.

"Please, don't—hold back I mean."

We kissed again after that and I let myself be swept away. Feelings I'd saved for an impossibly long time rose up. I wrapped my arms around his neck and wondered if I could let myself forget about Jimmy and fall for Doc. I wondered if my crush could turn into love. I let his kisses graze my neck and his hands smooth away my frazzled nerves, closer—much closer—to waking up the person I had glimpsed when I first woke up from my coma.

"Kyle, I . . ."

He placed a finger over my lips. "Sh-sh. Don't say it. It's too soon. Just feel it, Joy."

"Kyle—" I kissed him again. "I don't want you to think I'm ready to—"

"Don't worry," he said between kisses. "This is just practice."

"Practice for what?" I whispered.

"When you're ready, I'd sure like to show you."

His hands dropped to the curve of my hips, slid around to slip inside my back pockets and pulled me close.

Oh!

Thank goodness I'd bought those new jeans Ruthie made me try on.

"And I'd like to show you for a long time to come." His

breath was hot on my neck.

My knees went weak, just like in every romance novel I'd ever read.

Okay, I may not be young anymore, but I still had dreams of wedding dresses, steeples, and a nice long honeymoon. Preferably by the ocean. Could I have that kind of thing with Kyle?

A part of me, the part that loved Jimmy, wouldn't allow me to abandon myself just yet, but as Kyle's lips pressed against mine, his mouth warm and inviting, I glimpsed the possibility. I'd be lying if I didn't admit that it stirred a hope inside of me, and something else that I don't think had anything to do with hope. Like I said in the very beginning, I'm not a saint.

Chapter Twenty-two

"AUNT JOY, I thought you would fall for the mayor." Ruthie touched the roses from Kyle that sat in the center of Momma's big white table.

"You don't like Kyle, honey?"

"Oh, I like him. He's dreamy." She leaned in to breathe in the roses. Their fragrance was so sweet, the kitchen smelled like a rose garden.

"I'm just surprised. You and the mayor have some kind of . . . oh . . . I don't know . . . electricity when you're around each other." She smiled. "Like sizzles."

A bright blue blotch bled onto the poster board from the force I'd pressed the marker with.

"Darn," I complained. How had Ruthie ever gotten that impression? And how would she know it's the truth? Ruthie promptly took the marker and poster from me.

"It's okay. I'll fix it." She drew a tulip around the blotch and colored it in, adding a green stem. "There." She sat back.

"A blue tulip for the Tulip House."

We were at the kitchen table making posters for the big

fundraiser to top all fundraisers so far, which would be held at the Talley home. It would be a picnic style dinner with live country music and games for all and I was taking Reverend's advice and raising the price for dinner by a dollar.

The only sad part for me was, knowing that it could be the last party ever held at the house. The issue of the house had come back. The Lawyer, Mr. Littleton, had come over last week and urged me to make a decision. If we can't find someone to lease the land to, we might lose it. I refused to sell, but couldn't say no to a lease forever. My siblings and I just didn't have the resources to make the mortgage payment and pay back Momma's late payments and fees, as well.

"So what about the mayor?"

"We're friends, honey. You know that. You were here when he visited, but he's a widower. Sometimes widowers have a hard time moving on to someone new. I think maybe the mayor is like that, too."

"Every Sunday he asks how you are."

"That's what people in the ministry do, honey. He's the music leader, so he's kind of like a reverend himself. He needs to ask about everybody because that's his job."

"And he asks when I see him at Miss Donna's, when he's working on his car with Uncle River and Uncle Rory, and when I see him at the library."

My heart skipped a beat to think he cared enough to ask, but if he still thought about me the way that Ruthie had hoped, then he would have said something.

"We are friends," I said. "We'll always be friends."

"Do men come visit you a lot, when they're just friends?" Ruthie was standing at the window. I joined her. Jimmy was sitting in his over-sized truck, window down, talking to River and Rory in the driveway.

I kept my tone even. "Sure, honey. Friends visit."

"Will Kyle get mad if he finds out?" The truth was, I didn't know, but Ruthie's questions were making me want to pull my hair out. Jimmy had continued to visit, even after it became apparent that I was spending time with Kyle. I didn't think he was trying to get my attention. He was always looking for my brothers anyway. Or at least that's what I'd thought.

Maybe he really just wanted to know what I did with that dratted charm we hid in the chimney together. Could he still be thinking about it? Well, it was too late. He needed to forget about it, and so did I.

I'm glad it's gone.

But even as I thought it, the feeling that it could never be gone seized my chest, squeezing the air from my lungs. I breathed in, the way Daddy showed me when I had panic attacks as a girl.

Ruthie put her arm around me, and she sounded so mature that for a moment she could have been Nanette, instead of a teenage girl.

"It's not too, late, if you think you might have picked the wrong one." Ruthie capped her marker and stacked the signs neatly in the center of the table. "Do you mind if I go up to the attic and read for a while?"

I was relieved to have an opportunity with my own thoughts. "Sure. I'm just going to finish up the guest list. Grab some chocolate on your way up." The committee had been meeting regularly and we decided that in addition to inviting the community at large to the fundraiser, we should send personal invitations to individuals of some notoriety in the region.

I smiled as she called for Lucky to follow and trotted up to the attic.

"I'll just be reading."

And writing in your diary.

I wondered if I should take a look in there, just in case.

An engine roared and I turned back to the window. The boys watched Jimmy drive away before turning toward the porch. They both wore perplexed looks on their faces. I stood, placing my hands on my hips when they came in.

"What'd Jimmy want?"

"He said to say hi," Rory said. "He asked how you were doing."

"Why didn't he ask me himself?"

"He had to get back to work and didn't have time to come in."

River grabbed two beers from somewhere in the fridge that I'd missed. I hated having beer where Bobby could get a hold of it, so I tried to dump it out when one of my brother's left it behind, but somehow they always managed to pull a beer out from somewhere.

"So, what else did he want? Surely he didn't come out just to check on me." Rory and River shared a look, but they didn't explain it to me.

"You're not going to like the other reason."

"Spit it out."

Chairs screeched across the hard wood floor and the men sat down at the kitchen table, knees wide.

"He wants to buy this house," Rory said.

Anger prickled along the back of my ears. He abandoned me, kissed me while I was in a coma, kissed me while he dreamt of me in the balcony and forgot, and he doesn't care at all that I'm dating a man more than ten years younger than him. Now, he suddenly thinks I would let him buy the house? He could've had it if he'd married me. Crazy thoughts, I know, but I was so mad that strange things were flying around inside my head.

"Is he crazy? What's he want to do with it? Tear it down and build a new one? I mean, the repairs alone will be a fortune."

River took a long drink and set his can on the table. "He wants to save the house for you."

Me. Why?

I gave them an incredulous look.

"Oh, come on Sis. It's not a secret. You announced to the whole family that you made out with him in the church balcony."

A decision I regret.

"I'm dating Kyle."

"Good ole Doc," River said. I tossed my dish towel onto the counter and plopped down in the chair. I didn't feel like discussing my love life with the boys. I went for changing the topic.

"How much is he willing to pay?"

"As much as you need, Sis." River tilted his head back and drained his beer. The blood drained from my face.

I paced the kitchen. "That man drives me crazy. I don't trust him."

River raised his eyebrows. "Sit down. Let's think about this."

"No."

"Yes."

"I don't want to."

River stood and escorted me to a chair. I sat down, albeit begrudgingly.

Rory opened a can of beer and handed it to me. He didn't blink an eye when I took a swig. It tasted worse than I expected.

"I've never seen you this upset, Sis."

I drained the can.

"Me neither," said River. "What's wrong?"

I shook my head, but couldn't even begin to tell them. Jimmy hadn't marched into the kitchen, told me he loved me, and only then offered to help me buy the house.

Rory leaned forward. "What is it with you and Jimmy? He wants to help you out of this mess before the lawyer really starts giving you a hard time. He wouldn't offer that if—well, you know. If he didn't care or something."

Honesty with River and Rory? I couldn't imagine sharing such deep complexities with my brothers. Now, don't get me wrong. They're not stupid. They are just, well, as

I've said before, they're tool and dye sharp, not book smart. Of course, they might not be helpful about man troubles, but maybe we could settle something else.

"That's right," River said. "Maybe we can help you."

I belched. They laughed.

I thought about what they would do if I told them the truth about Jimmy, what happened to me—and to him, to be honest. The boys were staring at me, expectantly.

They were big boys. They were protective. And their cuteness really belied their capacity for anger. They might misunderstand what happened. Not even Jimmy with all his strength would be able to save himself from my brothers.

Scary.

It was best to give them something, but not that.

"I've been seeing Daddy a lot in my dreams."

"That's good," Rory said. I laughed, surely I misunderstood him. "Really, I mean it. I'm glad to know the old man is watching over you. Lord knows you are too much of a handful for your brothers to keep up with."

I punched him hard in the arm. My fist just bounced off, so I leaned over and gave him a big long hug and when I noticed Rory smiling, but looking a bit jealous, I hugged him too.

"So much has changed since we were kids," Rory said.

River scoffed. "But everything changes too slowly. Things move slower here than molasses, you know."

Oh sweet molasses. It sure does.

"But things do change," I said. "I mean, look at the new beautiful chimney you boys built. If Momma were here, I wonder if she'd put new charms in it?"

Both were quiet. The boys sat frozen, their beers clasped in their hands, boots planted wide on the floor, eyes staring at the hardwood. The breeze blew through the cotton curtains, lifting them like a ghost blowing in from the past. Rory shifted in his chair.

"Faith says we got to forget about all those charms and stuff. Says we should've never let the chimney get that way in the first place."

"Sweet positive Faith," River said. "You have a good wife. She would say something like that, as if we had a choice."

I guess River should've left it at that, but maybe he'd had one beer too many because then he said, "Someone like Faith wouldn't understand anyway."

"Someone like Faith?" Rory's eyes turned dark and stormy.

"Someone whose had a charmed life, without a chimney filled with them." River sat his can on the table beside the other empties.

Rory looked like he might hit River, so I placed my hand over his arm. "That's not true, River. Faith hasn't had a charmed life at all."

"Heck no, it ain't true. You all don't know it, but the first time she got pregnant, she lost it."

Holy Moses. How did I miss this?

I pressed my hand over my mouth while River clasped Rory's shoulder.

"Bro, why didn't you say something?"

Rory let one lone tear trail a path down his cheek. I'm telling you right now, there is nothing harder than seeing a big man like Rory cry.

"She didn't want me to tell anyone."

So, I'm not the only one who managed to keep a secret from the family.

"Why the hell not?" River said. What people didn't know about River was that as grumpy as he could be, he was nothing but a big pat of butter waiting to melt. Rory frowned.

"She thought there was something wrong with her. So, she's real worried about this one." His face hardened.

"She's hurt, too. All anyone talks about is stupid luck charms and Joy being crazy."

"What?" I lay a hand on his arm.

"Nobody's even given her a baby shower. You're all too wrapped up in your own stuff."

Rory never got mad for no reason. I wouldn't cry, no matter how ashamed I felt, because this was Rory's pity party and not mine, but I felt awful. It was true. This was just one more thing I'd not paid attention to before my coma, so wrapped up in my boring life was I.

"We're sorry," River said.

I searched for the right words, but they wouldn't come. I might as well have been back in my coma. "So sorry about the baby, and for not showing y'all we're excited about this one. Guess we were just waiting for him to come, honey."

"And her," Rory said. "Him and her."

"Oh my Lord!" I jumped out of my chair. River started

slapping Rory on the back, while I hugged his big old chest.

"Twins?"

"Twins!" River exclaimed. "That ought to be good luck, right?"

I laughed. "Not luck. Just a blessing."

"A miracle," Rory said.

"Yes, a doggone miracle," River agreed.

If Momma had been there, she, of course, would've given all kinds of reasons why Talley twins were a good omen, but none of us were saying it now.

Before the boys went back to work, Rory surprised me by turning the subject back to Jimmy.

"Sis, you got to patch things up with Jimmy. It's killin' him to see you and Doc hangin' out together."

"What?" That couldn't be true. Jimmy hadn't so much as called me and asked me to dinner since the night in the balcony. Either he really had been asleep, or he felt some moral dilemma about the rumors that were going around about that night, thanks to none other than my sister, and you can guess which one.

"It's true," River said.

"It's not."

"It is," Rory assured me. "Just think about it."

They each kissed me and walked out, leaving me to question everything I was starting to think about my relationship with Kyle. And apparently with Jimmy.

Ruthie's Diary

Dear Diary

Please don't think I'm a spy, but I overheard my uncles talking to Aunt Joy about the mayor, and it made me realize that I was wrong not to give Aunt Joy her box. Believe it or not, she took things better than I expected, when I finally did. I hadn't meant to wait that long to tell her, honest, but so much happened with the tornado and a bunch of other stuff that it hadn't seemed the right time before now. When I handed her the envelope and the box, she looked inside right in front of me. We were sitting on the front porch and as soon as she opened the box, she snapped it shut.

"Gross, isn't it?" I said, thinking of the tooth. That was one of the weirdest things about the charm Aunt Joy and Jimmy created. It didn't make any sense at all. A tooth, a silver heart with their names engraved on it, a little wooden man with a noose around its neck, and a carved snake. There were also a handful of letters and photos obviously put in there by Grandma Bess.

Aunt Joy said that stuff is from a charm she made when she was barely out of high school. She thought it would magically hide her secrets, which I have to say is silly. She said it seems ridiculous now, but that at the time, she was desperate. She kept the silver heart, but for some reason she let me keep the picture of her and the mayor. They were so young. Aunt Joy, so pretty and dressed in old-fashioned clothes, was sitting on the lowest branch of the magic apple tree. The mayor stood laughing with his arms out, as if to catch her. She said a friend of Jimmy's took that picture when Grandma Bess wasn't home. I put it in my Bible.

Aunt Joy said she wasn't mad at me for not giving her the box sooner. She said life was too short to be mad, but that she was relieved. I am, too, but I wonder what's going to happen now, with the mayor, and with Doc.

Ruthie

Chapter Twenty-three

SO AFTER MORE than twenty years, the charm was in the chimney after all, and safe-guarded by my own Momma who never said a word. In a letter she put in the box for me to read, she said, that because of the tooth, she had an idea of what had happened and why Jimmy and I would try our hands at making a dark charm. She said the charm wouldn't work, and that the only way to hide something like that kind of secret was to throw the evidence—the tooth—somewhere that nobody would ever find it. As for the wooden trinkets, she didn't know what we meant by including them, but I should just throw them in the well, too, because they were creepy and she didn't like them.

Momma. She had always liked the lighter side of magic, and nothing dark. As for those trinkets, except for the heart, I just wanted to forget about them, and the tooth, which Momma was right about. It was a bad thing to have hanging around. It was evidence, and the fact it had been in the box with a heart that had our names on it gave me the shivers. What were we thinking?

"Ruthie, come help me, dear." I held out the box I'd placed in the chimney all those years ago nodding at the question in her eyes.

"You are already mixed up in this. Might as well help me get rid of this awful thing. Let's go throw it in the well, where it won't ever be found."

Looking happy for the adventure, she grabbed my other hand and headed toward the front door toward the old well, but I gently pulled her back.

"I want to show you something, Ruthie."

She looked confused. "And then we'll go out to the well? Grandma Bess said you should put it in the well."

"Well," I said conspiratorially. "Let's just say that Grandma Bess didn't get to tell you all her secrets before she died."

I pulled open the basement door.

"We have to go down there?" Ruthie asked, her voice filled with dread.

"Are you afraid?" I teased.

"No." I knew she was lying. The last time she'd been down there was the night of the tornado, and that was enough to scare anyone, except me. Momma had taken me further into the bowels of the basement before and the need to dump those teeth and carvings into the well overcame any fear I might've had if I were smart enough to be afraid back then.

What were we thinking, Jimmy?

Actually seeing the items that had made up the charm we made and hid, only half believing and hoping that it would ward off the truth forever, reminded me of how young and naïve we were when we contrived our ridiculous idea. It was outrageous, of course, but an idea born out of fear and grief. An idea born out of immaturity and naivety.

And maybe stupidity, let's face it.

As we walked, I pulled strings dangling from light bulbs that zapped and flickered.

"It's cold down here," Ruthie muttered.

"It sure would be nice to have one of Carey's sweaters, wouldn't it?"

"She has one for every season."

I pulled Ruthie passed stacks of papers and one final bucket of charms left from the old chimney. Since the tornado, I'd been organizing the house, so it didn't look too bad anymore. The closets and trunks had been emptied and repacked. Grandma Bess's stacks of picture albums and scrapbooks had been organized on a shelf in the hallway. I'd even swept out the passageways behind some of the walls, sometimes imagining Daddy's voice was caught in those walls, and remembering playing hide and seek with my sisters when we were little. It was hard to believe Momma and Daddy let us play there.

"Look at this, Ruthie." This room had a real light switch and an old chandelier, something odd to be in a basement. It lit up the room, driving away all thoughts of ghosts or spiders. The room was adorned with dusty, moth-eaten, but stately looking furniture.

"Whoa," Ruthie breathed.

I picked up a handful of photos I'd found in a drawer

and set on the old coffee table in the center of the room. The first one was a picture of a man that looked just like Grandpa Talley beside what could only be outlaws.

"Is that?"

"No," I said. "It looks like your Grandpa, but it would've been a little before his time. "Must be a great grandfather or great uncle."

"That looks like Billy the Kid!" She said it in jest, but as we both leaned in to get a better look. We looked at each other with raised eyes. I didn't know if it was him, but it was fun to see Ruthie get excited. That girl needed some adventure and here we had enough of it in our home for her to write a book about.

My heart dipped a little to think of all this adventure being lost if we couldn't find a way to appease Mr. Littleton and keep the house, too.

"This kind of connection would explain the wild streak in your uncles," I said.

"Aunt Joy. You're teasing, right?"

I laughed, shrugged my shoulders. Ruthie's eyes grew wide as the moon.

"This way," I said.

"Where are we going?"

"Somewhere you can't tell the cousins about. It's too dangerous for the little ones."

We followed the tunnels behind the walls to a door in the floor, which I pulled open with an attached rope. I shined a flashlight down into the hole. I had to ask Ruthie three times to go down first. A shuffle in the corner made me jump.

Probably a mouse, right? Not a snake.

But I still prayed Momma's instructions were worth it to bring Ruthie all the way down here. All I needed was for the poor girl to get bit by a snake or a spider.

"Why can't we take stairs?" Ruthie asked.

"There aren't any stairs to this place, honey. This place is a secret."

"It's different than where we hid during the tornado?"

"It's just deeper in, honey." And damp.

The room was small, the walls bricked, and the air musty.

"The other side of this wall is the basement that everybody knows about, where we hid during the tornado. On the other side of that is the orchard, and of course beyond that and up the hill, the cave and The Spring of Good Luck."

"It's creepy down here." Ruthie's voice was a squeak.

"We won't be long." I motioned for her to follow me into a tunnel. Ruthie tip-toed behind. "This tunnel was built a long time ago. It goes pretty far back."

There was no electricity to the tunnel, so we followed my flashlight as we padded along, the cool air clinging to our skin. Finally, I came to an abrupt halt at the end of the tunnel, causing Ruthie to smash into me. I grabbed the wall to steady us both and I swear there was a minor earth quake that stirred the dust around us.

I flashed the light where the tunnel turned slightly and ended against a wall that curved into a half circle.

"This is an old water well," I said.

"Oh, wow. This is totally awesome." She peeked into the hole, but I pulled her back. It wasn't safe at all. "It must have been for the outlaws, right?"

"It makes sense to me."

I angled my flashlight down into the well before us. The light reflected off black water. I guess I don't have to tell you it gave me the creeps, but for reasons I couldn't divulge to Ruthie. My experience was that underground waterways held bad things, and for all I knew, some of those bad things might have drifted into this very well.

Lord, I hope not.

"Can we hurry? This is getting kind of scary."

"Why do you think I brought you with me? Hold the light, Ruthie." I pulled the pieces of the charm from my pocket, except for the heart, the photo I'd given to Ruthie, and the letters.

I stepped forward and Ruthie reached out to steady me.

"Thank you," I whispered, although I don't know why I was being so quiet. Nobody was down there but us. I stood at the well's edge, Ruthie's hand at my waist, and whispered, Lord, please make all this go away. Quickly, I tossed each item from the charm into the well—especially the creepy tooth. They landed with a plop.

"There," I said. "That's that."

We paused back at the bottom of the ladder.

"Aunt Joy?"

"Yes, honey?"

"The words you said when you were dropping things in

the well. Were those chants?"

"No," I said, laughing into the stillness at how much Momma had influenced Ruthie with her belief in magic and good luck. "Those were just prayers, silly." Prayers that those things would disappear into the well and never be found.

"What was the charm supposed to hide?" Ruthie asked.

"Something happened one day on the bank at Spavinaw Junction Creek. Something terrible."

Ruthie was silent, and then she asked the inevitable question.

"What?"

"I want to tell you, Ruthie. I do. But I need to tell some other people first and it's not going to be easy. Then, I'll tell you."

"It's something to do with why you and the mayor broke up, isn't it?"

I squeezed her shoulder. "You are such a hopeless romantic, Ruthie."

"Not hopeless," she corrected. "Just a romantic."

"Okay," I said, letting go of just a little, like handing one brick over and keeping the rest. "I used to be mad at the mayor, not for what happened that day, but for what he did after." I grabbed a hand towel and started wiping down the counters.

"You still are a little mad," she said knowingly, "I can tell."

"Yes, I am, but maybe I'm just being stubborn. What the mayor did long ago was because he was young and confused, just like me. He was hurt, too."

"You did something to him?"

Did I do something to him, too? Yes, I didn't let him go. I acted like I really was off my rocker by expecting him to know how to fix the past.

Out loud, I said, "What really happened, Ruthie, was that somebody did something to us, and all this other stuff is because of that."

"So you're going to forgive him?"

"Hmm. That is a good question, honey. That's a very good question."

Chapter Twenty-four

I'D HAD THREE cookies, even though my hips probably didn't need them, before I noticed Nurse Clara looked like she'd eaten a few too many herself. She sat on the edge of a chair in her living room still dressed in pink scrubs with her hands clasped tightly over her knees.

"What is it, Clara?"

"Girls, I should have told you this a long time ago, but now is the right time."

My sisters and I all leaned forward, confused about what big secret our childhood babysitter could possibly tell us.

"If it's about the house and all Momma's secret charms and stuff, we already know all about that," I said.

"Oh, that stuff," she said, with a dismissive wave of her hand. "I never let that bother me. Your momma was always a bit eccentric."

We girls nodded. How could we argue with that?

"What I want to tell you is more important. After I found out, I tried to forget about it. Seeing you girls around town, I always felt guilty, but didn't want to turn your worlds upside down." She bit into a new cookie. "When you showed up in my hospital, Joy, and I saw the tension in you, Carey and Nanette, I just knew it was time. Secrets always find their way to the surface, don't they?"

She peered at me, as if I should have known what she was talking about. It gave me an eerie feeling at the back of my neck, which I ignored. I was tired from waking up in the middle of the night from my own secrets, and during the little drive from the farm house to Clara's little house in the center of town, I promised myself that this would be a day of fun. Clara's positive attitude in the hospital had a lot to do with the change I felt, and I was determined not to let eerie feelings or signs of bad luck ruin this afternoon.

"What would you have to tell us that we don't know?" Carey asked, always the frank one.

Nurse Clara set her plate of cookies on the coffee table and stared at the cut flowers from Momma's garden. I'd wanted to thank her for the hours she'd sat by me in the hospital, even coming in on her own time. It had seemed pretty extreme that someone who didn't really know us would put in extra time, but I was convinced she was just one of those people, like a Good Samaritan type. It turned out that Clara, who really was a nice person, was also motivated by the past, just like so many of the rest of us.

"When you walked in to see your sister, Carey, the truth felt like a big ole rock in my chest. I knew it."

"Knew what," Carey asked, now intrigued.

I leaned forward to get a better listen and Nanette picked up her fourth cookie.

"I knew I had to tell you the truth, Carey."

Tell Carey the truth? Now, this was interesting.

Apparently, not everything is about me.

Carey sat, her spine straight, looking like a prim lady setting herself against unsavory news. It was interesting, and a little heartrending, to watch Carey's posture wilt a little with each tick of the clock on Clara's wall as she started telling us about her friendship with our mom, occasionally standing up to straighten her perfectly arranged knick-knacks on the sideboard and smoothing out the doilies and cloths draped on the antique furniture around the room as she talked.

"I feel like I've made myself at home with our new deeper friendship—which I admit I needed, been so lonely all these years by myself—and I'm not sure your Momma would like it."

For a moment I was distracted by her admission of loneliness.

This could be me.

I glanced around and noticed for the first time her three cats curled in little balls on furniture around the house.

This is me.

Not that being single is bad, but now that Doc had woken up my nerve endings, Lucky the cat wouldn't do.

Nanette waved her hand in the air, thank goodness pulling me out of my musings of me as an old lady with only a cat for company.

"I think she would love our new friendship," Nanette said. "Momma would especially be grateful for how helpful you've been to Joy."

I nodded. "I couldn't have made it without you, Clara. You were the only one who believed I would wake up."

Carey leaned forward and looked in my direction. "Nice way to rub it in, Sis."

I shrugged. I was happy Carey was trying to get on board with those who thought I was doing okay, but the fact was that she hadn't yet. Until she did, she would just have to take a dig from me every now and then, bless her heart.

Clara stopped beside a hutch and pulled an envelope out of a drawer.

"Carey."

Again, Carey, and not me.

I guess I half expected that Clara was going to spring something on us that had to do with my own secrets, that maybe Momma had told her about the charm or Clara had found out some other way. But as had been happening a lot lately, I found out during our little visit that it wasn't about me at all.

Carey had snapped to attention, her curiosity evident. Clara held the letter out to Carey.

"This is something I stumbled upon when I was babysitting for your mother one night. It was a long time ago. You were all so young and your Daddy had taken your Momma for a little overnight visit to Missouri. I was looking for something to read while you girls and River slept, and this fell out of a book." She shook her head. "Your Momma and I were good friends back in those days, so I was surprised she hadn't told me when she was pregnant. I guess some secrets are just too hard to admit." She gave me that look again that made me wriggle on the sofa.

Me and my guilty conscience, is what this is.

Carey took the letter gingerly and held it in front of her. Nanette and I leaned in to see what it said.

"To Reverend Michael Wilson," she read. "So, it's a letter Momma wrote to the Reverend. What could be so secret about that?"

"They're best friends," Nanette said. "Or were, I mean, after Daddy died, before she died." She looked sad.

"I didn't know the Reverend's name was Michael," I said.

"He's always lived in Spavinaw Junction." Nanette wore a confused expression. "Why would Momma write him a letter when she could have just gone to the church and told him?"

Clara didn't say anything as Nanette and I looked at her and then at each other, clearly not comprehending the gravity of the situation at all.

"Okay," Nanette said. "What is it? Is Daddy an outlaw or something? That wouldn't really be a surprise to any Talley."

Clara chuckled. We all laughed too, glad for the release of tension. Carey unfolded the yellowed letter, cleared her throat, and read aloud. The letter was apparently written when River was only an infant.

"Dear Michael: I don't know if I will ever be brave enough to give you this letter, but maybe someday I will have the courage to tell both you and Leroy the truth about us."

Us? As in Reverend Wilson and Momma?

I almost choked on my cookie. I placed it on the plate.

"There is no way Momma cheated on Daddy," Nanette exclaimed. "Momma and Daddy loved each other so much." She gave Clara the kind of dirty look she usually reserved for the Sheriff when he came around to check on Bobby.

"Nanette," I said, feeling protective of my favorite nurse.

"She's lying," Nanette exclaimed and it seemed to me like she had switched places with Carey: Nanette the complicated sister and Carey the reasonable one. Me? I wanted to protest, trust me, but after all that had happened between Jimmy and I, and then my scandalous relationship with Doc, I knew there was sometimes more to people than it first seemed.

"I think what Nanette means is that Momma and Daddy seemed so in love, it doesn't make sense." I placed what I meant to be a calming hand on Nanette's knee, but she surprised me by brushing it away.

"They did love each other." Nanette reminded me of a little girl trying to convince me Santa was real. She loved her husband, even though he had cheated on her that one time with a woman who served drinks at The Drunk Raccoon, and I know I don't have to explain what that place is all about. Certainly, sadly, Nanette knew.

"They did love each other," I agreed, sensitive to the fact she was sensitive about cheating, but then again. "But sometimes people lose their way, Nanette."

Believe me, I know.

How many times had I pined over a certain married man myself? Sure, I never pursued him, but how was I better than Nanette's husband? I admit it. I thought about it. Boy had I thought about it.

Carey lifted her head. "Maybe they were in love. That's why they stayed together."

"Then what does this letter mean?" Nanette asked.

"If you will let me finish reading it," declared Carey. "We will find out."

She stopped reading it out loud after that, so we sat quietly, fidgeting in our seats. I could hardly believe it, or that Carey sounded so calm, but the people I love kept surprising me all the time. After hearing that Momma had an affair with the preacher, we might have all thought nothing could be more surprising, until Carey slapped the letter and gasped.

"What does it say?" asked Nanette, but Carey had pressed her hands over her mouth. The letter floated to the floor and I snatched it up.

I read it aloud, my voice quiet in the small room.

"YOU PROBABLY ALREADY know what Leroy will figure out soon enough. Every time you look at Carey, you must see your eyes, your hair, and your smile. It must be obvious to you by now that she is your daughter."

A gasp erupted from Nanette, but to her credit, she didn't say anything. I looked at Carey who had always been so tiny compared to the rest of us, so blonde-headed, so, let's face it, so danged particular about every single thing, while the rest of us just liked to hang loose about stuff.

"You okay?" I asked Carey.

Clara, my favorite nurse, and now Carey's judging by the grateful look she gave her, had walked over and laid a hand on her shoulder.

"I was a little bit younger than your Momma and scared, girls, so I confessed to your Momma that I found the letter. She asked me to swear I would never tell anyone about it, but that I would deliver it straight to Reverend Wilson."

Realization flooded Carey's face. "You didn't deliver it, did you?"

"No," she said. "I couldn't be the one to break up your family."

"So he doesn't know," she whispered, a vulnerable look in her eyes. Nanette reached over and placed a hand on Carey's shoulder.

"Did Momma know you didn't deliver it?" I asked Clara.

Clara looked sad. "I don't think so. I never told her one way or another, though. And she never asked."

"Surely they talked about it," Nanette said. "Reverend Wilson took Momma for a walk almost every day."

"They did spend a lot of time together," I agreed.

A lot of time. Like people in love would do.

"I always knew something was different about me," Carey said. "I mean, look how different I look than you."

"What do you mean?" I asked, wanting to make her feel better. "I have red hair! How can that be? Maybe I'm not Daddy's either."

Clara shook her head. "Don't worry, Joy. You are."

"Of course you are," Nanette said. "You still have Daddy's eyes. And you get your red hair from the European blood in our family."

"But I," Carey said, "don't look anything like Daddy. "In fact, he's kind of old, but haven't you ever noticed that younger picture of the reverend hanging beside Jesus in the lobby at church?"

"I have," I admitted. Same hair. Same eyes. Definitely kin to Carey.

We all leaned closer to her, rubbing her knee, holding her hand, offering a tissue for the inevitable flood of tears, but they didn't come. Not one. Instead, she took the letter from me and waved it happily in the air.

"So this explains it," she said. Her eyes were bright as the quartz rocks the boys used to find in the woods and sell to the science teacher at school for a nickel.

"Carey, it's okay to be upset," said Nanette.

"We understand," I was quick to agree. "This doesn't make you any less our sister or any less Daddy's daughter. He still raised you while he was alive."

"But he helped raise you, Joy, even after he died," she said. "Even you saw him, Nanette."

"Oh, Carey." I suddenly felt a little bit embarrassed about all the times I'd seen Daddy when I was growing up. She smiled at each of us as if we were all a little slow on the uptake. And I guess we were.

"Don't you understand?" she asked. "This explains everything. It explains why I look different, why I don't get all the jokes you all find so funny, why I don't believe in ghosts, or care about the Talley charms, and—and maybe—" Now, I knew where she was going.

"And maybe," I finished for her. "It explains why Daddy never showed up for you." I should've been happy for Carey, but as I sat there listening to her blather on like an idiot, I felt sad. The longer I thought about it, the sad turned to mad.

So, that's why she has always been mean to me.

Recognition finally donned on Nanette who simply said, "Daddy. You think he never visited you because—"

"Because I'm not his daughter," said Carey. "Everyone else saw him at least once after he died, but never me."

Finally, I couldn't take it anymore. I stood, which was never a good thing when you were a Talley mad at another Talley. Recognizing the challenge, she stood too. One of the cats meowed and ran off. The other two eyed us, ready to make a quick getaway if need be.

"What?!" Carey demanded.

I just shook my head, thinking of the mountain of anger that Carey had built up inside of her, how she let it erupt at the worse times, and how it was always aimed at one person. Me.

"You know, to be named Joy, you sure are a Joy sucker sometimes. You always have to make everything about you." Her eyes flared, and I felt my cheeks blotch red because part of the statement was probably right, but it didn't change what I had just become crystal clear to me.

"Tell me, Joy. Can't you just be happy for me once in your life?"

"So this is why you've been so mean to me all these years?"

"I've been mean to you? What are you talking about?"

"Oh, come on, Carey. You're always out to put me in my place. Let's just face it. You're jealous."

"Of what, you being in love with a married man for all your adult life? Or for having an affair with a younger man?"

I gasped. "It's not an affair if we're both single."

"And you're lusting after the mayor? He's the music leader at church, Joy! You are no better than an adulteress!" She spat it out like the self-righteous snob she had become.

"That is low," I said calmly. "And it's not like he's a priest or something."

"Girls!" Clara tried to get between us, but Nanette stepped to her side.

"There's no use, Clara. When our family gets like this, best to stay clear."

"Low?" Carey asked, her hands planted on her hips. I planted mine the same. "Low is being the town spinster. At least I have a husband."

If she wanted low, I'd give her low. Looking back to that moment, I can't believe I did it. Before I could stop myself, I grabbed her pony tail. And let's face it, grabbing a girl's hair is like a man kicking another man in the you-know-whats. It's what you do when the other person doesn't want to fight fair, so with her ponytail in my fist I headed for the front porch. Carey had no choice but to follow.

I tell you what, it felt good to exact a little revenge on Carey, but once outside I let go. A cramp in my side reminded me I was on the losing side of forty and what had seemed like a good idea at the time, made me feel like an overgrown bully. Carey on the other hand was just getting revved up.

Why'd I wear a pony tail today?

I guess when you've been kicked and shoved too much in life the way Carey had been, you get sick of it, and boy was I ever sorry. It's as if all the anger and jealousy she'd stored up for me had been released by the revelation that Reverend Wilson was her father. She had me like that hunched over and screaming for mercy when I heard a car door slam and the sharp southern preacher voice of who else, but Reverend Wilson.

"What in heaven's name is going on here?"

"It's nothing to do with heaven," I assured him when Carey let go of me. The two of us adjusted our pony tails and stood side by side, much like we did when we were little girls caught running up and down the halls of the church. And that's when I noticed Jimmy standing at the preacher's side.

Holy cow.

He nodded, the slightest curve of his mouth turning up. My face flushed with heat, and I closed my eyes to hide my shame. I must have looked as crazy as Carey had made me out to be. When I finally had the guts to squint one eye at Jimmy, he was standing between Carey and me. He didn't get a word in edgewise before Carey lit in.

"Jimmy Cornsilk. Don't even try to interfere. Joy is not in distress, I am." She glared, not even looking at the reverend. Right behind her, Reverend was reading the letter that Nurse Clara handed him, only about forty years too late.

"I'm not interfering," Jimmy assured. "Just making sure you and Joy are okay." My heart turned into butterfly wings again. What was it about Jimmy saying my name that got me all excited, even though I had a boyfriend?

Acknowledgment.

Maybe that was it. Before, Jimmy never acknowledged me out loud. Our only interactions were necessary ones, glances, and electricity, which I probably had imagined many times in the past, but judging from the intensity in his eyes when he looked at me now, I wasn't imagining anything now. The question was whether or not the electricity was good or bad. All it takes is recalling Daddy's stories about being hit by lightning to know electricity doesn't always light things up for the better.

Jimmy touched my arm, sending a jolt up to the nape of my neck that settled in my chest, upsetting the butterflies again. Emboldened, I spat words at Carey.

"If you're in such distress," I said. "Maybe you should be the one to talk to a shrink."

Carey sulked, looked away for a moment, and then

bowed her head. "I'm sorry, Joy. I was out of line."

Dang it. Why does she always have to make it so I have to forgive her?

"Don't worry, Jimmy." She looked at me. "I'm not sending her off to the crazy house. That's just a rumor someone started."

That was a rumor?

"That's good," he said, his voice low and thick. "Because she isn't crazy." His eyes landed on mine. Locked.

I might be going out with Doc, but it hadn't erased the sparks that lit me up when I was near Jimmy, or even when I was far from Jimmy, but definitely not when he was standing twelve inches in front of me. I had a difficult time not wanting to reach out and lay my palm on his hard chest, turn my face up to his to finish that kiss in the church balcony that'd been all too brief.

Oh, heavens. I've got to stop reading those romance novels.

I tore my gaze away from Jimmy's to see Reverend Wilson staring at Carey, the letter floating down to his feet, no longer needed now that the truth for him and Carey was out. It was really something to see. Seeing his face transform from fear to relief to love gave me hope, too.

What if it would be that easy to tell my family the truth about Jimmy? I wondered if Jimmy was thinking the same thing as he looked at me in a way that I can only describe as tender. I wanted to throw myself into his arms, apologize for being angry, for being mad at his wife, for casting those longing looks at him during church when he was a married man, and most of all for never saying anything to him about my feelings in the past five years when he was all alone. Because who says that a woman has to wait for the man to speak first? For heaven's sake, I'm tired of waiting on my life to change.

I'm going to say something. Right now.

"Joy." I looked to Jimmy, thinking he might break this spell first, but it wasn't his voice.

Oh, no.

I turned slowly to face the road. Doc sat in his truck in front of Clara's house, windows down.

"Are you okay?" Kyle called to me through the truck window.

I attempted a smile. Was I? And more importantly, was Doc? Or had he seen the intense gaze between Jimmy and I, sensed the electricity all the way out to his truck. Lord knows, it was strong enough to zap anyone who had half a mind to look in our direction. Jimmy who had been looking at me expectantly, shifted an annoyed gaze toward Doc's truck. The way he rested his arms across his big chest seemed like a challenge to me, but I might have imagined it. It didn't seem like Jimmy felt guilty about anything.

Jimmy, for a moment the spitting image of my teenage boyfriend, looked at me with what I can only imagine was some kind of invitation in his eyes. My heart reached for his, but with a sharp breath I pulled it back.

I'm not a bad person.

Tearing my gaze from Jimmy, I walked quickly to Doc's truck, trying to look nonchalant.

"Hi," I chirped, sounding guilty and fake all at the same time.

"You need a ride back to the house or something?" Doc smiled, and I couldn't get a good sense if he was worried or not. Maybe I was lucky and he hadn't seen anything at all between the mayor and me.

"Sure. Let me tie a few things up. I'll be right back."

I hurried past Momma's dear friend Clara who'd walked down the sidewalk to say hi to Doc, conscious of his eyes on my back. Thank goodness everyone else had walked into the house. I could have kicked myself for not remembering Doc was coming to town today.

Inside, I brushed past Jimmy whose eyes felt like magnets as I swept up to Carey and Reverend Wilson. I hugged her, and to my surprise, her embrace was soft and warm.

"I love you," I said, and I meant it. "I love you no matter who your daddy is. And Daddy loved you too. I know he did."

She opened her mouth to argue with me on that note, but I held a hand up to stop her.

"Let's not argue, Sis. I'm tired of arguing." I reached out to pull Nanette into our circle. "Nothing can break us and the boys apart. You all are my family."

Nanette, who'd been surprisingly mute, started crying and Reverend Wilson produced a hankie from his pocket that I hoped was clean.

"But one thing is going to change," I said. I guess it was the tone of my voice that made Jimmy step out the back door, which was too bad because I would have liked for him to have heard.

"What's that?" Nanette asked.

"I've got to stop letting you all define me."

"But, Joy—"

I interrupted, which I'd learned was really the only way to get a word in edgewise with Carey. "I'm not blaming you anymore Carey. I blame myself. Just look at you with your new daddy. You don't care what anyone thinks. You love him."

She cast a shy smile to the reverend, who winked at her, looking happy as a raccoon with a belly full of crawdads.

"And you, Nanette. You are yourself every single day and you don't care what people say about you." She shook her head.

"Well, I should."

"No, you shouldn't," I assured. "And the boys definitely don't give a rip what anyone thinks. Not even us! They do whatever they want because they know we'll still love them."

That even elicited a giggle from Nurse Clara sitting quietly at her kitchen table having a glass of sweet iced tea.

"I have some thinking to do," I said, not able to keep my eyes from the back porch where I could see the back of Jimmy's head through the screen door. "But I'm just warning you all."

"Warning us? About what?" Carey looked worried.

I smiled, realizing I wasn't going to run anymore. Not from the accusing eyes of my siblings who would love me no matter what, not from the opinions of my parents who were gone, even though I'd seen Daddy's ghost more than once in my life, and not from the past, which was dark and scary, but over—or at least I hoped it would be soon.

"I'm just warning you all, another storm's coming, and I'm not going to run from it this time." I pictured myself huddled in the basement with Ruthie and River during the recent tornado, hiding, safe on the outside, but not inside my caged heart. That tornado had sucked the charms out of the chimney, but not the dark magic from inside of me.

They both looked baffled. I thought Carey was about to tell me I needed a nap and Nanette looked unsure of what to say. I ignored their anxiety and gave them each a hug, imagining I heard a click of the cage door around my heart, but it was only Jimmy's fingers around the handle of the screen door. As I walked through the living room toward the front door, I called out a thanks to Nurse Clara in the other room and walked past Jimmy, who stood like a pillar at the edge of the front door, out of Doc's view sitting in the truck waiting for me.

His hand gently encircled my elbow. I froze looking out the door at Doc, who was calling out to me.

"Are you ready, beautiful? Let's go," Doc called, as he waved through the open window of his truck.

I was about to step through the door, but Jimmy's hand was still holding my elbow. His touch was so soft, I could have easily stepped from his hold and out onto the front porch, but I froze for a moment, still looking straight ahead.

"I have the same question," Jimmy whispered beside me, his breath warm, tickling the side of my neck. I almost wilted, swayed toward him, and nearly melted into a pool of memories when I felt the smoothness of his cheek press lightly into mine.

I wondered how much of what I'd said to my sisters he heard after all. Taking a shaky breath, my elbow slipped from the curve of his fingers as I stepped out onto the porch and smiled at Doc, the man who had so recently saved my life, and walked away from the one who had discarded me years earlier. Why hadn't Jimmy spoken up earlier?

My heart was so heavy that day, as if the first signs of the storm were already upon us.

TURNS OUT, THE magic apple tree might not have been magical after all. Ruthie and I were picking flowers at the edge of the orchard in the cool of an overcast day, when we heard a huge rumble from the East of Spavinaw Junction. It wasn't the train. Since my Daddy was hit by lightning twice, no one has to tell a Talley twice to get out of its way, but before we reached the top porch step, a thunder clap ripped the sky wide open. We both turned at the same time, Ruthie and I reaching out to steady each other, before we wobbled off the porch. I've never seen a bolt of lightning up close, but when I turned to look over my shoulder, I saw its zap zigzag down out of the sky until it reached the top of the magic apple tree where it exploded, sending a spray of green apples into the air and splitting the trunk of the old tree from top to bottom.

Astonished, Ruthie and I stared at the tree that now lay open, its two halves arcing away from each other, its wound emitting smoke that circled up into the air, trailing up the way the lightning had come. Ruthie's short gasps captured my attention and I hugged her to my side.

"Don't be afraid," I told her.

"I'm not afraid, just sad."

"It is sad," I said, still recovering from the shock myself, but also not able to ignore a sense of relief that inexplicably opened inside of me. "But that old tree has served its purpose."

"Grandma Bess said it was lots older than her."

"It was," I agreed. "But I guess it has sheltered its last first kiss."

Ruthie's sharp intake of air made me smile. "Aunt Joy, how did you know?"

I squeezed her closer to my side.

God, I love this girl. Please give her something more than a fairytale someday.

"I'm Aunt Joy, of course."

"Of course," she whispered and leaned her head on my shoulder.

My guilt for having slipped again and read about her first kiss with Carl in her diary wasn't strong enough to wash away the privilege of sharing that moment with the closest thing to a daughter I'd ever have. That was another thing I realized as I stared at the tree stripped of its magic. After so many years as a so-called spinster, I wouldn't ever be a mother, but I was a darn good Aunt.

"It smells bad," Ruthie said.

"But it's not bad," I assured her, because I could smell

the change, so close were we to the lingering smoke. It was as if a giant match had just been blown out.

Ruthie's Diary

Dear Diary

So that's that. The charm is gone and I feel like a better person for giving it to Aunt Joy, so she could put it in the well like Grandma Bess said. Thank goodness I didn't lose that letter! That would have been terrible. And wow. I always liked the attic better than the basement, but I never imagined we had a well down there where outlaws used to hide! I can't wait to tell Kay when she gets back from her Dad's. And Carl. I bet he'll think it's cool.

Ever since Aunt Joy showed me the well, I've been thinking a lot about the mayor. It's hard to believe he was ever as cute as Aunt Joy says he was, but I guess she still thinks so. I noticed that he's sort of gotten old, and that started me thinking about the letter Grandma Bess left Aunt Joy and the picture of him and Aunt Joy under the magic apple tree. I know Aunt Joy is with Doc now, but last Sunday I thought I might just talk to the mayor, ask him when he was coming out to visit Aunt Joy again. I know it's ridiculous, but I did it spontaneously.

"Excuse me, Mayor?" I stepped in front of the ladies dressed in their squeezie shoes, shoulder pads, and wearing dark rouge on their cheeks. He smiled and gave my arm a squeeze.

"Ruthie. How's your Aunt Joy?" Right on queue.

"She's great. Busy with her Tulip House for Girls Foundation work."

He nodded. "She's really doing some good work."

I was just about to ask the mayor my question when mom's friend Mary Sue's purse caught my Bible and sent it flying to the floor. All I can say, is that sometimes God works in mysterious ways.

The mayor picked up my Bible and started grabbing

all the stuff that spilled on the floor: A purple book mark, a piece of lace Grandma Bess gave me when I was eight, a dried pansy from Aunt Joy that the mayor picked up delicately and placed back between the Bible's pages, a photo of . . .

Oh my word.

The mayor's eyes widened, then he smiled the way I think Prince Charming would smile. He stood, still holding the photo close, and handed me my Bible. I saw a lot pass over his face in that moment, and none of it was bad. I have to tell you that I realized at that moment that some fairytales take longer than others. Sometimes Sleeping Beauty doesn't just wake up and her Prince Charming is waiting right there. Sometimes, it seemed to me, it takes a while for Prince Charming to wake up, too.

Ruthie

Chapter Twenty-five

I THINK I always knew it would come to this, such a strange quirk that would free me from the secrets lost in the chimney once and for all. When I look back to the splitting of the magic apple tree, the fights with Carey, the twister, the coma, the fall from the roof, the reason I made that blasted charm and hid it in the fireplace with Jimmy in the first place, and even all the way back to the days when Daddy was still alive, I had this idea that it was my responsibility to take care of the whole gosh darn Talley family. I think my Daddy unwittingly put that weight on my shoulders.

"You have a good head on your shoulders, Joy. Take care of your brothers and sisters."

But that was when I was only a girl, long before I fell in love with Jimmy and our romance turned into a tragedy. Even though my brothers and sisters had all agreed to move on from their worries about the coma and my delicate state of mind, they still hadn't wanted to hear much about my coma vision, if you want to call it that, of Daddy holding the chimney brick.

You know what I hid in the chimney, don't you Daddy?

He knew, and while I wasn't one to consult mystics or psychics, I had consulted Nurse Clara. She just sipped her iced tea and said, "Maybe he pulled that brick loose, Joy, because your secrets needed to be free."

I was stunned. "Clara, I think you're right."

"So, what is the secret?" she said, reaching for one of the chocolate oatmeal no-bake cookies Ruthie and I'd made.

"Nice try," I teased.

She chuckled. We'd been through this before and she knew I wasn't going to tell her.

"I'll tell you soon," I said, which caused a surprised smile to spread across her face.

"I look forward to it," she said.

"But I have to talk to someone else first."

"Doc?"

"Someone else," I said. This caused her smile to turn down. She was partial to Kyle for obvious reasons. "I'll tell Doc, too."

"Well, I'm glad," she said. "After all, he is your boyfriend. He deserves to know before he shows you that ring I helped him pick out. Since his Momma died, he needed help, and—"

Her voice faded as my mouth hung open.

"Close your mouth, Joy. You'll catch a fly." I snapped it shut. "I'm so sorry, Joy. It was supposed to be a surprise."

Holy Matrimony.

I looked down at my hand, imagining the oversized glittery rock that Kyle would no doubt have chosen. I glanced down at my tattered blue jeans and blue cotton floral shirt and imagined myself in a gauzy white dress. And yes, it would be white, no matter my past. Thelma and Mary Sue could just go suck an egg if they tried to boycott my wedding because of a white dress. And don't think I'm joking. They'd tried it with other brides in our church before.

"Just forget I said anything about a ring," Clara said.

"What ring?" I smiled, but I knew I wouldn't forget.

These were the thoughts that haunted me in the morning hours as I prepared the house and my unruly hair for the big fundraising dinner party for The Tulip House for Girls. I was trying to decide between a twist and a pony tail when I heard a knock at the door.

"Come in," I called, knowing that at this hour it had to be one of my sisters, brothers, or Ruthie.

The knocking would not stop, so I pulled my hair into a pony tail and dashed downstairs, carrying the pair of sandals Carey gave me to match the yellow drop waist sundress I planned to wear during the fundraiser. It was going to be a good day. We'd never had a big party at the Talley home for as long as I could remember, even though its spaciousness and former grandeur seemed meant to entertain scores of people. Now it was run-down, but it had a new fireplace and a beautiful yard, so I hoped nobody would pay attention to the falling-down barn, broken shingles, or faded paint.

Spying brown hair through the triangular window, I hurried to the blue door and flung it open, thinking Kyle had arrived early.

"Hello, Joy."

I choked back my greeting. "Jimmy! I wasn't expecting you."

Holy Molasses.

His tall frame filled the doorway. His dark eyes peered down at me from a face that still made my heart flip over every time I saw him. Jimmy is one of those examples of a good looking man who just gets better with time. In his fist he held a single black-eyed Susan, its yellow petals bright against the tan of his fingers as he held it out.

"The daffodils stopped blooming," he said in explanation, and a part of me thought of how true it was for Momma, for Jimmy's wife, Fern, and for us.

I accepted the flower, noting how it bowed its head over my fingertips, and we stood there in the doorway staring at each other, me not sure whether or not I wanted to invite him in or step out onto the porch. I could see the former magic apple tree past his shoulder, its wound glaring at us from the orchard where it had once stood tall and full.

He turned and followed my gaze.

"It's a shame," he said. "It held a lot of memories."

The image of the photo, saved by Momma all those years, flashed in my mind like a slide projector. Tears prickled at the corners of my eyes and I looked down at my bare feet.

"Why are you here, Jimmy?" Oh, how I wanted to throw my arms around him, press my cheek against his chest again, but I refrained. "Because I don't have time to talk about the house right now. I have the fundraiser in a few hours."

Instead of answering, he asked to come in.

"I'll get you something to drink," I said, happy to disappear.

I placed the flower in a glass of water and took my time preparing a glass of tea sweetened with two full spoons of sugar, just the way I knew he liked it. He hadn't been out for iced tea on the porch since I started getting serious with Doc. At least I knew it looked like we were serious to everyone in Spavinaw Junction, and I suppose it did to Jimmy, too. If he had any doubts, he wouldn't after tonight, since I knew that Doc had a ring that said it was very serious.

Jimmy accepted the glass without meeting my eyes. I sat on the other end of the couch.

"I wanted to see how you're doing," he said. "We haven't talked much since that night in the balcony."

My iced tea swirled inside my chest.

"We've never talked about what happened in the balcony," he said, his eyes meeting mine.

My breath quickened.

"Oh that," I said, trying to look like I'd all but forgotten about that night. "Thank you for staying with me. It was a rough time for me." I don't know how I managed to say anything at all, because my throat was as dry as a creek bed with no rain in June. "I've been meaning to say that, but like you said, we haven't talked."

"Joy, I'm sorry I've been distant."

I laughed. I guessed he had no idea how funny that sounded, considering how distant he'd been over the years.

"There's something about that night that I wanted to ask you about," he said, staring at his boots. I studied them, too. They were black with intricate stitching along the toe and up the sides to reveal fancy leather work I could see just below the hem of his jeans. They were so shiny. I wondered how he kept them that way.

"I'm all ears, so shoot."

He cleared his throat and rested his elbows on his thighs. I noted how his arms strained against his shirt and how his legs set wide in front of him were still muscular through his jeans. That stirring thing in my chest swirled tighter. He was a runner, too. Yes, one more way in which he was near perfect. Who had I been kidding to think that this amazing person had missed me, his teenage girlfriend, over the years?

He chuckled, shook his head like he was about to say something unbelievable.

"I keep remembering this dream from that night in the church that we . . . kissed. It was a . . . vision I had, or something. But it was . . ."

It was what? Amazing? Awesome?

He stopped chuckling and looked at me straight on, so I decided to shoot straight with him.

"Not everything is a vision," I assured, thinking about my dreams during my coma, sleepwalking through memories, drifting through the present and the past and trying to figure out what was real.

"I didn't think so," he said, his eyes filled with meaning that I wasn't sure how to interpret.

"Kyle's going to ask me to marry him," I blurted, feeling a measure of loyalty to the man who treated me like a queen. "Clara told me he bought a ring."

Jimmy's cheeks darkened and he peered intently into the new hearth.

Lucky sat by the fire grate staring up into the chimney, and I wondered if he missed the mess that used to be up in there. I stood and shooed him away.

"Do you wonder what happened to it?"

He didn't answer.

"Oh, Jimmy. Why did we never talk about it?"

He sighed, his big shoulders defeated. "When I married Fern, I just hoped it would go away."

"It didn't for me," I said, hoping just a little bit to hurt him like I'd been wounded all those years ago.

"I didn't hear from you, so I thought you'd be okay." I knew he was sincere. "I was wrong, wasn't I?"

Hear from me? What was I supposed to do? Interrupt your wedding day?

"I wasn't okay. I needed you to come to me."

"I've known it, all these years, Joy." The way he said my name could still melt my heart, but I held my feelings about that inside. I needed more.

"Joy, I did . . ."

"You didn't do enough." I was surprised at the conviction in my voice. I could almost pretend I was tough.

"But, I tried . . ."

Tried? He is the crazy one. After all, his dad was lots crazier than mine.

I wanted to hurt him in that moment.

"What can I do now?" His eyes were intense, piercing. I had to look away.

"You owed me something . . ." I searched for words. What did he owe me? A promise kept? An explanation? "It was hard living with it on my own, not even having you as a friend when you were the only one who knew."

"Would we really have been happy that way?" My stomach tightened.

Absolutely not.

"And if we'd openly been friends, Joy, it would have constantly dredged up the past for Fern. And then there was Fernie. I didn't want our daughter to know how she came to be, to think she was a mistake. I only wanted her to know that I wanted her." His voice cracked and it occurred to me, with a certain amount of pain I'll admit, that no matter how he and Fern came together, they'd willingly had more than one child. They became a family and nobody had forced Jimmy to stay and be part of that.

Only then, as I thought about Fern and Fernie, instead of the secrets between myself and Jimmy, did I realize my mistake. Jimmy created a life with what he could salvage, while I'd lived in the past with the shadows of 'what might have been,' if that dark thing had never happened at the creek. Only when I'd acknowledged that part of the truth, did I reach across the gap to comfort him, as a friend; and I did want to be his friend, I realized. How could I be his enemy after what we'd been through together? I reached out, my hand trailing along the couch cushion, but he kept his hands clasped.

My hand lay there on the couch between us and I was about to pull back, my face tinged red with the embarrassment for my boldness, when his strong hand curved around mine. Friendship or not, a bolt of lightning snaked its way from my palm to my chest, but after that, I soaked in the goodness of it, the protection in his grasp, as if he'd reached out and caught me before I could fall off that precipice and back into the secrets of Spavinaw Junction Creek.

I want you back, Jimmy. But what about Doc?

I exhaled a long slow breath. His hand was warm and safe, just like I remembered, but, I reminded myself, without the romance. He still missed his wife. We sat there a very long time staring into the fireplace together, and my thoughts lingered on the dark memories that it represented for both of us.

"Are you glad it's gone?" I didn't turn to look at him, even when he squeezed my hand, and I didn't mention Ruthie's part in finding the secret or that I disposed of it in the well.

"Yes." A relieved whisper.

"Why did you come today, Jimmy?"

Why today and not years ago?

"To make amends, and to . . . I know I didn't do enough, Joy."

Enough? Try nothing at all.

"I want to make up for it now."

"I'm getting married," I said, "As soon as Kyle gives me the ring, so if you came to offer to buy the house again, there is no need. Kyle and I will take care of things." But even as I said it, I wasn't sure if Kyle wanted to be saddled with the house.

Jimmy let go of my hand. His sigh was deep, heavy with a regret that transferred itself to me. "To begin with. You're right. I did want to talk to you about this house, but it's not the real reason . . ."

"It was never for sale," I interrupted.

"I know," he said. "I just wanted you to know that I was only trying to help when I tried to get your brothers to let me buy it. I wasn't trying to take it from you. After everything that's happened, at least I could help save this place for you." He reached for my hand again. I moved to let go, but he held tight.

"I have the means, Joy, and it's the least I can do after what was taken from you." He let that sink in. My heart was wrung out with the memory of it, but I soaked it up like a sponge mop.

"And what I took, too, Joy." I nodded. That was fair, even though I was realizing in that moment that some of it had been my fault, too. I'd wasted my life based on a promise that I now knew he couldn't have kept. "But there is something else."

He pulled my hand to his lips and softly planting a kiss across our entwined fingers. My surprise must have been evident in the way my body quivered. It was probably a sin, a badly chosen moment, considering he still wore his wedding band and my hunky young boyfriend was about to give me one of my own. I held my breath for several heartbeats. Images of Fern, her gorgeous face gaunt with disease, flooded the moment. Ill at ease, I tucked my hands between my knees.

"I'm sorry," he said, his voice thick. I bit my tongue because there wasn't an appropriate response. I wasn't sorry. Just torn between the past and present. "I want to be friends with you, Joy."

"Okay." But nothing felt okay. I'd wished for just this moment over the years, but under very different circumstances. And I didn't want to just be friends. Now, we sat together by the fireplace that had once harbored our biggest secret, both of us mere husks of who we once were to each other. It seemed so much had been lost to each of us and getting it back was impossible. I was glad when he changed the topic.

"Fern knew some of the truth," he began. "And she told Fernie about it before she died."

So, Fernie had told Nanette the truth.

I could always tell from the way she stared at me with those beady eyes at church on Sunday mornings that she'd suspected something.

"She's been bugging me to make amends with you. She likes you. I guess you helped her through some stuff when you were her Sunday school teacher."

My heart warmed. Those were the days when I was so blinded in my faith that I handed out advice too freely, but I was glad I had helped. Now, my faith had been tested. For the first time, I felt it was real, but only after being shown true kindness from people I thought were my enemies.

I felt humbled, undeserving of compassion from Fern or her daughter Fernie.

"So, what exactly did you tell Fernie's mother, Jimmy?

He sighed, his chest rising and falling. I tried to block out memories of my head resting against his heartbeat on the banks of Spavinaw Junction Creek, in the church balcony, and oh let's face it, in my wildest fantasies.

"Mostly about the chimney, not about what my dad did."

My heart stopped for a beat.

"Of course, as we got older, she began to realize there had to be an excuse for what we did. She asked questions and made some accurate guesses. I didn't confirm them, but she knew in her heart, Joy. She was a woman. Things happened to her, too, before I met her."

I couldn't stop the feeling of shame. It burned my eyes and sprang from beneath my closed lids, to think that maybe Fern understood my pain, and that she had known, even as I'd sat with her to make amends during her final days. She never breathed a word.

"How long did she know about the chimney?"

"I told her the truth a long time ago, Joy. Even before we were married. She never stopped wanting to know the reason we did it. She knew it had to be terrible."

I was standing now, meeting his gaze at eye level while he remained seated. If the anger burning in my eyes wasn't what made him look away, I don't know what did.

"I trusted you."

"It was a stupid thing I did, telling her." He stared at his boots and for a second I wanted to hit him over the head like I'd have done to River or Rory when we were kids. "It haunted her throughout our marriage."

"Haunted *her*?" I planted my hands on my hips.

"We were so young, Joy. I did everything wrong."

He looked at me for understanding, but I just planted my fists harder on my hips.

"I'd been hanging around her a lot," he explained. "When I wasn't with you. I had cousins over in Jay where she lived and I just wanted to get away from the heaviness of what you and I went through here. I was drinking and—Fern was different then, more manipulating. And well, it's no excuse for how I abandoned you."

He looked down at me and his eyes were deep wells of anguish.

"I can't believe I failed you, Joy." And when he said my name, it didn't sound like 'happiness.'

"Did you love her?" I needed to know. Some folks might think I wasted my entire life on a silly teenage crush, but the truth is, it was more. The story was bigger, darker, and mattered more than anyone in Spavinaw Junction knew.

Jimmy stared at his hands, fiddling with his gold wedding band. I stared at his profile, at how his cheeks were slack in a frown.

"To say I have regrets wouldn't even begin to hold everything I've felt about the past, how we got to this." He raised his hands to encompass both of us. "I can't even tell you how much I missed you, but everything was set in motion. Once the wheels started turning, I just couldn't go back."

My resolve weakened. "You missed me?"

"Of course." He smiled, a guilty glint in his eyes, but then that sadness came back.

"Back then, Fern was obsessed with getting away from her family. Her home life was almost as bad as mine. You already know how bad mine was."

Oh boy, did I.

"Fern was going to get out of hers no matter what," he explained. "She was trying to get pregnant on purpose."

Of course, I already knew that. Everybody in Spavinaw Junction had known that.

"Not that it makes me feel any different about our daughter," he said, his voice growing stronger. "I had all these fatherly feelings going through my heart and I wanted to take care of that baby. In my mind, that included the mother of my child. Even if I'd realized she was using me back then, Joy, I think I would have married her anyway."

Well, why don't you punch me right in the gut?

"Because of the baby."

Of course. That's what people did back then. If there was a baby, the kids got married. Soul mates? Nobody asked.

You are such a good person, Jimmy. Not like me.

"She was already pregnant when you brought her to the church that day," I stated, thinking of the day she'd cast me that sulky-teenager, triumphant look in church saying, I won.

"She was pregnant then," he said.

My hands grew sweaty and I wiped them along the skirt of my dress. We didn't have an air conditioner in our house and I'd forgotten to open the big living room window to let the breeze in. I did so now and stood in the window letting the breeze blow in around me, the skirt of my sundress alternating in between clinging to my thighs and the breeze picking it up to swish around knees.

"But be honest, Jimmy. You'd already abandoned me weeks earlier in your heart." I turned around to face the truth that I'd been dead to since I saw Fern's pregnant belly. Still seated on the sofa, he raised his eyes to mine and I saw my own grief reflected.

"No," he said. He stood to his full height. "Not in my heart."

The heaviness of what we were digging up made me slump back onto the windowsill. I saw a younger Jimmy in my mind's eye again, trapped and confused with no adult to trust, a young man with problems that would've even been big for an older man. I, at least, had Momma and my brothers and sisters even if they didn't know what happened. I even had my daddy—at least a living memory of him if not an actual spirit.

"I'm an idiot, Joy. I let my emotions govern me." He walked toward the window.

Just like a politician.

"There's nothing wrong with letting your emotions

govern what you do for your baby," I said. I knew it was the truth. Wasn't I the beloved aunt of passels of nieces and nephews? If I'd lived for anyone besides Jimmy my whole adult life, it was for those kids. I may not have known what it was to be a mother, but I'd been a second mom to many. And Lord knows, they needed it.

"I did try to get a hold of you right before I got married," Jimmy said. Now this was a surprise.

"No, you didn't." I would have remembered. I would have gone running to him if he had been trying to reach me.

"I did."

"Maybe you remember it wrong," I said. "Because if you had, I would have wanted to talk to you."

"I'm pretty sure you didn't want to talk to me, Joy. But it was a long time ago. It doesn't matter now." But didn't it? The regret in his eyes told me that it did. I tried to remember what he was talking about. He was quiet, perhaps turning it over in his mind.

"The point is, I don't blame you if you thought I was the worst boyfriend ever, the worst man ever. I wasn't patient enough for you, Joy. I let you deal with that horrible . . . truth . . . by yourself. No man should abandon someone like that." He was standing in front of me now. The breeze picked up, billowing my dress and fluttering the curtains around us, wrapping us in a sort of embrace. "I don't blame you for—"

It was an entirely involuntary movement to reach out and lay my hand on his shoulder. My words came automatically, interrupting him in mid-sentence.

"You weren't really a man, Jimmy. You were a kid." I squeezed his shoulder, sorry for my anger, sorry for not ever thinking of what that terrible day had meant to him. "We both were."

He swallowed, obviously wanting to say more.

"My wife—"

The word wife made me flinch, so I pictured Kyle in my mind. After all, I was not free either, was I?

"She always thought I was still in love with you. It drove her crazy. I can't tell you how many times we argued over you."

It was my turn to stare at my feet in hopes that he couldn't see my feelings reflected on my face.

"It was awful to see how much she was hurt by everything, too." His pain was evident and for a minute I wasn't sure how to respond. Fern and I had talked during her last week on earth. We'd apologized for the distance that had always been between us. I replayed the conversation in my mind, trying to remember . . .

"I don't know if she was even happy," Jimmy said. "How could she have been?"

"I'm sure she probably was," I lied. It seemed the right thing to say.

I guess I knew, deep down, why Fern hated me, because it was the same reason I'd hated her. But with her lying in that hospital bed, the beautiful life Jimmy had afforded her not at all reflected in her cancer-ridden body, explanations were pointless. It had been enough to forgive and accept forgiveness.

"I FORGIVE YOU, Joy." Fern had reached her hand and I'd taken it in my own. Her arms were so skinny, nothing like the shapely arms she'd liked to show off in sleeveless shirts in church. Her eyes were hollow and dark, but she smiled. "I want you to really know it."

"I do," I said. She seemed to not hear me.

"I want you to remember this conversation, Joy. You're going to need to know it deep in your heart, that I forgive you for loving my husband for all these years. But it's true, I took him from you when you are the one he wanted to marry. Of course, he fell in love with me, but it took a long time. I blamed you for that."

"I'm so sorry."

"But when I figured out what his dad did that day, I forgave you for all of it. What a terrible thing to have to go through, Joy."

My heart had caught for a beat. She knew?

"If I had known," she said, but she couldn't seem to find more words.

"I forgive you, too, Fern." And I remember how my eyes had filled up for this woman who had hated me and I her. It had been confusing, emotion thick in the air.

"Thank you." She had laughed then, a hoarse, deep sound. "You know that silly saying, 'It is what it is'?"

I nodded, but I was starting to worry about her. I thought I needed to go get a nurse to help her relax, maybe give her some pain medicine, because I knew she hurt. It was all over her face, but I had no idea then that no pain medicine could've taken that away. She'd always seemed the luckiest woman in the world to me, to have the life I'd always wanted. It never occurred to me that anything was hard for her.

"It is what it is, Joy." She caught her breath. "And it doesn't matter anymore." She laughed again. "And it feels so good to be free of old grudges." She squeezed my hand, her grasp weak. "Come on, Joy. Admit it. It feels good doesn't it?"

I smiled and the longer she gently shook my hand, I started to laugh, too, just a little.

"It does." I assured her. "It really does. I. I'm sorry for being so mean, Fern. All those dirty looks, I'm ashamed."

She took a breath and gazed at me with a tiny smile.

"You do live up to your name, Joy. I think that in another life, we might have been friends."

"FERN AND I might have been friends in another life," I said. Jimmy looked surprised, but his sudden smile was grateful.

"I understand," I said. "You don't have to explain anymore." At least I'd never married, so nobody ever had to compete with his memory, the way Fern thought she had with mine. Thoughts of Kyle drifted through my mind and I wondered if I would ever tell him the truth about Jimmy. I wondered if I would even be able to be with Kyle after what I now knew about the past.

A part of my heart, obviously a very selfish part, wanted to ask, are you still in love with me? Instead, I said, "So in the end, you did fall in love with her."

He simply nodded and I tried to imagine when it had happened. What had he loved about her? But thinking about her laughter in the hospital, about her easy way of forgiving me, I think I knew. Had I not been so buried in my own grief and hate, I might have known that Fern had grown up, that she really had found a good life to escape to, and that she wasn't as unlikable as I thought.

"She was the best mother and a good wife, Joy." He said it as an apology, and that made me feel terrible. I told you, I am not always a good person.

"And I thought she only wanted to flaunt her perfect life at me," I confessed.

"Her life wasn't perfect," he said. "I admit," he said. "I wasn't a good husband at first. I was in love with you for many, many years—"

I turned away.

Breathe.

"I've always regretted that I left you, Joy, and especially how I did it." I felt his gaze entreating me to look at him, but I could only cover my eyes.

"Jimmy don't," I whispered, but I don't think he heard.

"I know this comes way too late," he said, his voice thick. "But I am so sorry."

Decades late.

"I did care what happened to you." He placed a hand on my back. I hunched forward, trying to fold myself away from the turmoil his words stirred inside my chest.

Fern's voice echoed in my head. "And I want you to know I forgive you. It wasn't your fault. It wasn't anybody's fault, Joy."

"Joy, do you hear me? I'm so very sorry," Jimmy said.

I'd once thought those words would make everything perfect.

Breathe. Just keep breathing.

My past and present had always been irrevocably intertwined with his, but painfully separate. And now he had apologized. I knew forgiveness was next, but I couldn't voice it just then. It had been easier to be angry at him.

"I'm really glad you and Fern found happiness."

"Oh, God," he said. "Me, too." I turned around and searched his eyes to see if he was sincere, or if he was some kind of player, messing with my heart, and his wife's memory, but the pain there looked real.

We stood in silence, and I was about to tell him that I needed to get ready for the fundraising party that evening, when some missing pieces moved together in my mind.

I sat down on the window sill, imagining how, in Fern's mind, I must have been a wild card who could have taken her husband away from her.

"I'm sorry you've lost Fern," I said. He twirled his wedding band. I decided I wouldn't tell him about my conversation with Fern in the hospital. At least, not yet.

"During her last days, she did her best to let go of anger and pain." He kept twirling that wedding band around his finger until I wanted to tear it off, but how could I be jealous of that anymore?

"She gave me—gave us—her blessing." He couldn't look at me.

"Blessing for what?"

"To make amends," he said.

I stood, twirled to face the window. How could I let him see my thrill, my shame, my confusion?

"Did you hear me, Joy?"

He placed his hands on my shoulders. I wilted.

"She tried to make me promise that you and I would finally talk about things." He shook his head. "I just couldn't. It felt wrong. She was my wife. I told her that the past was past, and that I didn't need to go back there."

My heart throbbed. "I guess I can understand that." And I really could.

"You know what she said?"

I nodded that I didn't.

"She said, 'You both will.'" My heart burst. It really did, just like in my coma in the hospital when I really felt my heart stop. He turned me slowly to face him, his fingers tipping my chin up, so he could see into my face. I couldn't stop the tears that sketched their way down to my chin.

"I wish that awful day was only a nightmare," I said. "I wish Fern hadn't gotten hurt, too. I never thought about anyone else being hurt. Not even you."

"It was a nightmare." His eyes were wells of regret. "And I would give anything to take that day back for you—anything."

Anything.

A sob welled in my chest and like a tidal wave of wretchedness, carried the last of my denial away. Even Fern wanted us to move on. I decided right then and there not to worry about inappropriateness when Jimmy pulled me close to his chest. Who was I anyway, to think I had some kind of reputation to uphold? I was a Talley. Nobody really understood us anyway.

"Please forgive me," he said.

"But you aren't the one who hurt me."

I let his wide arms wrap around me, acknowledging that on this earth, be it acceptable to Carey or the people at church or to Peter and Mary Sue and Thelma, Jimmy's knowing embrace was the only one that could hold all my hurt at that moment. His arms tightened and the movement made me think of Fern, wrapped in these arms, possibly every night that she lived. Had she really known all that had happened between us, to us, even this pain of mine, and still loved Jimmy?

"Did you ever tell anybody else? Maybe the pastor? Anyone?"

"No," he said emphatically. "I would never tell that." He stroked my hair. "But maybe you should, Joy."

We were swaying now, gently, like the branches of the apple tree when the breeze used to blow through its branches, and I rested my head on his chest drinking in Old Spice cologne.

"Who would I tell, and not go to jail?" Just the thought of exposing all that had happened made my heart race.

"I was thinking your family, for starters."

I pulled back slightly, to see his face. "You've surely heard about Carey's concerns."

"She's a tough nut, but from what Reverend Wilson shared with me after church on Sunday, I think Carey has changed, too."

"We all have, haven't we?" I dared to reach up, touch his chin. In response, he took my hands tenderly in his palms.

Lordy.

I didn't flinch, letting his hands slide softly around my waist, as if no time had passed since our first embrace at the creek. I whispered into his chest.

"There are some secrets I could never tell anyone."

"Maybe you could," he whispered.

"No."

He held me at arm's length and I had to look away from the intensity of his dark eyes. The sadness in his face was so genuine that I wanted to cry.

"If you're keeping that secret for me, Joy, you can let it go. I'm not afraid of the truth anymore."

I tried to imagine telling my family about what had happened to us—to me. And I realized that yes, part of my decision to keep the secret was for him.

"I'll stand by you," he said. "To be honest, it would probably free me, as well."

"Or send us to jail—if someone, maybe Carey, decides the right thing is to report a crime."

"Then I would go to jail—for both of us."

"Do you know what you're saying?"

His hand stroked my face. "Yes. I would protect you, Joy. That's what friends do. I will always be your friend."

We stopped swaying and his gaze trapped me. I wanted to stay in that protected space forever, where nothing had happened and we'd never been apart.

"Joy, no matter how you choose to live your life, or who you choose to live it with, I promise that I will spend the rest of my life making that day up to you."

"But it wasn't your fault."

His voice was gruff. "He was my father." And something about the way he looked reminded me of the coma dream I'd had, of how he'd been when we were young. All of a sudden I pulled back, only allowing myself to clasp his hands.

"I had visions, dreams of you in the hospital, Jimmy. I dreamed about when we were young, and it was like the bad thing had never happened."

Jimmy was very still, not letting me go, drawing long breaths and not interrupting.

"We were just in love like before." I looked away. "And you really saw me. And we were together. And still young. I wished it were real. All those coma dreams I had? What do you think they mean?"

He touched my chin and turned my face until I saw his eyes burning, like mine, with all that we had hidden.

"I think they mean we can't hide from the past anymore." His arms tightened around my waist and the old chemistry that had been smoldering just beneath our skin, ignited.

While my mind roamed its confusing corridors trying to find my way out of the past and into the present, Jimmy's hand wove through my hair. His hot breath lingered next to my ear. I knew I could pull away at any moment and there would be no anger between us. It is what a better woman, a saner woman who had a boyfriend about to propose, would have done. But at that moment, with Jimmy's breath warm against my neck, his lips grazing a trail toward my own, I went a little bit Talley crazy.

"When you looked at me every Sunday morning," I whispered, my voice breathy from the shivers shooting from the place where his lips touched the skin on my neck. "I always imagined, just for a second, that you had never stopped loving me—even though you were married."

There. I said it.

His hand slid through my hair and his smooth molasses voice whispered, "God forgive me; I never did."

When he slid his hands up my arms, over my shoulders, to cradle my face in his hands, my knees grew weak. One hand slid back around my waist and I was suddenly pressed against him, my body molded to his, just like in my romance novels, only better. His lips hovered close to mine—an invitation I'd longed for in so many dreams, his breath warm, enticing me to test, and then, taste. And so, I did, forgetting for a few minutes all about the fundraiser, or that Doc would be there any time.

Oh my Lord.

I didn't take him up to my bedroom and we didn't make love on the couch right then, but I'd be lying if I said it didn't cross my mind. Wouldn't that make my sister mad at me? So inappropriate for someone like you, she would say.

I will tell you this: Even compared to the kiss in the church balcony, the intensity of our breaths mingling, lips touching, savoring, and tasting; and our arms and hands just as hungry as our lips, has never been matched in any romance novel I've ever read—and I admit I've read a lot of them.

In the future, I hoped for long uncomplicated kisses that spoke of forever, but for that moment, the two of us couldn't get close enough to capture the past, or to sustain a future absent of each other, an intimacy that would never have seemed illicit had evil not shown up decades ago to meet us at Spavinaw Junction Creek. This delicious kiss was our confession, an apology, a promise of forgiveness, and ultimately a door opening that we would both need to walk through someday soon. That we would walk through it hand in hand was certain, but how we'd come out of it I was afraid to guess at that moment.

When we reluctantly pulled away, there were things that could have been said about loss and sorrow and the passage of time, but we didn't need to voice them. We simply parted, knowing that our future was changed. The next time we saw each other, we would be friends again, but I also knew that we could never be just friends. The memory of our past pierced between us, its sharp edges as glaring as the bolt of lightning that had split the apple tree in two leaving its torn trunk irreparable, but its thick twining roots still connected.

Chapter Twenty-six

A KISS CAN change you. It can turn you on the wrong track in which you break everyone else's heart to pursue your own wanton desires, it can set you back on the right track depending on how the kiss goes, or it can fling you right back in time. And time has a funny way of slowing down and speeding up at the most precise moments, doesn't it? I'd spent the better part of my life stuck back on the banks of Spavinaw Junction Creek, and all of a sudden, with one kiss from Jimmy, life decided to place a magnifying glass between me and the past. Through it, I could see every missed opportunity, each misunderstanding, and a complete set of circumstances that I'd misread—a life not yet lived all because of one horrible hour. I would love to give up that hour, but I wished I could turn back the clock and retrieve the thousands more that were lost.

You just can't get almost three decades of your life back. Heck, you can't get three days back. If my crazy coma experience had taught me anything, it was that the past can't be changed, yet, heaven-willing, I could turn the creek on a new course. I didn't have to fear the caves under the water anymore. They might always be there yawning their jaws, mocking me, but I didn't have to swim into them. I never had. I was beginning to see the world in a different set of eyes.

"Kyle?"

He smiled, freshly showered, from his place at the kitchen table. He'd been working almost non-stop for two weeks and shown up looking like he'd been working the late shift at The Drunk Raccoon instead of saving people, so I'd sent him straight to the shower. I fixed him something to eat and made a pot of coffee while the shower was going, every domestic action making me feel like the worst girlfriend in the world.

"I think this will be the best fundraiser we've had," I said. He nodded doggedly, and I realized he was still so tired that he was having a hard time following my excited babbling about the party agenda.

"It starts in two hours," I said, not sure he felt the same excitement I did.

He blew on his coffee before taking a large sip that would have burned my tongue, but I guessed that in his line of work he was used to drinking hot coffee fast. I sat beside him and smoothed a hand through his hair. I wondered if he would forgive me. He looked so tired, yet he'd come to help at the party anyway.

"I'm so glad you came."

"I wouldn't miss it," he said. "I love the big heart you have for helping young girls."

"And boys, too," I said.

"Who knows?" He shrugged. "Maybe someday The Tulip House for Girls will just be the Tulip House. I know that would make you happy."

I smiled at how well he already knew me. Only recently, did I understand that it was because I used to be one of those girls who needed help myself. And Jimmy could have used it, too. In certain ways, more than me.

"It would. And speaking of girls who need help, I have a really big favor to ask of you."

"Sure." He drained a third of his coffee in one gulp. "Anything."

My heart clinched. Could I tell him?

"I need to tell something . . . to someone I can trust."

"I'm your man."

"And a good one," I said, offering him a robust hug.

And I'm telling you, as cheesy as it sounds, if he'd pulled out that big ole ring right then, I might have thrown all plans to divulge the truth aside and married him. But he didn't deserve me like this. I had no doubt that Kyle would walk the journey with me, but I needed to walk it by myself.

"This thing you have to tell me, is it bad?"

"It's bad," I said. And just like that, I told him. I thought I might chicken out or that it would be harder, and it was, but I told him anyway. Surprisingly, I didn't cry very much, just stared at my hands and told the story to him in all its sad detail. When it was over, I looked up. A grey cloud slipped over his magnificent amber eyes.

"Oh, Joy. Baby." He drew me into his arms and then, yes, of course I cried, and I remember thinking to myself in that moment that this man could be my best friend. He had helped me through so much. Heck, turned me from town spinster to the woman with a hunky younger boyfriend! And not to diminish the boyfriend thing, but he had saved my life.

I could live with this man forever.

But then Momma's voice crept into the space between Kyle and me, reminding me that even though I'd told Kyle my biggest secret, I hadn't told him about Jimmy's kiss.

"Secrets always want to be told, and they won't stay hidden, Joy."

And then there was Daddy's ghost, who of course only ever said, "Breathe, Joy," and in this case was no help.

Oh, Momma and Daddy. Since you're both dead, can you leave me alone?

I really did want to ignore them and stay right where I was with the hero of all my romantic novels to take care of me, but as I settled into hunky Kyle's chest I felt something solid in his shirt pocket pressing against my shoulder. It felt about the size of a jewelry box, the size of box that might hold an engagement ring. It pinched into me, uncomfortable, reminding me that I wasn't Cinderella. Then Kyle kissed my cheek very tenderly, as if he knew I was about to break up with him, and that just made me cry even harder.

Chapter Twenty-seven

"THIS HAS BEEN the best fundraiser ever," said Mary Sue, who wore a great big hat like she thought she was living on a southern plantation. Beside her, Nurse Clara wore pink stretchy pants and an oversized top that was designed for a much younger, and to be honest, thinner, woman, but she looked cheery in it.

"That sure is true," said Clara. "Joy has outdone herself. Bess would be proud of her."

"We're all proud of her," Mary Sue said, and I was glad she didn't notice me behind the screen door. A compliment from Mary Sue was like receiving a pat on the back from your pretty, popular enemy. I guess even Mary Sue had a good side. I wondered, maybe she had her own secrets and hurts that made her the way she was, just like me. And just like one of my sisters in particular.

Carey, who was running around trying to get her kids and husband settled, wore a sundress like mine, but in a blue print. Nanette's, also handmade by Carey, was a lime green floral print and she was running around barefoot, because she said the sandals Carey bought us were too tight.

It was a good thing most of the folks had sent an R.S.V.P. because we might not have had enough food to go around.

People were there from the community, as well as some V.I.P. guests from towns in the surrounding area, all except for Doctor Kyle Christie, whose absence my sisters had not yet addressed. Watching the visitors milling about the property made me realize what a great place we had and I decided right then and there, we'd be having people out more often.

It's hard to say what the most popular part of the fund-raiser was. If you asked River or Rory, it would have been the fact that we had a beer for all the men if they wanted it—and a couple of the women, too. If you asked Bobby, it would have been the beer, too, if he hadn't been flanked by River and Rory all night waiting to box his jaws if he so much as took a sip; so instead, he enjoyed a bottle of Orange Crush and ate a good majority of the fried okra all by himself.

Ruthie was after the strawberry-lemon cake, but was as delighted as the little ones when she found out we'd also added watermelon wedges to the menu at the last minute. I couldn't help but laugh when I caught her spitting water-melon seeds in a competition with children.

The Talley children ran about being their usual unruly selves and showing off for the community's children. We'd never had a party at our house, and rarely visitors, so the kids in town had long talked wide-eyed about the 'haunted' Talley house. We allowed the kids to show their friends the interesting points of the property, including a trap door into the fruit cellar, a ladder up to a low balcony just over the kitchen, and a tire swing in the back yard, as long as they stayed away from the caves up above.

They even climbed about the fallen branches of the magic apple tree that we hadn't had the heart to remove yet. I'd seen River standing near it several times over the past few days, an axe in hand, but never wielding it. He'd brought a date along to the fundraiser. I watched as Fernie and River found reasons to touch shoulders, legs, and even clasp hands occasionally, and I couldn't help but worry and hope that it all worked out.

My baby brother Rory and his wife Faith had chosen a quilt underneath one of the peach trees to shield the babies from the sun as it was setting, and I'd taken a short break to cuddle the teeny girl, baby Hope. She'd been born with squinty eyes that permanently looked to the side because in the womb, her brother had cut off some of her oxygen supply, but she already had a smile that made you want to give her one thousand kisses.

"I hope you won't mind babysitting these babies, some," said Faith, cradling little Harley in her long slender arms. "Rory says you aren't going back to the shop and that you might have some time to spare."

I couldn't help but laugh at the memory.

"We're letting you go," Rory had said with a smirk on his face. When I tried to argue, he'd interrupted. "Go live up to your name, Sis. Life is short. Then you die."

"Well, yes," I said to Faith, passing the baby over to Nanette, who'd just handed baby Harley over to his mother.

"It does seem like I got fired with pay from the auto shop, so I can't use Rory as a reference."

She smiled. "He gave you a glowing reference already."

"Okay, then," I said, unable to hide my happiness.

Like I've said, who needs babies when you have nieces and nephews?

"Call me when you are ready to go back to work, honey." I carefully laid Hope on the blanket beside Faith. "I'd love to watch the babies."

River needed help handing out jars with lids, so I took a handful and distributed them among the children. The jars would keep the children busy catching fireflies when the sun set in the next hour. I handed out the jars in a hurry and stopped for just a minute to talk with Thelma, who was seated in her new fancy wheel chair, obviously enjoying the way that Mary Sue and Peter were flitting back and forth taking care of her. It is strange, but since her stroke, Thelma seemed to have finally found happiness. Peter and Mary Sue had insisted on becoming her unlikely roommates and taken over her house—and her care—as if it were their calling. They still held the singles group every week when Thelma was feeling okay and Thelma still helped us with The Tulip House for Girls fundraising.

"The strawberry-lemon cake is divine," said Peter, pausing to kiss me on the cheek and then leaning over to kiss Thelma's.

Like I've said. Sometimes a kiss can change your course in life. Bidding them all goodnight, I released a contended sigh. Everything was perfect for my exit. And no, don't worry. No matter what anyone says, I was never really trying to exit this world when I hung myself, at least not on purpose.

AT THE LONE stoplight in Spavinaw Junction, Jimmy turned west. We drove along the twisting paved road through hollows and trees until we came to the intersection that would lead us deeper into the country. Truth is, I was a little bit nervous. I wished I could scoot close to Jimmy and gather strength, but I was frozen on the opposite site of the truck. Instead, I listened to country music on the radio, as we drove further away from Spavinaw Junction.

Eventually, we took another turn down an unmarked road that led us to an attractive looking building that was all lit up and surrounded by gardens and out-buildings. My heart seemed to leap out of my chest, but for different reasons than it usually did when Jimmy was around.

Maybe this is a mistake.

Jimmy helped me out of the truck and collected my bags. We stood on the big front porch decked with barrels overflowing with colorful pink petunias. He planted a light kiss on my cheek, which made me wish I could smile. Would I ever get used to having Jimmy around?

"Are you sure you want to do this? Because we can leave right now. I'm behind you either way."

"No," I said. "I don't want to leave. This is something I should've done years ago."

"And you're sure they're expecting you?"

"Yes, I talked to the board director who connected me with the counselor in residence just this afternoon. It's all set."

He set my bags down and drew me into his arms. "Look, Joy." His voice was low and soothing. "I know I encouraged you to face the past, I didn't really mean you had to go this far. You don't have to do this."

"But I do," I said.

"Okay," he said, his voice filled with skepticism. "But if you aren't home in a month, Joy Talley, I am gathering up your brothers and we're coming to carry you right out of this place."

"Okay," I said. "Deal."

When he was finally satisfied I was staying there, he turned to the heavy ornate red-painted door with an elaborate ring of dried flowers hanging from it and rang the bell. After a while, we heard some shuffling inside and a bolt clicked. The door creaked open and a woman in her sixties with red hair and a hot pink sweat suit peeked out.

"May I help you?"

"Yes, I said. I am here to check myself in."

"You must be Joy Talley," she exclaimed. "We've all been waiting to meet you. Come in. Come in."

We stepped into the entryway and I admired the blue and white tiled floor. She ushered me into a living room where perhaps a dozen young women and girls sat around wearing sweats and pajamas.

"Girls. She's here. This is Joy Talley."

"Hi, Joy." They echoed.

The red-haired woman turned to me and held out her hand. "I'm Barbara," she said. "Welcome to The Tulip House for Girls."

Chapter Twenty-eight

I ADMIT IT'S not every day that a grown woman, okay, a middle-aged woman, checks herself into a home for troubled girls, but I was still a troubled girl inside. And besides that, I refused to even consider that I was really off my rocker. Sure, I had problems, if that's what you call having a ghost father, realistic visions during my coma, and a house full of teas, charmed chocolates, and—up until the night of the twister—enough luck charms hidden in a medieval-style chimney that we could have opened a shop painted blue and decorated with moons and stars, but as I got to know the girls living at the house over the next few weeks, I would learn it could have been much worse for me.

I'd kept my secret for so long that I almost started to think I was the only one with such a dark problem, but as the girls told me their stories, I realized I could've had to live their lives. At first I wasn't sure if they would accept me or not. It could have been a bit awkward with my being a little bit old—in their teen minds, totally ancient—but since the folks who ran the home had gotten to know me through the fundraisers I'd been facilitating, they decided to make an exception for my strange request.

"I knew your mother, Bess. She was special to us here."

"I remember the work she did to help," I said. "I just wish I'd paid attention to it when she was alive."

"You are now." Barbara smiled a big glittery grin.

At the Tulip House, I had my own room and unlike the girls, I could leave the house without a chaperone at any time without permission from a parent or from the state. Although, after my first counseling session, when I hinted at my problems, they highly discouraged my leaving before the thirty days were up. At times, I longed to leave and find comfort with my sisters, even my brothers, but I stuck to it. The only escape I allowed myself were a couple of phone calls.

Carey: "Joy, I am sorry! I feel like this is all my fault. I didn't really mean you should go to a place like that. Please come home."

Nanette: "Sis, is this because I didn't take up for you enough from Carey? I'm sorry."

River: "Are you nuts? You need to get your ass back home and be with the people who really care about you."

Rory: "I'm surprised you did this all by yourself, Joy. You know I wouldn't have let you go. Call me if you need me to break you out."

Jimmy: "I love you." And not even a word about what my stay here might do to him.

Be still my heart.

Jimmy's comment sent me back a few years to the warm banks and cool waters of Spavinaw Junction Creek, reminding me that the issues I wanted to deal with happened when I was about the same age as these girls. Maybe I was nuts, but this was the right thing. Besides, the only home like The Tulip House for adults was a hundred miles away and for more serious mental issues. Me? I didn't need that, as Doc had explained to me when I confessed my past to him. He had put on his doctor hat and assured me I wasn't crazy, helped me make the call to the Tulip House, and gave me a kiss goodbye.

Oh, Doc. I will miss you.

The emotion on Doc's face when I broke it off had shocked me. I don't know why, but the realization that he loved me was a surprise. Sadly, it hadn't changed my heart.

"You're going to be fine," he had said.

"So are you," I told him, but he looked doubtful, completely unaware of what a desirable man he was. He would have a girlfriend in no time, I had no doubt.

Me? I did think I would be fine. My stay was almost like a little vacation. It wasn't all relaxing, of course, but I enjoyed the change of scenery. I was given more responsibility around the house than the girls, since obviously I was more mature than them, but sometimes when we sat in group sessions and I listened to their stories, I realized they were wise way beyond their years, and many of them beyond mine. It made me wonder how such smart girls could end up there. I said as much in a group session one day, as we all sat around on couches in the den.

A brooding pregnant girl with pigtails turned the tables on me and said, "A bunch of us have been wondering the same thing about you."

I gave her a sad smile. "That's fair," I said. "I guess it's time to tell y'all my story, but it isn't easy to talk about it."

The girl said, "It'll be okay. We've been where you are. You can trust us."

Saddened by the girl's stark honesty, something inside me broke open.

"Okay," I began, my voice stronger than I would have expected, considering what I was about to say. "On the day that it happened, I was late meeting Jimmy at the creek."

WHEN I PULLED into the parking area at the creek, there was a truck parked beside Jimmy's and I remember hoping he'd made it to our spot before some fisherman took it first. I locked my car, anxious to get to him. He was supposed to bring the fishing rods, so I pulled out a blanket, a picnic lunch, and a couple of bottles of orange pop. Orange Crush was Jimmy's favorite back then.

Excited to see Jimmy, I jogged down the trail. When I got close, I saw his long wavy hair showing from beneath his ball cap and was about to call out when I heard yelling.

Hurrying through the trees, I saw Jimmy and his dad up ahead standing on the creek bank.

Why is his dad here?

I'd seen his dad one time before and had forgotten how huge and intimidating he was, but he had Jimmy's sinewy look and striking features with a wide chest and arms. I'd tried to say hello to him in Jimmy's driveway, but Jimmy had gunned the truck and drove right past.

"Don't ever talk to him again."

I'd laughed. "Don't be embarrassed. He's just your dad."

"He's a drug dealer."

I still believed, in those days, that everyone had a shred of decency in them. What I didn't know before the hottest day ever on the Spavinaw Junction banks was that while most people do have good inside of them, even addicts, Jimmy's dad was bad, even before he started dealing and taking his own medicine.

"Maybe he can change," I said.

"Evil people can't change. Don't talk to him. Ever. And don't ever come to the house looking for me. I shouldn't have brought you. Now he knows what you look like."

"Jimmy—" I protested, still not grasping why Jimmy was being so over-protective.

Jimmy's eyes had turned steely. "Promise me."

"Okay," I said. "Promise."

Now, my stomach flip-flopped to see his dad, a wicked gleam in his red-rimmed eyes set in a hollow face, towering over Jimmy. His muscles rippled through his shirt, a menacing sign of his physical strength over Jimmy's, while his hairy waist peeking out of his too short T-shirt had a malnourished look to it. I hadn't noticed that he looked like an addict before, but now I wondered. Was he high on some kind of drug at that very moment?

I paused behind a tree, peeked out. Jimmy stood tall, his chest out, ready to defend but when his dad started swinging, Jimmy cowered like a child, as if he'd been the brunt of this kind of beating before. I wanted to run and help, but I was so scared.

Come on, Jimmy. Get up.

The gravel beneath them crunched. I didn't know what to do as Jimmy's face opened up, blood puffing into bruises and trickling out of his nose.

Holy Cow!

At one point he clamped Jimmy's neck between his bare hands and Jimmy struggled for breath. Despite the terrified wobble in my knees, I was about to throw caution to the wind and run out when his dad let go, throwing Jimmy backwards.

"I'll ask you one more time, where did you put it?"

Put what?

Jimmy looked up from his hands and knees. Blood spat from his mouth and splattered red on the smooth, pale rocks.

"I told you. I didn't take your stuff. I don't even use drugs, Dad."

His dad growled. "Now that you're dating that red-headed slut, you getting all high and mighty on me, boy? You sell it to her?"

"She's not that kind of girl."

Jimmy stood, slowly, wiping blood from his mouth with the back of his forearm. The front of his white T-shirt was splattered with red dots.

I'm going to throw up.

I nearly cheered when Jimmy took a surprise swing. His

dad spat a tooth, ran his tongue over where it used to be, but he still stood like an oak, angrier than before.

The blow to Jimmy's face was swift. I blocked a scream with my fist. Jimmy tottered to the side and fell on the ground. My heart pounded like the locomotive that went through Spavinaw Junction every afternoon. All was quiet for a moment, then a grunt and more stomps across the gravel coming in my direction. The locomotive in my chest crashed. Even in my nightmares of falling into the spring, I had never felt that kind of fear—the kind that spikes into your chest and draws down through your belly and legs, and I haven't felt it since.

In an instant, Jimmy's dad strode past my tree towards the far away parking area. I froze. He hadn't seen me, so I waited. When I heard a motor engine roar to life in the distance, I bolted towards Jimmy's limp body lying on the creek bank. He lay twisted, like a ragdoll discarded by a toddler, and his long beautiful hair splayed on the rocks, a dark, damp, velvet lock of it covering his face.

"Jimmy."

I knelt, gently nudging his shoulder. His beautiful Cherokee skin was snow white, which wasn't normal at all. I placed my hand on his chest and was relieved to feel his heart beating, but he wasn't breathing anymore. Illustrations of how to administer CPR that I'd seen in a library book ran through my mind. I sealed his mouth with mine, hoping I was doing the right thing, and breathed into him.

I was so busy trying to get him to stir that I didn't even hear the truck still idling in the distance, or the crunch of gravel behind me, until long fingers wrapped around the back of my neck like a vice.

I sucked in emptiness, drowning in midair.

This can't be real.

I didn't have time to cry, or to reflect on how the situation resembled the crime novels that Nanette liked to read. All I can say is that for the rest of my life, I never read anything if it wasn't romantic and filled only with problems that were easily fixed by dashing heroes. Once you meet a real villain, it ruins suspense novels for you.

The villain in my all too real story jerked me like a puppet, my legs and arms flailing. A hand wrapped around my thigh and carried me through the trees where branches snagged my hair. I grabbed frantically at the tree trunks with my free arm, but I couldn't grasp any of them. The foul odor of what I thought must be whiskey, mixed with sweat, wreaked through my nostrils and I tried to hold my breath. His strength was super human. I tried to cry out, I really did, but as he moved over me like a storm cloud, he pressed his hand over my mouth. With each movement, my breath was taken, my innocence stolen.

I lay in the trees afterwards like the crushed beer cans discarded by partying teenagers on the forest floor around me.

"Now," the villain said, adjusting his zipper. "While my boy is sleeping, me and you are going to take a little ride where no one can find us."

I turned, pulled my knees up, fresh fear shooting through me like a shotgun shell. Faces of missing girls on

TV scrolled through my mind, girls and even boys whose bodies were found years later, if at all.

I sat up, thinking that if my head stopped spinning, I could run.

God. Please. Help.

When the villain leaned to snatch up his discarded ball cap, I saw Jimmy. His eyes were fierce as he rose up behind his dad, stealthy like a panther.

Oh, thank God.

EVEN THOUGH I'D later be brave enough to tell my siblings the same story and marvel at how supportive they would be, the reaction of the Tulip House girls was the closest I would ever feel to being understood. Our common troubles—some of them had been abused in the same way made me realize that my being drawn to Tulip House was no accident, although I couldn't have admitted my own need for help back when I made that first call to see how I could help them out.

When the girls dispersed, house mom Barbara asked me if I wanted to press charges for rape against Jimmy's dad. The question confused me, at first. I'd never even considered reporting what he did to me for a myriad of reasons that I couldn't tell Barbara. I hadn't even gone to the hospital after it happened, but, of course she had to suggest it, didn't she? It was her job.

"It was a long time ago," I said, still somewhat breathless from the emotion of telling my story. "I don't even remember all the facts."

"But you just told them to me and my girls."

Well, shoot. Why hadn't I expected this?

I reached a shaky hand to touch Barbara's, truly grateful. "Thank you for helping me tell the truth. I feel so free, like you said I would, but—I'll never cooperate with the police on rape charges. They would never be able to find Jimmy's dad, anyway."

She seemed unfazed by my words, as if she'd heard the reasons not to report a crime many times before from a hundred others girls. She then made a gallant effort to convince me to go to the police station with her, but I didn't.

You see, I knew why the police would never locate Jimmy's dad, but even without that knowledge, the word around town had been that he left his family decades ago and never returned, and then, everyone had just stopped talking about it. Nobody missed him, and nobody wanted to find him.

"Joy, I'm sure the police could—"

"Please, no," I said. "I don't want to."

She had looked doubtful, but nodded.

"This," I said, motioning to the walls around us. "This house is what I needed. It has saved me, and I'm so glad you don't have to close it down."

"Thanks to people like you," Barbara said, and she gave me a hug that for a moment made me miss Momma who had always hugged us kids, whether we thought we needed it or not—and I had always needed it.

The thought that I'd had a small part in helping the Tulip House stay open made me smile, but the experience had turned out to be so much more meaningful than the pleasure of raising money for a good cause. At first, I'd thought I would be a big help to The Tulip House for Girls, but in the end, the Tulip House girls had been the ones to help me, and—I hadn't even needed to tell them what happened to Jimmy's dad in order to finally feel free. Besides, after what he did to me, who would care what happened to him?

Chapter Twenty-nine

IT WOULD SURE make a nice ending if I told you that after I told the truth, first to the Tulip House girls and upon arriving back home, to my family, everything worked out like a fairytale, but that's not exactly how it happened. No matter Ruthie's fantasies about Prince Charmings and happily ever afters, we all know life isn't really like that, especially if you are a Talley.

As for my friends, I had to tell them something. Despite their imperfections, I was stuck with them, and them with far-from-perfect me, so I decided to tell the truth—most of it. I left the saddest parts out, but they got the gist of it and were sad anyway. Suddenly, they were inspired to confess and apologize for things I didn't even know they'd said about me, which strangely made me laugh out loud; and while they could never be expected to give up their gossip, I knew they wouldn't be spreading this bit of news around.

"Why didn't we hang out like this before?" I asked one night as I sat with them in my living room. Since our work for Tulip House had turned out so well, we started meeting weekly to perform small acts of kindness in the community, not just for Tulip House. This night we were busy crocheting scarves and mittens for children in need, while my brothers, Jimmy, and my quiet brothers-in-law were out in the back tearing down the old barn.

"Because you never invited us," Peter said. "And I was your best friend in high school."

"I'm sorry," I said.

Peter continued. "I loved Bess as much as everyone, but we all knew she didn't want to share her house, like she was hiding something."

"Maybe she was," Ruthie said, and I winked at her.

"Well," Mary Sue said. "I always supposed that whatever she put in those teas might have been what she was hiding."

"And those chocolates," someone said.

"Hey," I said lightly. "This is slightly off topic, but speaking of Momma, have I ever mentioned that I heard y'all talking about me at her funeral?"

"I knew it!" Peter exclaimed, and I loved him for it. "I didn't mean anything I said. I was just so nervous, crossing myself like a Catholic and everything."

Mary Sue, not looking surprised at the news, either, said, "We were so sad about Grandma Bess and there you were, our best friend, in a coma, kidnapped by your crazy brothers and sisters."

Your best friend?

"Crazy?"

"Well," Peter said. "They were acting crazy."

Thelma motioned with a curled wrist to her chest. "Meeeee? I was just meeean." And then, she laughed.

"You sure are, Thelma." Peter leaned over to kiss her on the cheek, but I was already there. If nothing else, that lady was honest and I respected her for it. No secrets, ever, where Thelma was concerned. Her stroke had not changed anything about her personality.

Carey lay down her scarf. "You aren't as mean as Nanette, Thelma honey; and now she's even a jailbird!" She playfully swatted Nanette's shoulder.

Everyone giggled. Carey was referring to our sister's recent night in jail. Who in the heck would've ever thought that a nice lady like Nanette would spend an evening in the same jail that had held her son overnight for drugs?

"The sheriff was lucky you weren't carrying your gun, but he rightfully deserved you running over his foot," Carey declared.

"Here, here. That's what the old bugger gets for selling drugs to a child," Peter said. "And it's not the first time it's happened, as everyone knows. Too many crooked cops in this county. Only a few good ones, like Officer Gray. I hope we get more like him."

I went back to my crocheting, thinking about how glad I was that Bobby was getting a second chance at a good future, thanks to his mom's foiling of his pot smoking habit and the crooked police who were selling it to kids. Course, I was getting a second chance at mine, too, and I'd let everyone know about it. The last time Reverend Wilson did the altar call like he did every Sunday with lots of bravado and encouragement, I even left the balcony and walked down to the front. It was nice not being stuck in a wheel chair for this one; and I admit it, I squeezed my cheeks together a little bit this time. There wasn't any reason to let what happened at Momma's funeral happen again. Reverend Wilson, who developed amnesia about such things, took my hand. Afterward, I sat in my regular seat instead of hiding up in the balcony. Jimmy did that little fist tapping his chest thing, which sent my butterflies to fluttering, and I didn't even have to feel guilty about it even more.

"Joy," Nanette nudged me. "The men are back. Should we set the dinner out?"

I set down my crocheting. "I reckon we should." I eyed Jimmy as he walked in. He held a hungry look in his eyes that I didn't think had anything to do with food.

Lord have mercy. Will I ever get used to this hunk of man?

Somehow we all managed to squeeze around Momma's big farm table and spent the next hour handing bowls of mashed potatoes and grits, green beans, platters of pot roast, and baskets of bread around the table. We followed dinner with three kinds of cake and two pots of coffee. I loved having so many people together in Momma's house, and I loved the way Jimmy kept casting me meaningful looks across the table. Out of habit, I glanced down at his left hand and lo and behold, his wedding band was gone. I blushed like a teenager on her first date.

WHEN ALL THE friends had gone home, and Bobby and

Ruthie took the kids out front to play Frisbee, I surprised the men by producing one beer each from the fridge.

"Joy," Carey said. "Do you really think we need to promote alcoholism in this family after all the trouble Bobby's been in?"

"Don't be dramatic. I'm not promoting alcoholism," I said. "I'm promoting taking a break after these men have been working hard tearing down a century-old barn for free."

"It's our barn," Rory pointed out.

"Doesn't matter," I said. "You still deserve a beer." I held one of the ice cold cans out to Jimmy, but he waved it away.

"Don't drink," he reminded me, and then, I recalled that he never had.

"I didn't know you didn't drink," Nanette said. "Can I have yours?"

"Jimmy's the church music leader," Carey said. "And the mayor. Of course he doesn't drink."

"That's not why," Jimmy said, stepping to the fridge for a Pepsi. He grabbed a few extras and handed them out to the rest of us who weren't really beer drinkers. "I don't drink because of my old man. Alcohol and drugs turned him into a crazy son of a . . ." He paused.

"Gun?" I asked.

"A crazy son of a gun."

Rory nodded. "Makes sense."

A silence that wasn't altogether uncomfortable, but just empty, settled around the room. I knew my brothers and sisters were thinking about the things that'd happened to Jimmy and me. After telling my story to the Tulip House girls, telling my family about Jimmy's dad was easier, but they still needed a little more time to get used to it.

Thank God, they don't know the whole story.

I was about to change the subject when River spoke up, asking a question that came completely out of nowhere. But River was never one to mince words.

"So, whatever happened to the son-of-a-gun, anyway?"

"I've always wondered the same thing," Rory said. "He disappeared a long time ago, right?"

Jimmy nodded, his eyes never leaving mine. It had been no secret in the community that his dad was not a good man, that he'd left his family numerous times, and that the last time had never come back.

"You ever hear from him?" Carey asked.

"He's dead," Jimmy said, shifting his gaze to the floor, and I couldn't stop the gasp that escaped into the room.

"I don't remember hearing about that," Nanette said. "When did you find out?"

Everyone stared, River pinning me with his gaze. He looked back at Jimmy, then back at me.

"Yeah, when did you find out?" I could tell River suspected more.

Darn it, River.

He was always the best at getting the truth out of people. All of a sudden, I felt like the ceiling was coming down on top of my head. River's voice was quiet, but clear in the abruptly quiet kitchen. Not even a clink of ice against an iced tea glass broke the silence when he spoke next.

"I've been thinking," he said. "Joy never really finished the story about that day. You kicked the shit out of him after what he did to our sister, right? And then he ran off?"

Jimmy's lips tightened, he stared harder at the floor. Nobody bothered to correct River's bad language.

"River," Nanette said. "Why are you asking these things?"

"Cut it out," Carey said.

River laughed, the sound scraping across the room. "I mean, if it were me, I would've killed him."

Rory leaned forward, his elbows on the table now, his eyes narrowing. "I would've killed him, too. Hell, I wish you would've."

My heart felt like it would burst through my chest. I stood, thinking about saying something to make them shut up, but Jimmy motioned for me to sit. I couldn't, so I started pacing, aware that my sisters were looking at me oddly.

River shrugged. "Please, tell us you killed that bastard."

Rory uttered the Lord's name in vain, which his wife opened her mouth to correct him for, then thought better of. Everyone else just looked at Jimmy, waiting for an explanation—a denial.

Jimmy's eyes locked on mine, and I was swept back in time.

"I did," Jimmy said, and the tornado that slammed the chimney into the ground not so long ago was back swirling in my head.

"No," I said, but then Jimmy was beside me, squeezing my hand, his eyes piercing mine, his head shaking almost imperceptibly. His lips brushed my ear and I heard him whisper, *don't.*

"I fought him," Jimmy said, "and in the struggle, he was stabbed. He died."

Everyone started talking at once. Would they stay quiet? Or would someone—maybe self-righteous Carey—feel like they needed to report a crime?

The tornado in my head grew louder. I imagined Jimmy in an orange jump suit.

"That's not what happened," I whispered, but no one was listening. I spoke loudly, drowning everyone out, which isn't easy to do in a crowd full of riled-up Talleys.

"That's not what happened."

The panic in Jimmy's eyes broke my heart. "No," he whispered.

But these were my brothers and sisters. I told them the truth—all of it.

I WOULD NEVER forget how the sun beat down on us as we stood on the banks of Spavinaw Junction Creek that day.

"Are you okay?"

I looked down at my bare feet, the rocks pressing into their soles, fresh memories of the attack in my mind blotting the beauty of the scenery that surrounded us. What was I supposed to say? That no, I had bruises where he couldn't see?

I peered at Jimmy, hoping he might see what I couldn't say. He gave me a long look, his eyes moving across my face and then he took in my appearance. His eyes darkened and I shrank at his gaze, ashamed. His glance moved to his Dad, to the evil villain, who lay where he had landed after spinning around and trying one last time to choke the life out of Jimmy.

I was afraid—could barely get myself up off the ground—but when Jimmy's eyes had rolled back in his head and he'd dropped the switchblade he was brandishing, I knew he was going to die.

I didn't think. I just grabbed the open switchblade. I thrust it into his dad's side, pulled it out, and dropped the knife.

Afterward, when Jimmy was okay, except a deep bruise developing along his neck, we stood helplessly facing each other, his dad's body ominously still on the rocks. I trembled, hugging my sides, as he turned away and emptied what seemed like everything he'd ever consumed. He wiped his mouth and I wondered if he would ever be able to look at me again. When he turned back, I saw a tear slip down his cheek.

"I don't know what to do." He choked.

He looked at me then, as if awaiting my instructions, but of course, I didn't have an answer.

"I don't know what you need," he repeated.

We stood staring at each other, worn out, as tattered and bloodied as our clothes. Images of all that had happened flashed across the sky, as if I was witnessing somebody else's nightmare. My legs were so tired. I felt the spontaneous strength that had been propping me up wane while my body swayed. Jimmy caught me and scooped me up in his arms. I remember feeling safe, because I knew the son of the villain in this story was a hero.

Jimmy stood cradling my exhausted body, turning in a circle, as if not knowing the way back to his truck anymore. I wanted to point him in the right direction, but it was all I could do to hang onto his neck. I remember being afraid I was hurting his bruised neck, but he never even flinched.

"I don't know what to do," he said, again. He shifted, to get a better grasp on my body, and carried me up stream away from the body, across the bank, and ultimately, down into the cold water that wrapped itself around us.

My feet found the bottom of the creek and Jimmy began scooping handfuls of water and washing the blood off my face. I closed my eyes, letting the flow of the water wash away the filth from my skin, but not from the place deep inside where nothing could reach.

"Your dad," I said, my voice dry and raspy. "I'm sorry. It's just—he was choking you. I didn't meant to—"

"Sh-sh."

I closed my eyes against Jimmy's sad gaze. "It's going to be okay," he said.

"Promise?"

"I promise."

I breathed in, a tiny bit of relief seeping into my heart, but when I opened my eye, I saw a large water moccasin slide out of the water and slither up a partially submerged tree. It coiled itself in the fork of a branch and then its slick, black body fell perfectly still, waiting, I imagined to strike.

It occurred to me that the snake must have swam right past as we stood in the water, perhaps looping around our legs even as it swam across the creek to find its waiting place. I was mindful of how it could have easily bitten us, so distracted we were with washing away the blood, but to tell the truth, we probably wouldn't have even felt it in that icy water anyway, poisoned as we already were.

MY SISTERS TRIED to press close after I finished our story, wanting to comfort me, but I didn't want to be touched right then. I gently pressed them away. Strangely, I was okay. I was fine, in fact. Even the idea of going to prison didn't bother me. I'm not saying it'd be easy—I look awful in orange—but I would do it.

River moved closer. "You saved yourself, Sis, and Jimmy. I shoulda' known." He sounded proud, which inspired a mixture of feelings in my chest. I'd never seen it that way. "So, what did y'all do with the body?"

I had never asked about the body and when Jimmy tried to tell me right after it happened, I hadn't wanted to know. All I'd focused on then was that crazy idea about making a charm dark enough and magic enough to hide our secret. I used all my knowledge from the stories Momma and Daddy had told me over the years. I was too traumatized and just not wise enough at that age, to know that by including a tooth that Jimmy had knocked out of his dad's mouth in the fight, I was essentially creating a box full of evidence against us and not a protective charm. I hadn't even thought about asking when Jimmy had picked up that tooth off the rocks. The carved snake represented the one we saw that day, and the man with the noose, his dad. I was glad I got rid of them.

"What did happen to the body?" I asked now, ready to hear the answer. Maybe Jimmy had buried him.

"Everyone knew your dad disappeared," Rory said. "But we all thought the mother f—" Faith punched him in the arm. Rubbing his arm, Rory finished, "We all thought the son-of-gun abandoned you, Jimmy."

"He did!" I defended. How much more can a boy be abandoned by having a father who did what he did?

"Joy." Rory's voice was soft now. "We know what you mean, but why lie anymore? We know everything else, that he was a monster. Nobody's blaming anyone. So what happened to his body?"

Jimmy who'd taken his seat at the table scraped his chair back, leaned forward, legs wide, hands on his knees. His dark eyes were thick with a building storm.

"I went back to the creek after I took Joy home. He was still there. Still dead. Once everything started to sink in, I got scared. I was just a kid, you know? Not that it's an excuse for what I did to cover it up. But I was just a kid."

"No better reason," piped up Carey's husband. Nanette's husband nodded as we all stared at them, even their wives. I'd always wondered if they even liked being part of our family. They never talked to any of us, even when they worked with our brothers.

"So, you found his body still there," River said, trying to help out. "You were scared, rightfully so, and then what?"

"I threw him in the back of the truck." He was silent for a minute, his jaw working. I wanted to get up and walk around the table, hold him, comfort him, but that's not how you treated a man like Jimmy. He wasn't needing my sympathy.

"Then what." River.

"Then I took him to your place."

"Our place." Carey stood. "Whatever for?!"

"Sit down, Carey." Rory held his hand up. He could always calm a storm.

"To throw him into the spring."

River shook his head, unbelieving. "Where Daddy's Spring of Good Luck pours back into the ground? You threw him into the bottomless cave?"

"I hope it's bottomless," I said, finally finding my own voice again.

Silence. Shifting. Breathing. Throat Clearing. And then, a sound I didn't expect. I looked up at River.

"Holy Hell!" And he was laughing. "You threw that devil into the hole?"

Nanette and Carey both shushed him. He waved their chastisement away. "Mother Fudger . . . into that bottomless cave?" He laughed so loud that I worried the kids might run in to see what was going on.

"Perfect," River said.

"What?" I looked at him to see if he was okay.

"I couldn't have thought of a better plan myself," Rory said.

"Rory!" Carey was standing with her hands on her hips. She might have unwound just a little bit, but it was obvious I needed to remind her about making some of those Whoopie pies with her husband.

River stopped laughing. "Can you think of a better way to have gotten rid of him, Sis?"

Her face turned red, she looked at me, and then something different than self-righteousness took over her face. They were talking about the man that took away my youth, after all.

"Did this man ever go to church, Jimmy?"

"Refused to hear the word," Jimmy said. "Hated the church. My grandma tried to help him, but he was mean to her, too. Mean to other people, not only Joy, in ways that don't bear repeating."

"So he didn't want to change?"

Jimmy laughed, but the sound held no humor. "Carey. I'm not just trying to justify what I did, but my dad wasn't one of those hard cases who wanted to change and just couldn't stick to it. He didn't try. He didn't want to. He never did. If you don't believe that, then you didn't listen to Joy on the day she told you all what happened."

"Well," Carey said. "In that case, I would've thrown him in alive." And at that moment, I believed the new Carey might have done just that. "I would've knocked his teeth out."

Nanette smiled, like a thought had just occurred to her.

"I think he did. That's why you had that tooth in that charm that you threw into the well, right?"

"How did you know I threw it in the well?" I hadn't told anyone about that, and I doubted Ruthie had either.

Nanette chuckled. "After Bobby's trouble, I started looking for Ruthie's diary. I finally found it up in your attic the other day. Found out that she's a good girl, but that you and her have been having some little side adventures this summer."

"True," I said.

"What I don't understand," interjected my sister-in-law Faith, "Is why I don't remember him being missing. I know I am younger than the rest of you, but seems something like a missing man would have been talked about over the years."

River shot Jimmy an apologetic look. "Nobody ever looked. I heard there were people glad he disappeared."

Jimmy looked sad as he nodded in agreement.

"And," Rory added. "Nobody cares."

"I do," Jimmy said. "It was wrong."

And this is when Carey became my favorite sister. Who knew her self-righteous, religious zealot attitude would really help someone someday?

"Jimmy, if you believe those words you sing every Sunday, you know you are forgiven." And to my surprise, Jimmy who'd never had much use for Carey, hugged her. She blushed so red that her husband at the other end of the table chuckled.

"So it's done," River said. "We're not gonna talk about

this again, agreed?" He stood and walked to the edge of the table, lay his hand on it. The rest of us joined him, ready to agree.

"Now wait a minute, all of you." Nanette held her hands up, palms out at her seat. Everyone pulled their hands back. "Is it at all worth telling the police now? Is it possible they might see that it was self-defense and nothing bad will come of this?"

The rest of us looked at her, deadpan.

"The sheriff around here just got arrested for selling drugs to your son," I reminded her.

"Okay," she said. "I was just trying to be the voice of reason. But I agree with all of you."

"Then get your butt over here," River ordered. "We're making a pact for Joy and Jimmy."

Rory thrust his hand into the circle. "We ain't telling no one."

We overlapped our hands on top of Rory's, Jimmy's closing over mine at the top.

We all sat silent for a long time after that, the boys shaking their heads, the girls smiling, and Jimmy and I staring at each other across the room, the distance that had grown between us over the years shrinking a whole lot more.

Chapter Thirty

FROM THEN ON, we Talleys lost our taste for the spring water that ran from the caves above our property. The Spring of Good Luck was now bad. Nobody ever mentioned the villain again, and I started reading my romance novels right out in the open. Carey never said a word about my scandalous reading choices. My only regret was that I couldn't read under the apple tree anymore, but thanks to my brothers, maybe the nieces and nephews will be able to someday. While I was at The Tulip House for Girls, my brothers had enlisted Bobby and his friend Carl to cut away the fallen trunk of the magic apple tree and all its branches, preserving the massive stump and stacking the logs along the side of the house to be used in our new fireplace. With its rings exposed, the tree finally revealed its age. It was indeed as old as Momma claimed.

"One-hundred and sixty-five," Ruthie told me when I'd arrived home. Such an old age for an apple tree in this part of the country was rare, but so were a lot of other things that had to do with my family.

In another part of the orchard, they had planted a new

apple tree. The part that made me smile was that Jimmy had gotten a cutting to propagate from Doc. It turned out that Kyle's own mother had a tree that was propagated from ours years earlier when Grandma Bess sold cuttings from the magic apple tree to make extra cash.

"Doc was happy to give it to us," Jimmy had explained. "With one exception."

"What's that?" I was nervous that Kyle would never forgive me for my choice.

"That you call it the miracle apple tree."

I tried the name on for size. "The Miracle Apple Tree. I like it, don't you?"

"I do," he said. "And with any luck, it will take off and live to be at least as old as its magic grandmother did."

I only hoped we could keep the property long enough for future Talleys to witness another old apple tree. Now that would be a miracle.

The sun dipped low in the sky as the porch swing cricked and creaked beneath me. For some reason, the house stood prouder these days, but I couldn't prove how I knew. Its blue paint still flaked around the edges and some of its lace curtain bedecked windows still needed replaced, but it had livened up with all the attention it was getting lately. I imagined it was happy to have visitors teaming inside again. No outlaws, just people stopping by for iced tea, strawberry-lemon cake, sugar cookies, and Carey's famous Whoopie pies that she finally got her husband to help her make. My favorite times were when the ladies, and always Peter, came over to crochet or brainstorm new ways to help out the community.

Chance and Marvel, new friends we'd gotten for our yippy little Daffy, livened things up around the place, too, darting back and forth across the yard and through the orchard where the branches grew heavier with fruit, chasing rabbits and sniffing out squirrels. Boy, I sure fell in love with those mutts fast. I can't believe we waited so long to get them. But of course, I did know. It was Momma. She had gotten rid of so many pleasures after Daddy died and spent so much time trying to fix us with her teas and worries. She worried about so many things.

But we're fine now, Momma. Don't worry anymore.

On the day Fernie came to visit like a prodigal daughter to apologize to her dad for being so distant to him since we'd been dating, we had dinner simmering on the stove and were sitting out in the shade of the porch like two old people, and I loved it. My eyes swept the orchard and I thought about how we'd at last found someone to lease five hundred acres to, which was better than having Jimmy pay all the bills. We Talleys might not be much in the eyes of the world, but we are proud. What of? Not of how our legacy looks on the outside, our proud century old house falling down around us, or our ancient apple tree now ready to fuel our fireplace that once was unusable, but sticking together was something to be proud of. We also have a history that nobody around those parts could match when it came to unique attention-grabbing adventure. And how many people can claim to have people who had seen the other side of this life and come back from it? It was still hard to believe I was one of those Talleys.

What I saw and heard in my coma happened, and it was a miracle, not magic. At least not the kind of magic Momma was thinking of. And it wasn't anything to do with luck. I think that Daddy's ghost had been trying for years to lift that thin curtain and give us a glimpse of heaven—to show us there was more than luck and magic. It's veiled from us, but it's just . . . right . . . there.

"Did I ever thank you for coming back to me, Jimmy?"

Beside me, his arm tightened around my shoulder. "Only fifty-three times."

"Is that all?"

"I reckon you better start on fifty-four now."

I tilted my face to meet his lips. Oh how many kisses have we missed? Only thousands more to go.

We heard Fernie's car coming down the gravel road before the dogs did.

"Looks like Fernie's coming for dinner," Jimmy said.

The dogs barked at the heels of her sleek black Camaro. Jimmy met her at the steps and gave her a kiss.

"You want some tea?" I asked. "Ruthie made some for us just this afternoon."

"River is waiting," she said, and shot me a shy smile. "I just stopped by to give you something he sent over."

I saw that she was holding a small satchel. Jimmy pointed to it.

"Whatcha got there, Sweet Pea?"

She pulled out several pages of a very old-looking book that had been bound together with a piece of twine.

"River found this when he was working on the chimney and threw it in his work bag. He wanted to show it to the girls because it was neat. But when we got to looking at it, we noticed it has something here on the back cover that looks a lot like a treasure map."

"A what?"

"And then I remembered that plaque that the boys found when they were cleaning up the chimney mess."

"Talley Luck is Well-treasured in this Home," I quoted.

Now that was unexpected, but I guess that secrets really do find their way out when they're ready to be told. By the time she left, I really did believe in second chances, and, maybe—buried treasure, too.

Chapter Thirty-one

"DO YOU SEE anything?"

"Nothing yet," Rory called up. But it's really not as deep down here as I thought. I can stand up in it."

River and Jimmy were bent over the opening wearing head lamps, while Bobby shined a Mag light down into the secret well in our basement.

"Just don't go poking around too much, because you're standing in a cave," River said. "And it leads to God only knows where."

And maybe to the bones of a certain villain, but we won't mention that.

I shivered. "Y'all be careful."

"I still can't believe that Fernie was able to find this map." Nanette's voice whispered into the half-light. "She is one sharp girl."

"That's what college will do you for," I told her, hoping Ruthie and Bobby were both listening.

"I can't believe there was a map in the first place," Carey said.

One thing is for sure. I'm hanging the plaque that says

"Talley Luck Is Well Treasured in This Home" between Momma's and Daddy's portraits in the living room. How would we have ever guessed the plaque meant there was really a treasure hidden in the well?

"Just be glad we made the connection when we did," I said.

"Do you see any snakes down there?" Carey called down into the well.

"No," shouted Rory. "Do you think I would still be down here if I did?"

"I can't believe Momma and Daddy never told us about this," Nanette said.

"Maybe they didn't know," Carey commented.

"Bobby and Ruthie," Nanette said, visibly shivering in the light of the dim bulb hanging from the ceiling. "I'm surprised you kids never found this well when you were little, as much as you disobeyed us by sniffing around the passageways."

Ruthie didn't mention to her mother that she'd already been down there with me when I tossed the charm into the well.

"I'm about ready to come back up," Rory called up, disappointment evident in his tone. "I haven't found anything."

"It was worth a try," I said, trying to keep my voice even. Even as my heart sank, I suddenly felt stupid for hoping the treasure was real.

"Easy for you to say," River muttered. "You're aren't the one holding the rope for Junior down there. He needs to stop eating Joy's pot roast."

"Coming up," Rory called, his voice echoing through the basement's depths.

Bobby held the light while River and Jimmy held tight to the chain ladder.

"Let's get you up." River groaned.

"So there's no treasure?" Ruthie.

"I'm afraid not," her mother said. "I know you kids are disappointed, but let's get Uncle Rory out of that hole and get outta here. It creeps me out."

"Maybe it's somewhere else," Ruthie said, still clinging to hope the way a child clings to fairytales.

"Honey, there's no buried—"

Just then we heard a clank and a splash as if rocks were falling into the well.

"Damn it," River exclaimed. We didn't correct his language anymore. If there was one thing that was probably never going to change in this family, it was Rory's and River's potty mouths.

Bobby turned to us girls. "A bunch of rocks fell out of the wall. One hit him in the head."

I rushed forward. "Is he okay?"

Rory, cursed from the bottom of the well.

"What do I have to do for someone to get me out of here?"

"The chain ladder broke," Jimmy called to him. "We'll get another ladder."

It took some time, but eventually the men managed to get a regular construction ladder down into the basement and into the well. It wasn't quite tall enough to reach the top, but the water was shallow enough the ladder would get Rory high enough the men could grab him.

"Wait," he called, and then, "Holy crap!"

I think we all thought of water moccasins as the men leaned perilously forward, ready to pull him to safety.

"Rory?"

Bobby angled the light down into the hole.

"What is it?"

"You all aren't going to believe this. Pull me up."

We women drew closer as they hauled him up. He wore a big goofy smile on his face and in his hand, he held up a small shiny, gold brick.

Heavens to Betsy.

"Found this behind the rock wall of the well," he said. "Our so-called Talley luck has been lining the god-forsaken well all this time."

I shivered, wrapped my arms around myself, closed my eyes.

Momma and Daddy, you would have loved this.

A shiver whispered up my arms and to the back of my neck. I swear I heard Daddy murmur behind me.

"You can breathe now, Joy."

Chapter Thirty-two

I'M STILL BREATHING, so I obviously didn't kill myself. I'm glad my sisters and brothers finally let go of that notion. I do want to say that sometimes I'm tempted to think I'm still in my coma and that I never woke up, but every time I walk out onto Momma's porch and the sun hits my face, I know that I am awake. I can see the orchard, its trees empty of leaves that have long blown away in the wind that came with winter and the baby miracle apple tree sheltered from frost with a layer of gunny sacks and hay arranged by my beloved to protect it until it is strong enough to weather a winter on its own. I guess we won't know until spring if it's going to make it, but I have this feeling that it will.

After finding the treasure, we were able to pay off the outstanding mortgage.

Take *that*, Mr. Littleton.

Now, we can afford to have our ancient house restored instead of torn down. I like to think Momma and Daddy would be happy to see how things have changed. I know Momma might be sad about the changes to the chimney, but she'd be glad to be free of all the luck, which is so undependable. Course, I think she is free of all those worries and superstitions now, having gone past that narrow gate the Reverend, her once lover, told her about, and where Daddy, who must be a saint, was allowed to wait for her. Jimmy swears that the angels there will sing better than him, but I don't know. He's pretty good.

Now, don't get me wrong. I'm not judging Momma and Daddy, or even the Talley people for being so superstitious. In fact, I honor them, and let's face it. We're rich now, and I can't thank our ancestors enough.

"We're rich," I whispered to Jimmy when he walked out on the porch and wrapped a blanket around my shoulders.

"Yes, you are," he said, wrapping his strong arms around me. "But you don't need to go getting all high and mighty about it, Joy."

I laughed. "I can't help it. Have you ever been poor?"

"Well . . ."

"Never mind." Sometimes I could just kick myself for my stupidity. I knew he was poor when he was a kid. Poorer than I was, for sure. At least I had been rich in family. He hadn't even had a father to speak of.

Believe me. We never spoke of Jimmy's father, not even when we paid to have the Spring of Good—or rather, bad—luck sealed up. Bobby was pretty upset about that, although Ruthie said nothing. I had expected her to be upset because of the magic water and all, but she had silently nodded when I mentioned our plans to seal up the hole where it poured into the ground.

"For safety reasons," I told them.

Bobby and Ruthie's boyfriend, Carl, helped Jimmy, River and Rory seal that hole with a cement barrier. Jimmy made a flower bed above it, filling it with rich dirt that he planted daffodil bulbs in. I couldn't wait until spring when they would bloom at the same time as the Dogwoods and Redbuds, and then each year the daffodils would multiply until the box overflowed. Maybe I would separate the bulbs and hand them out to Bobby and Ruthie for their homes someday, and then later to the little ones. I couldn't wait until then.

Of course, you know that every fairytale, if fairytales were real, has to end in a wedding. And so did mine. We got married two days before Christmas. Since we aren't short of change anymore, Jimmy bought us one of those light up nativity scenes and we put it out in the front yard, along with a great big star at the top of the house. I just want to say right now that I've had enough of roofs and chimneys, so I didn't volunteer to hang that thing, and I made sure not to look when Bobby climbed out on the balcony, up on the shingles, and suspended that thing from the roof; but I loved that you could see it far down the road, lighting the way to our home in the country.

They also hung evergreen boughs and tinsel all over the house inside and out, and a ball of mistletoe from a string suspended from the ceiling. Mistletoe just happens to be the Oklahoma state flower, by the way, so I don't even want to know how Bobby came up with the great ball of it, but it was beautiful and every time someone turned around, kids and all, they had to kiss someone. Dozens of stockings hung from the mantle and around about the house, one for every Talley. In the corner was a big empty pickle barrel decorated with ribbons and bows where instead of wedding gifts for us, people could drop in gifts for the girls at Tulip House. I smiled at how full it already was.

Above the mantle hung the biggest, gaudiest wreath that Carey and Nanette could make and then there were the trees. While we might not have useless charms hidden in the chimney anymore, we were happy to have baubles and belles hanging from Christmas trees all over the house. We didn't have just one Christmas tree, either. We had them upstairs and down to make up for all the Christmases we had missed having together. When Jimmy said he wanted that many trees and why, I worried about Fernie's feelings, that it would seem like we were discrediting her family's past Christmases with her mom, but she didn't mind.

"We had him for all those years, Joy. Give Daddy his trees he missed with you."

I couldn't help but hug that girl, even though, just like her mother, she shrugged away from affection, from everybody's except River's, of course.

We stood in front of the mantle for the ceremony and Reverend Wilson officiated. I loved him for it. Out of everyone in the world, he knew how Jimmy and I felt to have endured so many years, so close, yet so far apart from each other. I was reminded of this once during his sermon when he looked up and his eyes landed on Momma's picture. Reverend Wilson's eyes alighted on Carey, who stood with Nanette beside me, he flashed her that wrinkled smile, and then rested his watery blue eyes back on me.

Behind him, our friends from all over town—including Miss Donna, Peter in a tuxedo that I swear was from our prom, Mary Sue, Clara, and Thelma in her wheel chair looking smug, as if she had always known this would happen—were scattered about the house, the older people, wrinkled Cherokee faces and white scruffy chinned farmers that were such a big part of Spavinaw Junction, were all seated in Momma's lace bedecked furniture. Lots of them had even dressed in red, gold, and green in honor of our Christmas wedding, which is saying a lot for the adults of Spavinaw Junction who live in boots, jeans, and snap-down western shirts most of the time, and I mean many of the girls, too.

Ruthie and Bobby were both dressed up for the wedding, Ruthie having made her own red velvet dress that she dazzled in and a matching miniature Santa hat that she'd tied on Lucky's head, and even River and Rory wore red shirts. They didn't like them, I could tell, but by gosh, they were wearing them. Made me love them even more.

Of course, my precious friend, Doc, did not come. That would've been too weird for everyone, but I'd heard he was dating someone that Fernie introduced him too. She'd said the woman was from Colcord, just a few miles over and was a pharmacist from a good family.

Jimmy cleared his throat and I realized my mind had wondered. Tears threatened to spill as it hit me that Momma wasn't there to see my happiness or Daddy to give me away, but somehow I knew they saw.

Jimmy looked at me expectantly and I realized it was time for me to say those age old words, 'I do', but I didn't, at least not yet. Instead, I held my breath, savoring the moment for as long as I could. And for a moment, I was in the hospital again, drowning in memories, hearing the nurses and doctors say that I was lost; and Daddy, having always watched over me like the best father ever, was leaning over me, whispering in my ear back into the furthest reaches of my memory where I was back on the cliff behind our house in the dark. I was just a little girl again, lost in the hollows, perched on that cliff's edge above the caves—and then Daddy broke through the fog of my nightmare and he plucked me up in an embrace, saying, "You can breathe now, Joy. It's okay."

Okay, Daddy.

And so, I did, and then said, "I do."

Epilogue

Dear Aunt Joy,

I have been meaning to give you this letter. Grandma Bess left it for you when she left mine. I know you will never believe that I forgot to give it to you when I gave you the others stuff from the chimney, so I hope you will forgive me and simply accept it now.

Love,
Ruthie

I FOUND THE letter in the bottom of my stocking long after everyone had gone home, even Ruthie and Bobby, from our wedding.

"What's that?" Jimmy asked.

"A letter from Momma." I sat on the end of our bed.

Our bed!

Jimmy had one hand on a suitcase that he was about to carry downstairs. We were going on a honeymoon. I didn't know where. It was a surprise, but the bar was set pretty low since I had never been further than Tulsa in all my life.

It said *My Joy* on the front in what I recognized as Momma's handwriting. The envelope was sealed shut and when I held it to my nose, I smelled Elmer's.

Ruthie. Bless your heart, honey. I would have shown you, anyway.

I opened the envelope carefully with a letter opener from my dresser. Jimmy watched as I read a slip of paper that slid out. It was short, just a note.

Dear Joy,

I found this in the garden attached to the gate where I knew you waited for Jimmy at the same time every night before hiding with him in the apple tree (Yes, Dear, I always knew. I am your mother). I was devastated about what obviously happened to you (I figured it out when I read his letter, honey). And while I have since come to understand that Jimmy must have been a victim that day, too. At the time, I believed he was a bad influence on you.

I didn't want the letter falling into the wrong hands, and yet I could not bring myself to destroy it, either. Most of all, I didn't want you to go away, so I hid the letter from you. I hope you find it at the right time. I'm sorry for keeping it from you all these years. With Love,

Momma

I pulled the folded letter from the envelope. My name was written on the outside in a hand that was less familiar, but a lingering memory of song lyrics written to me in Jimmy's hand tugged at the outer reaches of my mind. I looked up at my husband whose eyes were locked on the letter.

"It's from you," I said.

He let go of the suitcase. It landed with a bang that echoed through the quiet house and sent Lucky skidding from the room.

Joy,

We have done a terrible thing, but I am glad my dad is dead. I know for a fact you are not the first person he hurt like that, but I hope you can find satisfaction that at least you were the last. I have replayed that day over and over in my head and I'm convinced he deserves where he's at . . . washed right down to hell, I hope.

But what I did to you, my Joy, my happiness, is worse than what we did to that devil. I am sorry. I am so sorry. I don't know how to tell you how wrong I was for abandoning you, for getting Fern pregnant. I cannot find the right words. Even my songs die when I try to explain to you why I broke my promise. I don't even know why, myself. I only know I am an idiot, I am worse, and I don't deserve you anyway.

I don't expect you to believe me, after what I have done, but I've never loved another girl and I don't want to marry Fern. I will die if I have to marry her. You are supposed to be my wife, Joy . . . only you.

If you can forgive me, I am begging you, please take me back. Please meet me here tomorrow night, same time we always do. We can run away and get married. We can go see the world together, just like we planned. Maybe you won't mind if the baby visits us sometimes when it's born, but I want to marry you. I have to hold you again, Joy.

I will be waiting here at the garden gate tomorrow night. Please, please forgive me.

Please take me back. I will be waiting.

I Love You, My Happiness.

Jimmy

I folded the fragile letter, its crackle the only thing breaking the silence. Jimmy sat down beside me on the bed and we both stared into the mirror, our images reflecting back the years that had passed since the note was written.

So many years.

And all this time I thought he just didn't want me.

"Momma found your letter."

A shadow darkened his caramel face, and suddenly each narrow wrinkle that splayed from his eyes and down his cheeks represented all the roads that'd led him away from me.

"All this time," he whispered, but he didn't finish his sentence.

I wanted to scream, to cry, to mourn our loss. In my mind, I ran through the house, turning over all the Christmas trees, wielding Momma's picture across the room, turning over the grandfather clock, ripping the silver tinsel down, and even—forgive me Lord—turning over the glowing Nativity in the front yard with a huge blow to their heads, and then pausing to set baby Jesus aright. I did used to be a Sunday school teacher, mind you, and I wasn't always coveting Jimmy as he sang my favorite songs on stage, only some of it. Okay, a lot, but that's not the point. In my mind, I ran out to the orchard then and yanked up the miracle apple tree and flung it high into the night sky, and then I screamed—louder than I have ever screamed.

In my mind, I'd just thrown the biggest temper tantrum in the world. In reality, I sat calmly on the bed, staring at my middle-aged self in the mirror, until Jimmy turned his hand over, opening his fist, his palm waiting. I pressed my palm against Jimmy's. His fingers encircled mine, and then I found his eyes in the mirror. I saw him as he had been back then, face smooth and tanned, dark hair loose and wild, and eyes wide open with hope. I pictured him standing at the garden gate.

"How long did you wait?"

"All night." He cleared his throat, looking down at our hands. "I went back the next night too. Five nights in all."

So he hadn't given up, like I thought.

"I would've gone with you," I choked.

He nodded.

"I would have gone anywhere with you."

He couldn't speak, but he let go of my hand and tapped his fist once to his heart, and then twice.

"Anywhere," I said, desperate for him to know.

I watched him, my heart seemingly unable to beat, and I didn't know what we should do next. He must have been heartsick to know that I had never received the letter, that my not showing up was not a rejection, and he had married Fern anyway. I waited as the truth sank in, wondering if he might be angry at Momma, if he might even cry—I know I would have—but instead, he turned to me and smiled.

How can he smile?

But he did, and then he stood, picked up the suitcase, and grabbed my hand. He pulled me from my seat on the bed and crushed me to his chest, his kiss carrying me through the garden gate in my mind and back into the present.

"Let's go," he said, his dark eyes bright with a spark that I remembered from my coma dream.

"Now. Go now?" I was wearing my robe, and nothing underneath it. "I thought we were leaving in the morning."

"Now," he said. "Let's go now."

"Okay," I agreed, my heart starting to beat again. "Right . . . right now?"

"Right now."

And in less than five minutes, the suitcases were in the bed of the truck, I was riding gunshot beside Jimmy and we were bouncing down the dirt road, the dogs chasing us toward the highway. Confident Ruthie and Bobby would take good care of them I rested my head on his shoulder and barely counted my blessings before I was asleep. When I awoke hours later, after one bathroom break—yes still in my robe!—I was, besides still naked, carried over an unfamiliar threshold in the arms of my lover.

My lover!

My lover looked at me as my sleepy eyes cleared. He was waiting for a response.

"It's kind of small," I said, my feet still dangling over his arm because he refused to put me down.

"It is."

"The Christmas tree is a little sparse. Is that a starfish on top?"

"Looks like a starfish."

"The fire place looks a little funny."

"It's one of those newfangled electric ones."

"It doesn't even have a chimney!"

He shook his head.

"The kitchen is tinier than what I'm used to."

"We won't spend much time cooking while we're here." He playfully tugged at my robe.

I heard a long sigh sweep through from the back of the cottage, like a wind blowing up from the hollows at home.

"Where are we?"

He carried me through the little house toward long sheer curtains that reached toward us in the cool morning breeze, out the French doors, and sat me gently down on a wooden deck. There was only blue as far as the eye could see. Salty air hit my face and the whoosh of waves bearing down on a sandy shore leading right up to a steep stairway off our deck filled the air around us.

The ocean! Just like in my favorite romance novels.

"You always said you wanted to see it."

I walked to the edge of the deck and leaned over the railing, arms wide. Jimmy's hand encircled my waist and pulled me back, but I didn't complain. I wasn't known for having the best balance, now was I?

"There's so much air!"

"And room to breathe," Jimmy said.

I breathed in;
And maybe for the first time ever,
my lungs were full.

Acknowledgments

My readers have been very patient waiting for *Waking Up Joy*, so I thank all of you first. I hope you will love the Talleys. Thank you to my excellent editor and dear friend, Amy Sue Nathan, who believed *Waking Up Joy* should be published a long time before it was. Thanks to Agent Chip MacGregor for insightful feedback and constant encouragement, to Jane Porter and the folks at Tule for choosing *Waking Up Joy* to be part of the amazing Tule Publishing Group, and to Lee Hyat for a beautiful cover.

Also, thanks to my husband Albert who is my biggest supporter, and to our kids. I'm so proud of you Jake and Dawson for the extraordinary young men you have become, and am glad you never complain about Pizza. Hannah, this gift of writing flowed from mother to daughter, but you had to accept it for yourself. Keep writing, dreaming, and finding your own voice. I am incredibly proud of you.

Huge thanks to the people of Northeastern Oklahoma for inspiring my imagination. Someone else needed to let everyone know that not all of Oklahoma is flat. Spavinaw Junction is fictitious, but the traits of humbleness, kindness, and generosity in Oklahomans are real. Thank you Donna Jane Harper for promoting my earlier novels at *Colcord Grocery* and at *S&P. Miss Donna's* is for you. Special thanks to my early readers and cheerleaders, and especially to Lori

Gardner, Heather Day Gilbert, and Barbara Gray for reading the final.

I am also grateful to my brother Troy Gray and sister Cheri Kaufman and their families. We do not have the same problems as the Talleys, but we love each other as much. Thanks also to my mother-in-law Nancy Forkner for always being supportive of my work and to all my friends for putting up with cancelled coffee dates during deadline time and giving me encouragement.

Thank you to my parents, Dennis and Barbara Gray, for recognizing early on that I was going to be a writer, and calling me one. I have amazing parents.

And finally, thank you to Dahn Benzen Dunivent Shelton. A more genuine fan was never had by any author. I have not forgotten the day you came to my book signing pulling your oxygen tank and told me that yes, you were aware of what was going on during your medically induced coma. Thank you, Dahn. Our coffee date was a pleasure, and when I went to tell you about the new book, I learned you had passed away. R.I.P.

About the Author

Tina Ann Forkner is a Women's Fiction writer and the author of *Rose House* and *Ruby Among Us.* While she was born and raised in Oklahoma, lived in England, and attended college in California, Tina makes her home in Cheyenne, Wyoming with her husband, three teenagers, and two spoiled dogs.

For the latest news from Tule Publishing, visit our website at TulePublishing.com and sign up for our newsletter!

Made in the USA
Lexington, KY
03 April 2015